I0719859

# THE CAPTAIN & THE QUEEN

## PHILLIP VEGA

***The Captain & the Queen***
Copyright © 2018 Phillip Vega
All Rights Reserved

This book or any portion thereof may not be reproduced without the express written permission of the publisher, except for the use of brief quotations in a book review and certain other noncommercial uses permitted by copyright law.

This is a work of fiction. Names, characters, places, and incidents either are products of the author's imagination or are used fictitiously.

First edition 2018

Published in the USA by *thewordverve inc.* (www.thewordverve.com)

eBook ISBN: 978-1-948225-52-6
Paperback ISBN: 978-1-948225-53-3

Library of Congress Control Number:  2018956599

~~~~~

***The Captain & the Queen***

A Book with Verve by *thewordverve inc.*

*Cover design by A.L. Lovell*
www.beechhousebooks.com

*Paperback and eBook formatting by Bob Houston*
http://facebook.com/eBookFormatting/info
~~~~~

# Table of Contents

# PROLOGUE

"**I**t's *you*! I'll *kill* you!" yelled the ninety-something-year-old man. His wineglass shattered on the floor as he picked up his steak knife and lunged for my throat.

*Sigh!*

*Here we go . . . again!*

Why the hell did I agree to coming to this wedding?

"Father, no!" Callie yelled as she and others held him back.

*Oh, right . . . the girl.*

"Let me go! I'll *kill* him!"

Looks like I've still got it, even in my fifties.

You're probably asking yourself, *what the hell is going on*? Well, to answer that, we need to go back a few months. Hell, who am I kidding? How about a few decades?

It all started with a ping.

***

*Ping.*

Helen Doherty tagged you in a post on Facebook.

*Helen Doherty? Jesus, I haven't thought about her and Aaron in forever. I thought they'd retired from the Dramatic Arts Department at my old prep school years ago. I wonder why she tagged me.*

I clicked on the hyperlink, and staring back at me in black-and-white was my seventeen-year-old self in all my high-school senior-year glory. I was on stage, dressed to the hilt as Puck, from Shakespeare's comedy, *A Midsummer Night's Dream.*

*God, was I ever really that young? And look at all that hair. Even in black-and-white, it's wavy and all jet black, no beard, and not a spot of gray.*

The caption read, "Happy Birthday, Ron Park," who was also tagged in the picture, dressed as Theseus, Duke of Athens. *I remember Ron. Good guy.*

*Hung out with that chick, Nina Ruiz.*

Helen posted a few photos from the play, so I thumbed through them. After all these years, I could still picture her walking around during rehearsals, taking action shots.

The seventh picture in the series hit me like a thunderbolt. After all these years, seeing her standing poised and elegant, dressed as Hippolyta, queen of the Amazons, still moved me. Even in black-and-white, her flawless olive-colored skin and almond-shaped, blue eyes glowed. And her wavy, long, brown hair . . . Man, how I'd enjoyed running my fingers through her hair.

So pretty, breathtaking.

How is it possible that I can still smell her perfume after all these years? Hints of flowers, musk, and lust.

I can still remember seeing her for the first time. It was the first day of my senior year—class of 1987—at our boarding school on Long Island. My best friend, Matt Salvatore, and I were on our way to football practice when her father's shiny black Mercedes barreled past us and parked outside her dorm. And then out stepped this stunning Greek beauty.

She stood there, staring up at the building with a look of uncertainty, as girls milled about her, entering and exiting the dorm. I couldn't stop staring at her. I literally halted in my tracks, slack-jawed. Matt bumped into me.

"Dude, what the fuck? We've got practice," he said with a tinge of annoyance in his voice.

I just gestured subtly with my chin. Matt followed my eyes and then laughed to himself, shaking his head.

"Dude, it's never gonna happen. She's way out of your league. Hell, she might even be out of *my* league." He chuckled.

"What do you mean? She's not out of my league," I said without taking my eyes off her.

Matt laughed again and gave me a playful shove. "C'mon, let's go."

As we walked toward the gym, I couldn't stop looking back at this beautiful girl.

Designer suitcase in hand, she wore a navy-blue overcoat over a pleated blue-plaid skirt, crisp white shirt, white headband, white socks, and shiny black patent-leather shoes. She looked like a prep-school poster child.

There was a vulnerable elegance about her. She must have felt me staring, because she turned and looked right at me. She arched a shapely eyebrow and smiled. It was subtle. One of those beneath-the-lashes smiles, with a slight upturn of the sides of her mouth.

At that moment, my heart melted. I literally gasped for breath.

Then, a man, who I assumed to be her father, pulled up beside her. He followed her gaze and was not happy to see me standing at the end of it.

"Calista! This way. Come!" he barked.

She frowned immediately, faced the building, and followed the man inside.

"Calista," I whispered with a smile.

*I had her first name. And a smile.*

*That's a helluva start.*

# 1 - The Players

It was the fall of 1986, my senior year at a Long Island boarding school in a town called Stony Brook. Lionel Richie was dancing on the ceiling, while Aerosmith and Run DMC were showing us how to "walk this way."

I was a day student, who, unlike other senior day students, still rode the bus to school, even though I had a perfectly good two-tone blue 1983 Chevrolet Caprice Classic sitting in my driveway, and a part-time dishwashing job to cover my expenses . . . *not that I'm bitter.*

Anyway, it was the perfect late summer/early fall day. The sky was a bright blue, with barely a cloud in the air, and full of possibilities.

Like other incoming seniors, I was ready for the year to be over before it even started. I had done well on my SATs in the spring, so I didn't retake them in the fall. My college applications were ready to go. The only things missing were my current transcripts and signed checks from my parents to cover the application fees.

According to my college advisor/guidance counselor, Mr. Andrews, I had chosen well and shouldn't have a problem getting into any of the colleges on my list.

On the first day of school, Matt and I grabbed our seats in the second row for our first-period class with Mr. Berry, who proceeded to bust Jean Paul Michael's balls, as he and his best friend (and fellow Latino) Emilio entered the classroom.

*Damn, looks like Emilio broke his hand. I wonder how that happened? I guess that means no football for him this year. That must be one hell of a story. Can't wait to hear it later.*

After the final bell rang at 3:15 p.m., I hit my locker and loaded up my backpack before heading to the gym to change for football practice. Matt met me on the way, and that was when I first saw the beautiful Calista.

"C'mon, bro. We've got practice," Matt said, elbowing my side.

When Matt and I entered the gym, we noticed Coach Connor's door was shut, which was unusual, especially for the first day back. He typically maintained an open-door policy, welcoming anyone who passed to come in and say hello. *Must be in a meeting or something. Whatever. I'll be seeing him soon enough out on the field.*

"Hey, B," I said as we walked by one of our classmates who was heading to tennis practice.

"Hey, guys," she replied with a friendly wave. Her high blond ponytail bounced from side to side as she headed toward the exit.

*Man, she's cool. I'm going to try to get to know her better this year.*

Practice and tryouts went as expected. Since we were a small school with a limited selection of players, most everyone made the football team. It really boiled down to which squad you ended up on: varsity, junior varsity, or one of the select few hybrids, playing on both.

I'd been starting at tight end on offense and played cornerback on defense since my junior year, and I didn't expect that to change this year. Sure enough, I had no real competition for either position. Just a pair of sophomores, who would probably start on the JV team.

Matt, on the other hand, had a couple of guys trying out to play quarterback. In his mind, he was our "star" quarterback, so I felt the competition would be good for him. I loved the guy, but, hey . . . humility is not a bad thing.

Of course, Matt ended up as starter, anyway. Though he *did* get a bit nervous when Josh Doyle, a junior, drilled me with a beautiful spiral ten-yard pass.

At six-one, two hundred ten pounds, and hands the size of hams, Matt wouldn't be outdone by Josh. He took the next snap and threw a fifteen-yard perfect spiral right between the numbers, eight and three, to yours truly, and I made sure to catch it.

I knew my audience.

Matt and I were members of a small Latino community at our school. While I was a dark-skinned, dark-haired Dominican, which I got from my mother's side, Matt was a brown-haired, light-skinned Cuban, taking after both his parents.

Due to his strong personality, you either loved or hated Matt. Clearly, I was a fan, and we got along great most of the time. I also got along great with his girlfriend, Gillian "Gill" Thompson, who was an athlete as well—a cross-country runner.

They were one of those "beautiful" couples. They looked like a preppy-

version of Ken and Barbie, if Ken were Cuban and Barbie were a short-haired brunette.

Gill stood about five-four with wavy, brown hair that she wore short, just past her ears, meeting her jawline. She had brown eyes, and a sprinkling of freckles dotting her nose and cheeks, which complemented her heart-shaped face. She came from a wealthy Connecticut family.

She was waiting for us outside our locker room after practice.

"How was practice?" she asked as she grabbed Matt's hand when we'd exited the locker room.

"Brutal," Matt whispered, and I had to laugh. "What the hell are you laughing at? You were saying the same thing a minute ago."

"Dude, *tomorrow's* going to be brutal," I said.

Gill frowned. "What's happening tomorrow?"

"Coach is gonna *kill us*. He *promised*," Matt groused and then gave her a few tidbits of what Coach had said.

Her eyes went wide. "Oh my gosh, is that even legal?"

"Who knows? All I know is I'm not overeating at lunch tomorrow," Matt said.

"Yeah, no shit." I snickered as I pushed the bar on the exit door.

As fate would have it, someone on the other end was pulling it open at the same time, causing me to tumble out the door.

"Whoa!" I yelled as I splashed onto the pavement.

In tandem, I heard, "Holy . . ." (Gill), "Dude!" (Matt), and "Oh!" (the girl who had opened the door at the same time as me).

"Oh, I'm so sorry. Are you okay?" she asked as I came to my knees and accepted her helping hand.

*The scent of flowers, musk, and lust . . .*

I lifted to my feet and brushed my hands on my pants. "Yeah, I'm fine. No big—" My words caught in my throat.

It was her. *The Goddess* with the daddy-grumpy-puss.

I felt the warm rush of blood fill my cheeks. For the first time in a long time, I was speechless. Fortunately, Matt snapped me out of it.

"Dude, you okay?" He and Gill were inspecting me for damage.

"Yeah, yeah, guys. I'm fine. I'm fine." I sucked in some air and shook it off.

*Shit, my knee's killing me. Am I bleeding?*

"I'm so sorry. I didn't realize you were on the other side of the door," said the blue-eyed lovely.

I assured her everything was fine, trying to play it cool, but on the inside . . . *Yow!* My heart was dancing like a pair of Dominicans doing the merengue.

"Hi, I'm Gillian Thompson," Gill extended her hand, "but everyone calls me Gill. You're the new girl who moved into room 127 today, right?"

"That's me. I'm rooming with Marnie Elliott." She shook Gill's hand but looked at me when she said, "I'm Calista. Calista Christos, but everyone calls me Callie."

Gillian threw a thumb in Matt's direction. "This is my boyfriend, Matt Salvatore, and this—"

"I'm—' I interjected, wanting to introduce myself.

"Miss Christos?" It was Coach Connor, approaching us with a clipboard in hand.

*Hey! Can I get a word in here, people?*

"Yes?" she replied, turning toward Coach.

"Good, you're right on time," he said. "Follow me to my office."

Calista Christos—now I had her last name, too—slipped past us and followed the coach back into the gym.

"Excuse me," she said on the way. "It was nice meeting all of you."

"Yeah. Um . . . It was, uh, nice—" The door shut before I could finish.

I felt my shoulders sink.

*Nice . . . to meet you, too.*

"You okay?" Gill asked gently.

"Yeah." I sighed while staring at the door.

Matt just shrugged. "Okay, well . . . mañana," he said as he walked Gill to her dorm.

"Yeah, mañana," I replied, heading toward the line of buses waiting for students to board.

God, I hated riding the bus. Have I mentioned that already? It took me an hour to get home every night, even though I lived fifteen-freaking-minutes away. It made no sense, but it wasn't worth the argument with my parents.

As I sat in my seat, lost in thought, someone rapped on the window. It was Matt.

"Want a ride home?" he asked through the thin pane of glass.

He knew me so well.

"Hell, yeah." I gathered my things and exited the bus, pronto.

Like me, Matt was a day student.

"You got Gill all tucked away?" I teased as we walked to his car.

"As best as I could. She had a tough practice today, too. But I got my smooches." He winked.

*Of course you did.*

"What was with our practice today?" I said as he pulled out of the lot.

"Dude, it sucked. I can't believe what they're making us do tomorrow."

"Yeah, no shit. You never see the guy's soccer team doing stuff like that."

"Buncha pussies," Matt said, and we both howled with laughter as he turned up the volume to our favorite local rock station, WBAB.

We jammed for a minute or two to the latest Bon Jovi song, and then he asked, "So, now that you know her name are you going to actually speak to her next time you see her?"

"I guess I *was* kinda speechless, huh?"

"You could say that. That's why Gill had to step in and help you out. She's pretty hot, bro. Good thing I'm with Gill," he teased.

"Fuck you."

He waved a dismissive hand at me and laughed.

I said, "Well, I'm going to definitely be talking to her tomorrow."

"If you don't, I'm sure someone will. You can bet on it. Hell, the minute Jean Paul sees her, he'll be on her like *stink on shit,*" Matt said.

He was right about that. Jean Paul Michaels was a friend and fellow senior at our school. He was captain of the soccer team, built like a brick shithouse, too, and chicks dug him.

"I'll definitely talk to her tomorrow," I replied.

*Because if I didn't, someone else would . . . and I saw her first!*

# 2 - Welcome Home

Fifteen minutes later, I was home. My house was a comfortable two-story home—four bedrooms, two-and-a-half baths, and a two-car garage—in the town of Stony Brook. It sat on a quarter of an acre of flat land, which was easy to mow with our John Deere tractor-style mower.

Matt, on the other hand, lived in this uniquely designed, three-story, modern split-level house, surrounded by tall oak trees, overlooking a stream that eventually fed into the Long Island Sound. It was in the upscale incorporated village within Smithtown called Head of the Harbor.

I loved hanging out at his house. It was like being in a mini-castle right there in the lowlands of Long Island.

In his long and winding driveway usually sat a Suburban with a trailer hitch for their boat, a pair of four-door Mercedes Benz S-Series cars, which his attorney father and realtor mother drove, Matt's Volvo, and his hot sister Kate's Honda Accord—when she was home from college.

Yeah, they had money, but were the most down-to-earth family you could meet—a close-knit Hispanic family with a welcoming demeanor.

Throughout the years, I'd been to their summer home in the Hamptons and fishing on the Sound—his parents treated me like a son, while Kate treated me like a little brother, dammit. Did I mention she was really hot?

With all the things they had going on over at their place, their home always seemed so peaceful. My house, on the other hand, of late, was everything but.

My dad always seemed . . . I don't know. On edge. He was an aeronautical engineer at Grumman, the well-known government contractor that employed many on Long Island. He'd been there since the latter part of the '60s, working on various airplane programs. Lately, though, he'd been more stressed than usual. Apparently, there were rumors of massive layoffs coming down the pike if they didn't secure one particular government program. This worried both my parents, even though my gut told me my dad would be safe.

After all, he'd been there for years.

He had seniority. He was turning fifty soon. Yeah, he was safe.

My mother was a nurse at Mercy Hospital in Smithtown. Like my dad at Grumman, she'd been there for years, working her way up the ladder. She, too, had seniority.

Still, their constant worrying seemed to cause a constant tension at my house. Some days, it felt like we were walking on pins and needles.

Consequently, I chose to avoid my parents as much as possible, going directly to my room and closing the door behind me. I just couldn't stand the perpetual black cloud floating over our house.

That particular evening, though, Dad caught me when I came in.

"Hey, Champ! How was the first day of school?" he asked, sounding unusually pleasant. But I knew it wouldn't last long.

"It was . . . *okay*." I was tired from practice and not much in the mood to elaborate.

He nodded his head as if he understood what my tone and simple response meant.

"So, you had a tough one, too, huh?" he asked.

"Yeah. We got a bunch of homework already, and practice was tough. Tomorrow, we're running three miles in full gear, *before* practice even starts." I knew I was whining, but I couldn't help it. Now *I* was contributing to the black cloud.

*Jesus, it's friggin' contagious!*

My dad chuckled. "I remember those years. Enjoy them while you can, kiddo. Before you know it, you'll be turning fifty and worried about layoffs, like your old man." He tapped his chest.

"Okay, Dad. I'll try."

"Dinner's in the kitchen. Mom's working till eight."

"Okay. What's for dinner?"

He grinned. "I made chicken almandine with a side of roasted garlic potatoes and asparagus."

"Yes!" I replied with a fist pump. Now *that* was something to celebrate.

My dad loved to cook. He was a natural. It must have been his engineering mind. He seemed to know what spices went together—just naturally. He'd often say that cooking relaxed him. It was his stress-reliever. And I was grateful for it.

Mom never complained—I mean, who would? To be frank, he was a better cook than she was, and she was no slouch. She knew her way around the kitchen as well. My Ta-ta, or grandmother, had taught her well. Her pollo guisado, mofongo, and tostones were the best in the world.

Food-wise, I was in the middle of paradise, basically. An American dad and a Dominican mom. All we were missing was an Italian aunt, and we'd have the grand trifecta!

"Well, go wash up and grab a plate, Champ," he said as he headed to the family room to watch television.

"I sure will. Thanks, Dad."

And I did.

As I inhaled the incredible meal, I watched TV with my dad. He told me about his day—none of which was very positive, in his mind—and in between mouthfuls, I gave him bits and pieces of my day, leaving out the part about being splayed across the sidewalk as the hottest girl in the school apologized for startling me. He didn't need to know his son was a spaz.

After dinner, I went to my room and did my homework, which seemed to last forever. Mom pulled into the driveway around eight o'clock. She popped into my room in her dress whites—nurse uniform—on her way to their bedroom to change.

"How was your first day?" she asked.

Like I had with my dad, I told her it was *okay*. I pointed out all the homework they'd handed out and received a bit of sympathy. Mom was like that. Maybe it was the nurse in her.

"Sorry, hijo," she said, as she caressed my cheek and kissed my forehead. "Be glad you are in school and not having to deal with the real world just yet. You never know when you might lose everything." She snapped her fingers. "Just like *that*."

I rolled my eyes, but not so she could see. *Here we go again.* "Uh, yeah. Thanks, Mom."

"Comiste?" she asked.

"Yeah, I ate. As usual, Dad made a great dinner. I left you a few morsels." I snickered.

She put a hand on her hip and popped an eyebrow. "Uh-huh, you better have. Okay, I'm going to change and get some dinner. I'm so tired."

"'kay, Mom. Enjoy."

"And don't stay up too late, okay?" she said as she left my room.

"I won't," I replied as I begrudgingly pulled out my next assignment.

*AP calculus! Ugh!*

# 3 - The Funeral

The rest of that first week flew by like a breeze. It was full of schoolwork, football practice, and homework. Wash, rinse and repeat. One thing it did not include was me talking to Callie. I'd totally pussied out.

During our AP calculus class, Gill gave me an update on our newest student, since they both lived in the same dorm. She was getting to know Callie, or at least, getting to know *about* her. One thing she learned was that Callie's father was a prominent muckety-muck in Greece, who seemed to travel a lot for work.

"So, when are you going to talk to her? Do you want me to introduce you?" Gill asked at the end of the week.

"No, I've got it," I replied with a bit of faux confidence.

"Well, you better hurry up. We have the back-to-school dance on Friday. It'd be a good chance to get to know each other."

"Yeah, I know, but I'm working all weekend—that includes Friday nights."

"Oh. Well, that sucks. What hours are you working?"

"Friday night from eight till three in the morning, Saturday from five to midnight, and Sunday from eleven to six. Mr. Anagnos knows I'm back in school, so I don't have to work as late on Sundays anymore."

She made a face. "God, you'll never have a social life with that schedule."

"Tell me about it," I mumbled.

***

That Friday night, it poured, and the diner was basically empty. I preferred it when we were busy. Time flew by. When we were slow, things just dragged, and Mr. Anagnos would "find things for me to do."

Sure enough . . . "I'm not paying you to just stand there," he said and then instructed me to go to the walk-in cooler and start rotating things. As I rotated the food, if I found anything expired or near expiration, he wanted me to put it near the front of the cooler, so he could "review it."

Which meant he would see if he could salvage anything before being forced to throw it away. He would create a "Special" for the next day based on what was salvageable, and if it sold well, he'd put it on the menu as a regular item.

After I finished rotating the food, he handed me a bucket of hot water with bleach, so I could scrub down the walk-in. It was disgusting. I cleaned off dried milk, cheese, and a few experiments I didn't recognize. It was exhausting, and I couldn't wait to get out of there.

The weather cleared up on Saturday and Sunday. I was looking forward to some downtime in between diner duty. I slept in on Saturday and ambled down for a late breakfast when my dad informed me it was too wet to mow the lawn. *Today.* However, *tomorrow*, I had the option of getting up early or taking care of it when I got home from work. Nice, right?

*I mean, I know we have a riding mower, but damn. It's not like I'm working all weekend at the diner or anything. Sure, I'd love to mow the lawn!*

But as bad as my weekend was, Monday at school was worse. I found out that two of my classmates had been in a horrible car accident over the weekend. The girl I'd said hi to on our first day of school, when Matt and I were walking into the gym—Britt-Marie Karlsson, also known as "B"—had died, while that bitch-on-wheels (*Sorry, God, but she is*), Mary Ferguson, who apparently was driving, was in a coma, but alive.

B's funeral was held mid-week. Her death impacted everyone at school. The black cloud that seemed to perpetually sit over my house had expanded and now stretched over campus as well. The somber factor was high, to say the least.

Now, B and I hadn't been close friends, but we were friendly to each other. She was supposedly the smartest student in school, and she always seemed happy. She had a glow about her, you know? B was one of those people who seemed beautiful both inside and out.

And just like that, she was gone. Her light snuffed out.

*Just like that.* My mom's words came rushing back to me.

A few of us went to the funeral. Matt, Gill, and I rode together in Matt's car. The place was packed. Our classmate, and her boyfriend, Emilio was a mess. His family was tight with the Michaels family, including Jean Paul and his twin sister Hannah. They were all there, too.

I'd heard Emilio and B were dating, but I never realized how serious it was. That made the tragedy even worse. It touched so many people. Changed us all, at least a little bit.

At the end of the service, they all just huddled together—B's family, Emilio's family and the Michaels family—holding on to each other. Like they were gathering strength from one another. It looked so . . . I don't know.

Intimate.

After the funeral, instead of going home, Matt, Gill, and I drove to the diner, which was in Setauket. Mr. Anagnos was surprised to see the three of us dressed so formally, with somber looks on our faces.

"Hey, kids, why so glum? Who died?" he joked.

"One of my classmates," I replied between gritted teeth, giving him an angry look.

His cheeks went red, and he immediately apologized, ushering us to a table and assuring us the meal was on the house.

I felt a little bad for being such an ass to him, but not too bad. After all, he *did* make me clean out that sludge from the walk-in the other night.

Anyway, not a good couple of days.

# 4 - Year of Renaissance

The day after the funeral, the headmaster held an assembly to address the tragedy. He talked about coming together and leaning on each other so that we could move forward.

Matt, Gill, and I sat together, still feeling numb and morose, like most of the rest of the school. We didn't even want to be there, frankly, but the headmaster was right: sticking together as a school was important right now. It was time to *circle the wagons*, as my Dad would say during times like this.

Suddenly, Gill nudged me. I gave her a questioning look.

"Front row, over there," she whispered, gesturing with her head.

I followed her gesture and saw Callie. I'd barely seen her since that first day, and I definitely wasn't thinking of her at that moment. However, as I gazed at the side of her face, I was reminded of her magnetic pull.

As I stared, Callie suddenly turned and looked at me.

I almost gasped. I mean, that was the second time—she seemed to *know* when I was looking at her. Our eyes locked, and I felt like a deer caught in a pair of beautiful, almond-shaped blue headlights.

I didn't know what to do. Should I turn my attention back to the headmaster? Should I continue to lock eyes with this gorgeous girl?

She must have sensed my trepidation and let me off the hook, giving me a brief smile and then turning back to the headmaster.

I did the same.

*Oh, Sweet Jesus.*

You could hear a pin drop as the headmaster wrapped up the emotional gathering with words that really hit me hard. He said, "If there's one thing we can learn from this tragic event, it's this: Life is precious. We never know when The Lord will call us home. Miss Karlsson led her life with purpose and was an exceptional role model for others. And while she excelled in many areas, she excelled, most of all, as a precious child of God."

People were crying openly now, faculty and students alike. Matt held Gill as she sniffed and tears ran down her cheeks. Hell, I felt a lump in my throat, too. The headmaster himself could barely finish.

"I encourage all of you to search for your purpose. Get outside your comfort zones. You're given only one life. Make the most of it. Do it for yourselves. Do it for Ms. Karlsson. Do it for The Lord. Let this be your year of renaissance." He inhaled a deep breath and let it out slowly. "Let us pray."

After the obligatory "Amen," we were dismissed. As we slowly and quietly snaked out of the auditorium, I could tell I wasn't the only one thinking about that message.

*Year of renaissance, huh?*

Matt headed in one direction for class, and Gill and I went in the other.

"Penny for your thoughts," Gill whispered as we walked to class.

"I don't know."

"You don't know what?"

"What he said. You know, a year of renaissance," I replied, head bowed as I walked.

She nodded but didn't say anything else for a long time. Then, "She sure is pretty."

I looked up confused. "What?"

Gill lifted her chin, gesturing ahead of us, where Callie walked, alone.

I sighed out my words. "Yeah, she sure is."

"I saw you two staring at each other."

"I have no idea what you're talking about."

"Uh-huh. I think she might like you," she said in a sing-song manner.

*Play it cool, play . . . it . . . cool.*

There was silence between us for a couple of beats, but then my coolness broke down. "You think so?" I asked excitedly.

"Only one way to find out. Go talk to her." Gill shoved me forward, but we were already in front of our classroom.

*I will! I will!*

As I sat in class, all I could think about were the words of my headmaster. They seemed to play over in my head.

*"Search for your purpose . . . Get outside your comfort zones . . . Let this be the year of your renaissance."*

I wondered what that meant exactly. Like, what would that look like—for me? It was my last year of high school. Now was not the time to be getting out of my comfort zone. Aren't I supposed to skate through my senior year, then do the college thing? Nah, I've got to stick to my game plan, or as Dad would say, "stay the course."

Besides, what could I really do "new"? Try out for the choir? I couldn't carry a tune if it came with a rope and handle. And like I'd ever try out for a play. That wouldn't happen in a million years.

*Nah, I'll just stick to the plan. That's my purpose. To fulfill the plan. Play football in the fall, basketball in the winter, and baseball in the spring. Go to college. There's nothing wrong with that. It's a good plan. A solid plan.*

*Still . . . hmmm . . .*

# 5 - Lasagna Dinner

The headmaster's words continued to haunt me. I couldn't help but feel like he'd been talking directly to me. I couldn't let go of the idea that there was something more for me to do than what was already on my roadmap.

After practice, instead of grabbing a ride home with Matt, I took the bus. I needed time to think. I greeted the bus driver, who gave me her usual kind smile, and hopped up the steps, found a seat, and settled in. My head pressed against the cushiony back of the bus seat, while my eyes gazed at the parking lot.

That's when I spotted Callie. She was alone, coming out of the auditorium with a book in her hands. Man, she was beautiful. She was . . . magnetic and didn't even know it.

*I should hop off the bus and go talk to her.*

But I didn't. I don't know why. Maybe I was just too shy or just too comfortable in my seat. Or maybe my brain was as tired as the rest of my body.

Plus, what would I say? *"That was some assembly today."*

Yeah, that'd be real smooth. Nah, I was just fine watching her from the bus.

***

An hour later, I walked through the front door and found Dad asleep on the couch in front of the television. It was just after seven, and he was already asleep.

*Guess you had a hard day again, too, huh?*

Instead of waking him, I followed the scent of homemade lasagna, meatballs, sauce, and garlic bread waiting for me in the kitchen, with one slice missing from the lasagna. Everything was still hot; steam floated to the ceiling.

*Man, I love it when Dad cooks Italian. This meal is just what the doctor ordered after a day like today. A bright spot in a shitty day.*

I cut a cheese-filled, massive square of lasagna, three large meatballs, a few pieces of garlic bread, and a tall glass of milk before escaping to my room. As I carefully made my way up the stairs to my room, I glanced at my dad, sleeping his stress away on the couch, while *The Jefferson's* played on the TV.

My heart ached a bit as I watched him from the stairs, his chest expanding and contracting while he slept. There lay my dad, a latter-day Atlas, seemingly carrying the weight of the world on his shoulders, yet he came home from a presumably crappy day at work and created this delicious meal for his family.

*I don't know how he does it, but I hope I grow up to be just like him someday.*

I ate the delicious meal and did homework while listening to WBAB playing quietly in the background, doing my best to stay focused . . . and failing miserably. All I could think about was the girl.

*C'mon, it's not a big deal. Just walk up to her and say hi. Stop being such a pussy.*

*It's not like talking to her is outside my comfort zone.*

*Ha! Yeah, not much.*

*Sigh!*

*Is she what my headmaster was talking about? Is she my renaissance? Her dark, wavy hair, amazing blue eyes, long legs, great smile . . .*

I shook my head free of the crazy thoughts and went back to my homework.

*Tomorrow.*

*Yeah, I'll talk to her tomorrow.*

# 6 - The Fates Intervene

Of course, the moment I saw her the next morning, I turned tail and walked the other way.

*You pussy!*

Fate, however, had plans of its own.

After a routine morning of classwork and homework assignments, lunchtime came. My senior year, I was the work job captain in the kitchen. This meant that during the second of two lunch sessions, I worked behind the scenes in the kitchen, assigning students to various jobs, like cleaning pots, to washing the silverware, to running the professional dishwashing machine, nicknamed, "the machine," to putting everything away and making sure things ran smoothly.

As lunch wrapped up, and students started arriving at the back window to receive their clean sets of plates, glassware, and silverware for dinner, I happened into the room, carrying a hot stack of plates, still steaming from the dishwasher. As I did so, someone called out to me.

I heard, "Excuse me."

I recognized her voice immediately. The sound of an angel. I almost spilled the stack of plates as I quickly turned around. There, framed in the window, staring at me with piercing blue eyes and white smile, was Callie.

I set the stack of hot plates in a plate rack. "Oh, hey. Uh . . . Callie, right?"

*Real smooth there, champ!*

"Yeah, that's right. And you're . . . ?" Callie started.

"Hey, Captain! Can we get out of here?" That was Jackson Bennett, a junior working on my crew.

I tried to hide my annoyance at the interruption. "Yeah, sure, Jack. Have you put everything away and made sure your area is all cleaned up? You know the drill."

"Yeah, it's all done," he replied with an eye roll.

"Cool. Yeah, go ahead." I turned back to Callie. "Sorry about that. So, how can I help you?"

"Well, *Captain*, this is my first time having to set the table for the next meal, and I'm not sure what I need to get. I was told to come back here and that *someone* would help me," she said playfully.

My nerves took over, and I just stood there, nodding and staring.

She cleared her throat, and raised her eyebrows, bringing me out of my daze.

*Jesus, man! Respond!*

"Oh, right. Uh . . . sorry about that. Yeah, sure, I can help you," I said as my brown face turned beet red.

*Get it together, man!*

She bit her lower lip and giggled, knowing the effect she was having on me. I took a deep breath, turned, and started gathering her dinner set: plates, silverware, napkins, and glasses.

"Thanks," she said.

"No problem. Here, I'll help you." I swallowed hard as I grabbed the stack of plates and glassware.

This wasn't my first time at the rodeo. I knew what I was doing. At this point in my scholastic career at this school, I could set a table for ten in my sleep.

She picked up the silverware and napkins. "Thank you, Captain."

I followed behind her, enjoying the view as we walked to her table, along with her scent. It was a subtle blend of a warm tropical breeze and teenage lust.

Okay, maybe the last part was just me.

It took us no time at all to set the table. She followed my lead as the afternoon dining room crew swept the floor.

She turned to me with her hands on her hips, smiling. "That wasn't too bad."

"Nah, not when you have help," I joked.

"So, *Captain*, what's next?"

"Well, uh . . . nothing, that's it. We're done."

"Oh, okay. Well, um . . . thanks."

She dropped her head and started to turn away.

*Idiot. Don't let her go.*

*I won't. Leave me alone.*

*Idiot.*

As I ignored my internal battle of wits, I managed to say, "Yeah. Sure. No problem."

"I guess I'll see you later," she said with a half-smile as she grabbed her things.

"Yeah . . . okay, um, I'll see you later."

*Talk to her, you pussy!*

But of course, I didn't. I just stood there and waved as she walked out of the dining room. I shook my head, went back to the kitchen to grab my stuff, and then headed to class.

I don't know why I was so tongue-tied. I've talked to plenty of girls at school. Hell, I speak to Gill all the time and never get tongue-tied.

I better man up soon, or someone else will, and I'll miss out on my *renaissance*.

# 7 - Walk Me to Class

After gathering my stuff from the kitchen, I left the dining hall and made my way to my next class.

As I exited the building, to my surprise, I found Callie sitting patiently on one of the benches near the entrance, soaking in the afternoon sunshine, as if she were waiting for someone.

It turned out that someone was . . . *me.*

"Hey, Captain. Care to walk me to class?"

*Yes, please!*

I guess she knew how to take the bull by the horns.

"Sure, I'd love to. Er, um, I mean . . . uh, sure. Where you headed?"

"Physics with Mr. Digman."

*Physics.* The way she said it was so . . . I don't know.

Sexy.

"Physics with Digman, huh? Cool. I took it last year. What are you learning?" I asked as we walked.

"Newton's law of attraction," she whispered flirtatiously and grinned.

*Gulp! Is it getting hot out here?*

"Oh," was all I could get out.

It was a perfect fall afternoon. The sun was shining, the sky was blue, the birds were chirping, and the squirrels were scampering from tree to tree as they gathered nuts and berries.

I kept stealing glances at her while we walked and talked. Well, she did most of the talking. It's not that she wouldn't let me get in a word; it's just that I liked the sound of her voice. That and the fact that I was tongue-tied.

There was something so unbelievably perfect about her. I don't know if it was her modest outfit of a light-blue blouse and navy-blue skirt that fell just below her knees. Or the way she held her dark hair away from her beautiful face with a black headband.

Or the way, her pillowy lips glistened in the afternoon sun as she gestured with her hands as she spoke.

"So, how do you like school so far?" I asked.

"It's okay, so far. It's nothing like my last school."

"Oh yeah? Where'd you go?"

"I went to an all-girls Catholic school in the city."

*All-girls Catholic school? Yikes!*

As if she'd read my mind, she added, "Yeah, we had to wear uniforms and everything."

"Why'd you change schools?"

The moment the words left my mouth, something about her demeanor changed. She went from this bright, smiling girl to a withering flower. It was bizarre, and I immediately felt terrible for having asked the question.

*Did she get kicked out or something?*

"Didn't mean to touch on a sore subject," I said with sincerity.

"Yeah . . . I mean, it's okay. Let's just say, my father, in his infinite wisdom, decided that I needed to get out of Manhattan and come here instead." Her tone had a bit of an edge to it.

*Yep, I hit a nerve. Note to self: don't mention it again.*

"Sorry," was all I could think to say.

"It's okay. It's not your fault. What about you? How long have you been going here?"

I shared with her my tenure at our school. I told her all about the decent teachers, the ones to watch out for, and the cool places to hang out on and off campus. I glanced down and noticed she was carrying a yellow-and-black striped script book that read *A Midsummer Night's Dream by William Shakespeare* on the cover.

*I guess she's into Shakespeare.*

"Well, here I am," she said as we stopped at her classroom door. "Thanks for walking me to class. I enjoyed talking to you. *Finally*." She emphasized the last word and grinned.

I just had to grin, too.

"Yeah, me, too," I said, a bit embarrassed.

"So, what are you doing after school?"

"Football practice. What about you?"

"Cross country, even though I hate running." She giggled, and it was such a magical sound.

*Man, I'd love to kiss those pillowy lips.*

"Okay, everyone. Grab your seats." That was Mr. Digman, the physics teacher.

Callie gave me a quick wave. "Gotta go."

I returned the wave. "Yeah, okay. See ya later."

"I'd like that," she said, causing me to step backward and trip over my feet, nearly falling on my ass in the hallway.

She giggled and waved again as I straightened myself out and shook my head before heading to my class down the hall.

She'd like that. Nice!

# 8 - What'd She Say?

The rest of the afternoon, including football practice, flew by. Matt had told me that Gill and Callie were partnered up on the cross-country team and that Gill would put in a good word for me. While I appreciated it, I was also a little worried. Gill's history to date for playing matchmaker had been disastrous.

Of course, that other girl was nothing compared to Callie. Frankly, all the other girls at school were nothing compared to Callie. Regardless, I was anxious to hear "the scoop" after practice.

Between running, passing, and tackling drills, I would look over at the cross-country team to see if I could spot Gill and Callie. Of course, every time I looked, they were nowhere to be found.

If it were the springtime, it'd be easy to spot them running around the track in their short-shorts and t-shirts, sweating up a storm. But this was cross-country season, which meant they went on long-distance runs around the local community, dressed in sweats from head to toe.

By the time practice was over, I was exhausted, but not so much that I didn't want to find out what, if anything, had been said. I quickly showered and changed. Gill usually waited for Matt after practice, so I knew she'd give me the skinny.

But was Gill waiting for Matt after practice today?

*Of course not.*

I damn near punched the wall.

"Dude, you have to let me know what she said," I told Matt as we left the gym.

"Relax, man. I will. I will."

"You better."

"Tell you what—I'll stay tonight for dinner and get the skinny from Gill. Then I'll call you when I get home. Cool?"

I gave him a high-five. "Yeah, cool. Thanks, bro."

Day students could stay for dinners at the school as long as they dressed appropriately.

Matt said, "Not a problem. I'll just borrow a jacket and tie from one of the guys."

"Yeah, okay, cool. Smell ya, later." I gave his shoulder a fist-bump and headed for my bus.

"Smell ya, later."

"Hey, don't forget to call me," I yelled back as I neared my bus.

"I won't," he said, rolling his eyes before disappearing into the distance, presumably to hunt down a jacket and tie.

# 9 - The Skinny

The hour-long bus ride home seemed like days. I just wanted to get home, wolf down dinner, and wait for the call.

*Gill better not have said anything stupid about me, like, "He's funny, but not that funny." Or, "He chews with his mouth open, and picks his teeth when he eats." Because that* had *happened, but only that one time. I had a friggin piece of meat stuck in my molars. What was I supposed to do?*

*Argh! Why does this stupid bus ride have to take so long? Why do we always have to go the same way home every night? I only live a few minutes away from school! I could walk home faster, for chrissakes!*

When I finally stormed into my home, I was *hangry*—equal parts hungry and angry—not the best combination for a teenage boy, or anyone on the receiving end, for that matter.

To my surprise, I found my father once again sleeping on the couch, with the television on and remnants of his dinner on the coffee table in front of him.

*Jesus, Dad. Again? I guess he had another hard day at work. Yeah, well, get in line. I'm starving!*

Dad had made his world-famous meatloaf with a side of mashed potatoes and fresh broccoli with homemade cheddar-cheese sauce.

It took me longer to make my plate than to eat the meal—I'd inhaled it. I spent the next hour sitting in my room, pretending to do homework, but I couldn't keep my eyes off my digital alarm clock, waiting for the phone to ring. The radio played softly in the background.

Time dragged by. I could almost hear the tumblers advance like loud bass drums as the minutes crawled away.

*Boom! Click . . . buzz . . . boom!*

I tossed my homework aside, turned the radio off, and put my television on, but even that couldn't distract me. I began pacing my room. Eventually, I got tired of looking at the four walls of my bedroom and ventured downstairs toward the kitchen, to place my dirty dishes in the dishwasher.

As I passed the family room, my dad was waking up.

"Oh, hey, buddy," he said, stretching and rubbing the sleep from his tired eyes.

*Man, Dad, you're really starting to show your age. Is that more gray hair?*

"What time did you make it home from school?" he asked between yawns.

"Got home around seven."

Every cell in my body wanted to blow him off and sit by the phone in the kitchen, to wait for Matt's call, but I stayed put.

"Wow, you had a longer day than I did."

"Yeah, I guess," I said, slowly inching my way toward the kitchen.

"Oh, hey, did you eat? I made—"

"Meatloaf," I finished for him, then gestured at the plate in my hand. "I just finished eating."

"Oh, yeah, right. Sorry, buddy. I guess I'm getting old," he said with a pinch of sadness. I guess he sensed that I wasn't up for talking, because he turned back to the television and added, "Well, don't let me keep you."

*Crap.*

"No, it's okay," I replied as he sat down on the couch. "How was work?"

"Let's just say, I had a long day."

"Sorry, Dad." And I really was. If anyone needed to catch a break in life, it was this guy.

"Meh . . . it's okay. Listen, Mom will be home soon. Why don't you go put your dishes away and make her a plate?"

"Yeah, okay," I said with a small grin, before heading to the kitchen, which was where I wanted to be.

"Thanks, buddy," he shouted after me.

After putting my dirty dishes away, I made up a plate for mom, covered it with aluminum foil, and placed it on the stove.

Then the phone rang. Finally. I guess God was waiting for me to act selflessly before answering my prayers.

"I've got it," I yelled to my dad as I grabbed the receiver. "Hello?"

"Hey, dude, what's going on?" It was Matt.

"Dude, what the *fuck*? What took you so long?" I whispered, practically hissing into the phone.

"Dude, calm down. I told you I'd call you. I just got home a few minutes ago."

"Yeah, okay, fine, whatever. So, what happened? What'd she say?"

"Well, you're not going to be happy."

My heart sank. *Great! Just fucking…great!*

"How come? What happened?" I asked.

"Well, apparently they didn't talk about you during practice."

"Oh." While that was disappointing, it wasn't the end of the world. *Wait for it . . .*

"But after practice, on their way back to their dorm, they *did* talk about you."

"*Oh?*" I squeaked out and then cleared my throat. "I mean, oh?"

"Ha, yeah. Gill said Callie brought it up, actually."

"Really? So, what did she say? What did *Gill* say?"

"Callie wanted to know if you were gay," he said.

"*What?*" I shouted.

"Everything okay in there, buddy?" my father called out from the family room.

"Yeah, Dad. Everything's fine." I then turned my attention back to the phone, where I could hear Matt howling in laughter.

*Yeah, yeah, ya got me. My mouth was open. Asshole.*

"Ha, ha, very funny, asshole. So, what did she *really* say?" I asked.

"Man, you're easy." He laughed some more. "Anyway, she wanted to know the usual stuff, like how well Gill knows you, where you live, and if you have a girlfriend."

*Yes!*

"Oh yeah? That's cool. So, what'd Gill say?" I replied, trying to sound nonchalant.

"'That's cool,' huh? Uh-huh. Anyway, she told her she's known you for a while and that you're a nice guy, blah blah. Oh, and that you didn't have a boyfriend . . . I mean, girlfriend!" He cracked up again.

I just rolled my eyes and said, "Cool. So, what else did she say?"

"Nothing. That's it. We all sat together for dinner, so I had to wait until afterward to get the scoop. Callie's pretty cool, actually. Maybe too cool for you."

"Yeah, yeah, whatever. So, what was she like at dinner?"

"Normal dude. It was school dinner, not different than lunch, only with ties and families."

"Okay, okay, fine. So, what should I do?"

"Well, Gill thinks you should ask her out before someone else does."

"Who else? Is someone hitting on her?"

"Yeah, dude. You know how this place is. The moment there's fresh meat around here, the wolves pounce."

Matt was right. New students stood out at this place like a sore thumb. And if they were hot like Callie, even more so.

"Shit. Yeah, all right. I'll figure it out," I said.

"Dude, what's to figure out? Just go up to her tomorrow and ask her out."

"Yeah, yeah . . . I know. I know. I will."

But that's the thing. I *didn't* know. I wasn't good at talking to girls or any of this dating stuff. I'd never really had a girlfriend. I wasn't like Matt, full of confidence. I remember the first time he saw Gill. We were standing at our lockers, and she was coming out of class. He had smacked me in the chest and said, "*Damn*. See ya."

And just like that, he walked away from me and right up to her, smiled, and turned on the Latino charm. She fell for it hook, line, and sinker, and they'd been together ever since.

Yeah, I wasn't like him. I wasn't suave and smooth.

I was just, well . . . *me*.

# 10 - Might As Well Jump

It took me forever to get dressed the following morning. I was nervous about going to school. I knew the minute I stepped foot on campus, Matt and Gill would be expecting me to ask Callie out.

I didn't want or need the added pressure. I was literally the last one off the bus that morning when we arrived at school. The moment I hopped off, I scanned the area for one of the three. Fortunately, I was in the clear. No one was waiting for me, so I walked straight to my locker, dropped off my stuff, and then went straight to the bathroom . . . to hide . . . I mean, to use the restroom.

Instead of stepping up to a urinal, I entered the farthest stall from the door. The handicapped one. I don't know why I was so nervous.

*I mean, what's the worst thing that can happen? I ask her out, and she says no. Or she* screams *no and then runs off with her arms flailing.*

*Or I ask her out, and she pulls out a grenade, pulls the pin, stuffs it into my pants, and I explode on the spot as she runs away, screaming. Of course, I'd be dead, so it's not like I would have to deal with the embarrassment. I can hear it now . . .*

*"What happened?"*

*"He asked out the new girl."*

*"What was he thinking?"*

*"I have no idea."*

*"What did she do?"*

*"She blew his ass up!"*

*"Damn! What a way to go."*

The first bell rang, reminding everyone we had five minutes to get to our first class, so I took a deep breath, flushed the toilet, even though I didn't do anything, checked my look in the mirror, and headed off to class.

Unfortunately, I had Gill in my first class, and the moment she saw me walk through the door, she smiled like the cat who ate the canary. She then gave me the head-nod, indicating the desk next to her was open like I was blind or something.

Internally, I rolled my eyes, but outwardly, I smiled back and slid into the seat next to her. Gill was the worst at keeping secrets. Talk about a weak poker face. She wore her emotions on her sleeves, and the moment I sat down, it started.

"So . . . what's up?" she asked, all sing-song.

Of course, both of us knew exactly what was up. Still, I just shrugged. "Not much. What's new with you?"

"Oh, 'not much,' huh? So, you have nothing *special* planned today?"

*Jesus, she's worse than a dog with a bone.*

"You know . . . the usual."

"Uh-huh. So, when are you going to ask her out?" she asked, throwing the skunk on the porch.

Allyson Fredricks turned around to face us. "Who are you asking out?"

"The new girl, Callie," Gill replied.

"Oh, wow. She's pretty," Allyson said, giving me the once-over.

"I know, right? But, I think they'll make a nice couple," Gill whispered.

Allyson shrugged at first but then nodded her approval.

I felt like a side of beef on display at the market.

*Um, ladies? I'm sitting right here!*

"Yeah, I guess. So, when are you going to ask her out?" Allyson asked as I felt other eyes looking our way.

"Yes, please, tell us all. When are you going to ask this lucky girl out?" Professor Michaels asked.

*Oh, Sweet-Jesus-on-a-stick! Seriously?*

"Uhhh" was all I could get out, which caused my classmates to snicker. I just turned red and slump down in my chair.

Professor Michaels coughed loudly and said, "Right, so, if we're done with managing your social life, let's have everyone turn to page fifty-seven in our textbooks."

I felt like I'd just died ever so little inside.

*Fuuuuuuuuuck Me!*

When class finally ended, I turned to Gill, who had been trying to catch my eye for the last forty-five minutes, and hissed, "I'm going to ask her out *later.*"

She just smiled and nodded, like a triumphant child who won first place at a talent show. I never realized my social life was so important to her. Maybe having me around as the third wheel all the time was starting to grate on her or something.

*Who knew?*

The rest of the morning went off without a hitch. It wasn't until lunchtime that it started to hit me. I knew I'd run into Callie, so that was when I started getting really nervous. The good news was, because of my work job, I could hide in the kitchen. The bad news was, she also knew where I'd be, and I sensed she'd be waiting for me after lunch.

It wasn't like I felt like the whole thing was a setup or anything. Like someone was playing a cruel joke on me. I liked Callie. There was something about her. I don't know. I definitely wanted to ask her out. It was just that I felt like everyone on campus knew about it, too, and my life was on display for the whole world to see.

Like I was living in a fishbowl, with people tapping on the glass and pointing at me

How does that Don Henley song, *Dirty Laundry*, go again? *"Kick 'em when they're up. Kick 'em when they're down."*

That's how it felt. Like people were waiting to kick me, regardless of Callie's answer.

During lunch, I popped my head out of the kitchen area and quickly scanned the dining room to see if she was there.

Sure enough, she was. Her back was to me, and she was chatting away with someone sitting next to her. Suddenly, she turned and looked right at me, as if she could feel me staring at her. I was caught red-handed. But I didn't care because at that moment…she smiled at me.

And it wasn't just any smile. It was a killer smile. Her head tilted slightly, as she bit down on the tip of her manicured thumbnail.

It was like her pheromones had shot straight across the room and encompassed my very being.

I felt my eyes open a bit and dilate.

*Holy shit.*

I smiled back, gave a quick wave, and ducked back into the kitchen to hide some more.

As lunch wrapped up and members of my crew asked to leave, I slipped on a rogue knife lying on the floor and fell flat on my ass in the silverware room.

*Fuck!*

"Oh my God, are you okay?" I heard someone trying to stifle a laugh as I composed myself.

I stood and turned.

It was her. She must have witnessed the whole thing from the window and rushed into the room to check on me. Our faces were inches from each other, and I instinctively pulled my head back.

*Yep, this is the guy who's about to ask you out, in all his glory. Sigh!*

She put a hand to her mouth, giggling. "Man, you just can't seem to catch a break, huh?"

"Yeah, you could say that." I grinned and brushed myself off.

"So, I heard you wanted to talk to me," she said, playfully punching me in the arm, with the side of her fist.

*Gill! I swear to God, I'm going to* kill *you!*

She tilted her head slightly, bit down on her manicured thumb, and raised an eyebrow. "So, what do you want to talk to me about?"

*Man, you're pretty.*

"I, uh..." was all I could get out before people started to come to the window for their silverware, plates, and cups.

*Jesus, I really can't catch a break, can I? You know what? Fuck it!*

"Here, let's go over there," I said, taking her by the arm. I walked her over to the far corner of the dining room, next to the coffeepots, which were full of hot coffee for faculty and seniors.

I turned to her and stared into her eyes. She returned my gaze, raising her perfectly shaped, thick, black eyebrows, her nostrils flaring slightly, in anticipation.

"I, uh, was wondering, you know, if, uh, you, uh, wanted to, um, you know, go out w..." I stammered.

"Yes," she replied quickly.

*Oh, thank God.*

"Really? Um, I mean, that's cool."

"You're so funny." She smiled and grabbed my hand, giving it an affectionate squeeze. "So, what are you doing after school?"

"I have football practice. What about you?" I asked, knowing she had cross country.

"Cross country."

"Want to hang out after?" I asked.

"Yeah, I'd like that."

"Cool. Can I walk you to class?"

"Sure, Captain."

"Cool. Let me go grab my stuff. I'll be right back, okay?"

She nodded, still smiling.

With that, I went back into the kitchen, dismissed everyone, grabbed my things, and met her at her table.

As I approached, she smiled again—something I was sure I'd never get enough of—and then she made a funny face, crossing her eyes and sticking out her tongue. It was equally cute and funny, which made me laugh, which made her laugh.

I smiled and stuck my tongue out at her, but I didn't cross my eyes since I don't know how. *I'm one of those.*

"Ready to go?" I asked as she stood.

She took my hand in hers. "Yep."

And just like that, we were officially *going out.*

# 11 - She Said Yes

"So, where you headed?" I asked as we walked, still holding hands.

"AP Bible English. What about you?"

"Um, AP Chemistry with Mr. Clayton," I replied.

*Man, she has soft hands.*

While PDAs—public displays of affection—were a big *no-no* at our school, you could hold hands. And there we were, doing just that. You'd think I'd feel self-conscious about walking around campus, holding hands with a girl. But, for some reason, this just felt . . . right.

If people were staring at us, I never noticed.

When we arrived at her classroom, she said, "So, I guess I'll see you later?" She bit her lower lip after she said it as if she were nervous.

*I'm glad I'm not the only one.*

"Yeah, definitely," I whispered.

Of course, neither of us moved. We stood there, staring into each other's eyes, smiling. The stunning blue of her eyes just drew me in, and I felt like I could stay like that forever.

Her eyes reminded me of a picture I had come across once, as I was thumbing through a copy of *National Geographic*, looking for an article. Her eyes were the same color as the Caribbean Ocean after a summer storm. They were bright blue, full of life, and electricity.

Simply put, they were stunning. She was stunning.

"Excuse me," someone said from behind me, bringing us out of our euphoria.

"Huh? Oh, yeah, sure. Hey, Karen." I stepped aside so Karen Whitaker could pass.

"Hey. Not a problem," she replied, smiling as she gave us a quick once-over before going on her way.

*Dirty laundry! Sigh!*

"I better get to class," I whispered to Callie.

"Okay. I'll see you later." She squeezed my hand and winked at me, shooting electricity through my body.

I watched her for a moment as she entered her classroom and found her seat, glancing over her shoulder to make sure I was still there. I was, and she smiled.

Then I headed down the hall to my class, where I met up with Matt. He'd saved me a seat at the back of the classroom. The moment I sat down, he nagged me for an update, clearly Gill's influence on him.

"Yo. So?" he said, the moment I sat down.

No preamble. No *"Hello, friend, good to see you. How are things?"*

I just rolled my eyes. "Can I at least get my notebook out?"

"No. So, what happened? Gill's been yapping about this all morning." He shook his head as if he couldn't take another moment of the discussion.

*Oh, I'm sorry.* You're *annoyed? How do you think* I *feel?*

"Everything went fine," I whispered.

"Nice. So, what happened?"

"Nothing. I asked her out after lunch, she said yes, and I walked her to class."

He leaned back and crossed his arms over his chest, smiling and nodding with approval, like a proud father.

*Jesus, you happy now?*

"Good. That's good. Glad to see I'm rubbing off on you," he teased.

"Yeah, like a rash," I replied with a snicker.

"So, are you two going to hang out after practice?"

"Yeah, probably."

"How're you going to get home? Won't you miss your bus?"

This was a valid question that I hadn't considered yet.

"Dude, I have no idea. I'll figure it out."

"Cool, dude," he said, as we fist-bumped.

I was still new at this whole boyfriend-girlfriend thing, and it never occurred to me to track Callie down after class and walk her to her dorm. It was a rookie mistake, as Matt called it when he asked me during practice.

Fortunately, Callie was waiting for me after practice, standing next to Gill outside our locker room.

"Hey," I said the minute I saw her.

"Hey, yourself, Captain."

"Captain? Did you make Captain, this year?" Gill chimed in.

I looked at her like she had three eyeballs. "Uh . . . no. It's an inside joke."

*Hey, check it out. Dating one day, and we already have an inside joke.*

"An inside joke, huh?"

"Yep," Callie replied, placing her hand in mine.

We smiled at each other and walked away, leaving Gill to wait for Matt, who was busy bullshitting in the locker room with one of our teammates. Matt had many good qualities, but thinking of others wasn't one of them.

"Sorry for not waiting for you after school," I said as we stepped outside the gym.

"That's okay. You're here now, and that's all that matters." She gave my hand a squeeze.

As we walked up the parkway toward her dorm, I kept glancing at her and smiling. I couldn't help it. She was so . . . Callie.

We talked about our respective days. It was like we were old friends or a couple that had been together for years. It felt so natural. She felt so natural. I'd known it from the first time I saw her.

"I'll be right back. I'm just going to drop my things off in my room." Callie said as we stepped into her dorm lobby.

Before walking away, she looked around quickly and softly kissed my cheek. It was unexpected. I didn't even have time to react. She kissed me, smiled, and went to the side door, presumably leading to her dorm room. I just stood there, grinning and holding my cheek.

Girls flowed in and out of the lobby while I waited for Callie. No one said a word to me. They just walked by, smiling, as if they were in on a joke. I guess news of my relationship status had made its way around campus.

*Jesus, that was fast. Friggin' dirty laundry.*

I thought about how I was getting home that night. I guess I had a pensive look on my face, because when she returned, she asked, "Is anything wrong?"

*Not anymore.*

Seeing Callie immediately took my mind off my worries. She looked prettier now than when she'd left. She'd changed out of her track sweats and put on a pretty blue-patterned dress, and brown penny loafers. Her wet hair up was in a ponytail, accentuating her swan-like neck, which I wanted to nibble. She also had put on a bit of makeup, using eyeliner to give her eyes that Egyptian cat-eyes look, a light shade of lipstick, and some perfume. She was the complete package. The real deal.

"Hello? Cat got your tongue?" she asked, bringing back to my senses.

"Hmm? Oh, sorry, right. Nothing. Nothing's wrong." I took her hand and led her outside.

"Are you sure?"

"Yeah, yeah. It's just that . . ." I started

"Just that *what*?"

I gave her a sheepish look. "I don't know how I'm getting home tonight."

"Oh, that's right. I forgot. You're a day student. I guess there aren't any subways you can hop on, like in Manhattan."

"Yeah, no. The closest train station near my house is the one at the end of that parkway." I pointed to the parkway leading toward Route 25A, which was perpendicular to my school. The train station was at the end of the parkway, on the other side of Route 25A.

"Well, I don't want to get you in trouble. The buses are still here. If yours is up there, I'm sure you can still catch it." Callie said.

"Are you kidding me? No way." I said, putting a smile on her face. "I'll figure it out."

"You mean, *we'll* figure it out."

"Right. *We'll* figure it out."

She thought for a moment, then asked, "Doesn't Matt have a car? Maybe he can give you a lift home?"

"Yeah, maybe," I said, looking around for Matt. "You know what? Let's not worry about it. I'll just call home, and ask my dad to pick me up."

"Are you sure?"

"Yeah. Plus, it's not like I don't have a car sitting there in my driveway," I said with an edge to my voice.

"Let me guess. Your parents won't let you drive your car to school."

"How'd you guess?"

"Because my father is controlling, too," she said, rolling her eyes, which caused me to recall the first time I saw her and her father.

"Ah. Well, my parents aren't really controlling. They just don't '*see the need*' for me to spend money on gas if I could ride the bus, even though I have a part-time job."

"Really? What do you do?"

"Wash dishes at a local diner. I've been doing it now for about two years." I wanted to move away from this subject. I was probably getting close to boring her to death. "So, what do you feel like doing?"

In response, she put a wicked smile on her face, causing me to gulp, which caused her to giggle.

"Uh . . ." was all I could get out.

She giggled and playfully slapped my arm. "Well, I've got about an hour before dinner. Want to take a walk? You can show me the local sights." Then she reached up and brushed some strands of hair away from my face.

*So sweet.* "Sure," I said.

# 12 - The Cook's Tour

We walked past the buses, down the parkway, and toward Route 25A. On the way, we chatted about everything and nothing, all at the same time. She told me about her classes, which ones she liked and which ones she didn't.

I enjoyed the sound of her voice. She had a unique accent. One I couldn't quite put a finger on. Unlike my Long Island accent, hers was . . . I don't know . . . *worldly*. It wasn't Southern or foreign. It was feminine and sophisticated, like she was well-traveled and had picked up accents along the way, all meshing into a sound that was unique to her.

I also liked the way she walked. She seemed to glide across campus, like a ballerina. She certainly could have been one. She was about five-seven, shapely in all the right places, yet couldn't weigh more than a hundred ten pounds. There was something fragile or delicate about her, even though she was well toned.

And I loved the way she smelled. Her scent was fresh and clean, not overwhelming or overpowering, like some perfumes. Some of the girls on campus practically bathed in their perfumes. You could smell them before they turned the corner. In some cases, it was like someone had punched you in the face.

*Pow!*

But that wasn't the case with Callie.

She smelled . . . elegant. She *was* elegant.

She was so different from the other girls who went to my school. I mean, it's not like there weren't other rich girls going to my school. We had plenty of them. And we also had girls from other countries sporting accents.

Maybe it was the way she carried herself. She had a confidence about her that I wasn't used to. It was like she held the secrets of the universe or something. Like she was vulnerable and invulnerable at the same time.

Hand in hand, we walked to the nearby plaza, stopping first in the deli, which reminded her of her local bodega in Manhattan.

The moment we walked in, I made a beeline for the coolers in the back of the store and spotted my favorite drink.

*Mmm . . . Snapple!*

"So, what strikes your fancy?" I asked, causing her to grin wickedly.

*What strikes your fancy? Is this the eighteen hundreds? You're an idiot.*

"Oh, they have Snapple. I love Snapple." She grabbed a raspberry iced tea flavor.

Which was my favorite flavor, too.

*Sweet! She's hot and has great taste.*

I snagged two bottles, and said, "Yeah, I love Snapple, too. Are you hungry? Want a candy bar or something?"

"No, just the Snapple. Thank you."

"No problem." I smacked the bottom of the bottle, grabbed a Snicker's Bar for later, and paid for our things. I checked my watch and noticed we still had about forty minutes to kill, so I continued our tour, hitting a few more shops.

I made sure to point out the local dry cleaner. I remembered Gill mentioning it once, so I figured it might be necessary for Callie as well.

At the end of the plaza was a local pub called the Park Bench. It was popular with the locals, as well as the college students and graduates from my school. It was *the place* to go on the weekends, if you were legal, or had a good fake ID, which I didn't.

"So, what's this place?" Callie asked as we walked past.

"This is 'the Bench,'" I informed her, as we looked through the large glass picture window overlooking the street.

"Is it a fun place?"

I shrugged. "It's supposed to be. I haven't been in."

"*Oh*? So, you don't have a fake ID or anything?" she asked with a gleam in her eyes.

"Uh, no, not really. I mean, I've been to clubs and stuff out in the Hamptons, but I never got proofed. I went with people who knew people, if you know what I mean."

"Oh yeah, I know what you mean," she said with a knowing smile. "If I didn't go out with my older sister, who knew *everyone*, I'd get proofed all the time."

*Older sister? There are more of you?*

We proceeded to exchange club stories. I told Callie about my adventures in the Hamptons over the recent summer with Matt, Gill, and Matt's hot older sister, Kate. Of course, I left out the *hot* part.

She was surprised to hear that Gill was able to spend time at Matt's place over the summer. "She doesn't seem like that type of girl, ya know?"

"She's not," I replied defensively. "I mean, it was cool. Matt's parents were there the whole time, and they didn't really allow them too much *alone time*, if you know what I mean."

"You mean like we're having now?" She waggled her perfect eyebrows at me.

"Uh . . . uh-huh," I stammered, causing her to giggle.

"So, you were saying?"

"Right, yeah, so, Gill crashed with Matt's sister, and I crashed with Matt."

"Sounds like it was a fun time."

"It was."

She shared her adventures of club-hopping in Greenwich Village. She made it sound so cool. There were biker bars, gay bars, punk bars. You name it, and it was available in the Village, she told me.

*Gay bars?*

"When I was with my older sister before she got married anyway, I'd get in everywhere. But when I was with my friends, we'd sometimes get turned away, even though we offered to pay the cover charge . . . and begged." She chuckled and winked at me.

"I can't believe someone would turn you away. They must have been crazy. I can't imagine anyone telling you no."

She popped an eyebrow. "It's been known to happen."

The last stop on our tour was the local pizzeria. It wasn't as good as the one near the triplex in Stony Brook, but, in a pinch, it worked just fine. It was better than Domino's or Pizza Hut.

"So that's it," I concluded with a smile. "If you need a slice, you now know where to go."

"Mmm, good to know. I *love* pizza."

"I'm with you, sister."

"Sister? You think of me as your sister? Eww."

"What? No! It's just an expression," I quickly replied. She elbowed me in the ribs, laughing.

*Oh, she was joking. I'm such a spaz.*

"You're so easy to tease," she said and then hugged me, which felt so good.

I checked my watch and noticed it was getting late, so we headed back to campus. Callie slipped her arm around my waist, and I put mine around her shoulder as we walked up the parkway. There was something so comfortable about her. She fit just right.

As we walked back to campus, she said she wanted to learn more about me. Where did I grow up? Did I have any brothers or sisters? Stuff like that.

"Nope, I don't have any brothers or sisters. I'm an only child and grew up here in Stony Brook."

"That must have been nice, growing up here," she said, with a bit of melancholy in her voice.

"It was. What about you? Do you just have the one older sister?"

"No, I also have an older brother. They're both married and have kids already."

"Wow, *that* must be nice."

"Yeah, it is. They both married young and had children right away, just the way my father wanted." Her tone changed on those last few words. And not in a good way.

*I think we struck a nerve.*

"Really?"

"Yeah. My brother married his—what do you call it here?—college sweetheart, right after they graduated college, and my sister married during her junior year of college. She didn't even finish." she said with a somber tone, like it made her sad. "She just married and got pregnant right away."

I nudged her playfully. "Is that what you're planning on doing? Getting married young and start having babies?"

She stopped and stared at me, her blue eyes penetrating my soul. "You're not asking me to marry you already, are you?"

*Uh . . . What?!*

"*What?* Uh, no. I, uh, was . . . just asking. In general. I mean, it's not that I wouldn't—"

She saved me from further humiliation by interrupting me. "Calm down, Captain. I was just teasing you. Wow, you really *are* easy." She giggled.

*Oh, thank God!*

"C'mon. Walk me back to my dorm before you have a heart attack."

We kept on walking, and she continued to share stories about her siblings, nieces, and nephews. You could tell, she adored her family. She became very animated when she talked about them.

"What about your parents?" I asked.

It was like a chill fell over the entire campus.

*Is it getting cold out here or is it just me?*

Callie's entire demeanor changed. One second, she was laughing and animated, talking about her beloved nieces and nephews. The next second, it was like someone threw a wet blanket on us.

"I don't really want to talk about *them* right now, okay?" she replied quietly.

*What the . . . What did I say?*

I didn't know what had just happened, so I simply said, "Um, yeah, sure."

As we quietly walked toward her dorm, I pulled her to one of the many benches located across campus.

"Callie, listen. I'm sorry if I said something wrong earlier. I didn't mean to bring up . . . anything."

"It's okay. Can we just talk about it another time?" she said, trying her best to smile but failing miserably.

*Way to go, putz! You had to bring up her parents. You couldn't just listen to her stories.*

# 13 - Our First Kiss

As we sat on the bench, I put my arm around her and held her close. We didn't say a word. She just slowly nuzzled her body into mine and took my free hand in hers, making small circles on the back of my hand, with her French-manicured thumb.

I felt so badly about upsetting her. I didn't know what to say or do to make it better. Where's Jiminy Cricket when you need him?

I know I was just getting to know her, but there was something different about Callie. Something . . . I don't know . . . familiar and comfortable, yet electric about her. I felt it the first time I saw her across campus. I felt it as we quietly sat on the bench.

She just felt so right.

"Hey, Captain?" she whispered.

"You know you can call me by my first name, right?"

"I know, but I like calling you *Captain*. Don't you like it?"

*Sweetheart, you would call me Shithead, and I wouldn't complain.*

"No, not at all. I mean, no . . . it's fine. I like it."

Hopefully, one day soon, I won't be so tongue-tied around her.

"Okay, good." She sighed and snuggled closer. "Thanks for showing me around."

"Sure."

"And for not, you know . . . pushing me," she said. "You're very sweet." She leaned in and kissed me softly on my cheek.

Feeling her lips against my cheek, ignited every nerve-ending in my body. "It's okay," I whispered. "I'm not that type of guy. You know, the kind who pushes."

She pulled back and stared up at me with her dazzling blues.

"Oh, really? What type of guy *are* you?" Her tone was flirtatious.

"I, uh . . ."

The way she looked up at me with her electric-blue eyes, shapely arched brows, and flirtatious smile damn near blew me off the bench.

"You, uh . . ."

And just like that, she leaned in closer, smiled, tilted her head slightly, and planted those pillowy lips onto mine.

Kissing her felt like I was caressing a velvet mitten or something. Her lips were full, rich, silky soft, and smooth, with a hint of Raspberry Snapple Iced Tea.

*I knew it was my favorite flavor for a reason.*

I held her in my arms and didn't want to let her go, there on the bench, under the cover of one of the mighty trees that covered our campus like a canopy. We were lost in our own little world, until . . .

*"Whoo-hoo! Nice Kiss!"* someone shouted from one of the windows of the boy's dorm, which overlooked the bench we sat on.

*Oh, fuuuuuck me!*

Embarrassed, we quickly uncoupled and went flush.

"Oh, my God," she said, quickly standing up, ready to bolt.

"F-you!" I shouted, flipping the finger to the small group of guys standing at the window and applauding.

Of course, this didn't deter our admirers. The catcalls continued as we quickly slunk away. I wrapped my arm protectively around her until we got to her door of her building. She gave me a hug and a kiss on the cheek.

"Thanks for tonight," she said as students walked by us, entering and exiting the dorm.

It suddenly felt like we were standing in the middle of Grand Central Station.

"Sure. Thank you for the, um . . . you know."

"Kiss?"

"Yeah, that."

"It was nice. I can't wait for the next one," she said, wiping my bottom lip with her thumb.

*Yes!*

I kissed her thumb and said, "Me, too. I'll see you tomorrow."

We hugged and parted ways, even though it was physically painful for me to do so. As I watched her walk into her dorm, my current situation hit me like a ton of bricks.

*How the hell am I going to get home?*

*Dad's gonna kill me.*

# 14 - Calling Home

The only free phone about available at this hour was in the kitchen-staff manager's office. I used it to call my dad, who answered after the third ring.

"Hello?" he answered, sounding tired.

"Hey, Dad, it's me. I, uh, missed the bus. Can you pick me up?"

After a sigh, he acquiesced and told me to wait for him in front of the auditorium, at the end of the parkway, referred to by many, as *the quad*.

As I left the office, I ran into Sharon, the kitchen staff manager, and second mother to many.

"Hey, Sharon, I hope you don't mind. I had to use your phone. I missed my bus and needed to call home for a ride." I said.

"Missed your bus, huh?" she asked with a smirk. "So, what's her name?"

*Damn, she's good.*

"Callie. How'd you know?"

"Oh, honey, you think you're the first day student to miss the bus and use my phone?" she said with a laugh. "You keep forgetting how many years I've worked here."

I just smiled and nodded.

"Well, here . . . take a piece of carrot cake with you before you leave," she said, handing me a napkin filled with homemade carrot cake.

*I guess she* has *done this before.*

I thanked her and left through the dining room, just as students started piling in, along with family members and faculty. Everyone was dressed appropriately, except for me. I stuck out like a sore thumb, dressed in my regular school clothes—no tie or blazer.

I ran into Gill at the front door. I had been hoping to run into Callie as well, but no such luck.

"So, how did it go tonight?" Gill asked with a subtle smile on her heart-shaped face.

"Good," I replied with a smile of my own.

"That's it? Just *good*?"

*Inquiring minds want to know, apparently.*

"Yeah. It was . . . I don't know . . . you know . . . *good*." That was all I wanted to say about it. Not because I was ashamed about our kiss or our conversation or that I'd upset her. I just wasn't the kiss-and-tell type of guy. Also, I respected Callie's privacy.

Gill just gave me a look of confusion.

I shrugged.

She sighed and said, "Okay, champ. Listen, I've got to go inside. I'll talk to you tomorrow."

"Later." I waved and started to walk away.

"Oh, hey!" she called out.

I turned. "What?"

"Do you have the phone number for the dorm?"

"What do you mean?" I asked.

She walked toward me while rolling her eyes and shaking her head.

"What do you mean?" she whispered to herself, as she approached me. "I mean, do you have the phone number for *the dorm*. You know, in case you wanted to *call her tonight*?" She emphasized the latter part like she was talking to a first-grader.

*Ohhhhhh . . .*

The lightbulb in my head flickered on. "No. I never thought to ask her for it."

"Okay, listen, I don't have time for this. Just give me a piece of paper and a pen," she said, snapping her fingers.

I took out a notebook and pen from my backpack and handed them to her. She opened the cover, and on the inside of the cover, she wrote in big letters the name of the dorm and the phone number.

"Here. Now, why don't you give her a call tonight, say around eight o'clock," she suggested, handing me back my things.

I nodded. "Okay, got it. Call her tonight at eight. I will."

She patted my arm and smiled. "Good boy. I've got to go."

"Thanks, Gill."

"Yep. She'll get you trained up soon enough." She giggled as she walked away.

*Trained? What am I, a dog?*

About fifteen minutes later, my dad's car drove up the parkway and met me in front of our auditorium. I had been sitting on the stairs as I waited for him, thinking about the evening and the kiss.

It really was a good kiss, regardless of the wolf whistles.

My father's headlights pulled me out of my Callie-trance.

"Hey, bub. Missed the bus, huh?" he asked as I got in.

"Yeah. Sorry, Dad," I replied, feeling the appropriate amount of guilt.

"It's no big deal. Heck, it gets me out of the house and off the couch. You hungry?" he asked.

*Seriously? Am I hungry? I'm always hungry. It's like I have a tapeworm or something.*

"Yeah, I could eat."

"Let's hit McDonald's."

*I got to make out with Callie and get McDonald's? All in one day? Does it get any better than this?*

# 15 - Grumman

As we drove to McDonald's, Dad fidgeted with the radio, which was unusual. He always had it on one of two AM channels, but now he was flipping through the popular FM channels.

"Dad, you okay?" I asked as we drove down Stony Brook Road toward Nesconset Highway.

"Hmm? Yeah, son, why?" he asked, as he finally settled on a station.

"You're, um, I don't know…"

"Yeah, son, I'm fine. I'm fine."

But I wasn't convinced. He seemed distracted, "off" somehow.

We turned right onto Nesconset Highway and made it to McDonald's a few minutes later, just as the latest Van Halen song played in the background.

*Sammy Hagar's not too bad. I never thought I'd like him as much as David Lee Roth. Go figure.*

Instead of hitting the drive-thru, we pulled in and parked. Dad and I ordered the same thing. A Big Mac, fries, Coke, and hot apple pie, which I fully expected to burn the roof of my mouth when I bit into it. As usual.

"So, how was school today?" Dad asked as we sat in a booth.

"It was okay." I opened the Styrofoam shell to my Big Mac and poured my fries into the opposite side of the shell.

He was doing the same thing. "Good, good," he said.

It was like watching a mirror. We were literally doing the same things, almost at the same time—opened our Big Macs, poured our fries, took a sip of soda, ripped open the ketchup packet, drenched our french fries, picked up a fry, and ate it. Then, we each took a bite of the Big Mac. Wash, rinse and repeat.

"How was work?" I asked.

The moment my question left my mouth, he began to squirm a bit in his seat. He furrowed his eyebrows as he chewed his Big Mac, like he wanted to tell me something but didn't know how.

"It was okay. And everything will *be* okay, so don't worry."

*What do you mean, everything will be okay and not to worry? What the hell does that mean?*

That's when reality reared its ugly head.

"We lost our program to Northrup," he said.

*Oh, no, no, no . . .*

"So, what does *that* mean, Dad?"

He sighed deeply and brushed his hair back, "It means, I lost my job today, champ."

The words just lingered there between us, silently taking up the space in the booth.

*Oh, fuck!*

A knot immediately formed in the pit of my stomach. It felt like someone had punched me in the gut. I was at a loss for words. A million thoughts raced through my mind. School, football, Callie. I thought about Mom and Dad— what will they do?

*What about our house? Does this mean we're going to have to move? Does Mom know? Am I going to have to drop out of school and go to public school? Do I need to get a full-time job?*

"Does Mom know?" was all I could choke out.

"Yeah, champ. She knows."

"Oh, Dad. I'm so sorry." I took his shaking hand.

Biting his lower lip, he seemed to be fighting back a tear. "Thanks, son."

We sat there for several minutes, silent, staring into space, looking for answers that wouldn't come. Finally, I struck up the nerve to ask the question I knew he had to be dreading.

"So, what are we going to do, Dad?"

"I don't know, son. I don't know." He sighed. "But things *will* work out. Trust me, okay?"

*How does he know things will work out? No, they won't. Things never work out. Not for us, they don't.*

"They offered me a good severance package, so between that, my retirement savings and your mom's salary, we should be okay for a few months. In the meantime, I'll start looking for a new job," he said and then cleared his throat, before taking a sip of soda.

"What about school?"

"What *about* school? Nothing's changed there, at least for now. We take things a step at a time, okay? So, don't worry. *Please.*"

But I did worry. I worried about everything.

Clearly, neither of us were going to finish our food, so Dad suggested we take it home and finish it there later. I just said, "Okay," and closed the Big Mac container, mixing the burger with my ketchup-laden fries.

We arrived home about fifteen minutes later. Neither of us had said a word in the car. I just stared out the window, pretending to listen to the radio. The moment he pulled into the driveway, I hopped out of the car, went inside, and walked straight up to my room.

My poor old man. As an adult, I think about that moment and feel a bit ashamed. I should have offered him a shoulder to cry on. Given him an ear so he could share his concerns. Provided him a measure of support.

Instead, I'd selfishly abandoned him in his time of need and went straight to my room, shutting the door and world behind me. I dropped my backpack on the floor, jumped onto my bed, and cried into my pillow, thinking only of myself.

I wasn't ready to take on the world just yet.

*I knew things were bad, but not this bad. And what about Mom? What was she going to do? Would she leave Dad? Would they get a divorce? Where would I live? God, this really sucks.*

# 16 - Did You Forget to Do Something?

The following morning was no better than the previous evening. Mom checked in on me when she got home from work, as usual, but I told her I wasn't ready to talk, so she left me alone.

On the bus ride to school that morning, all I could think about was Dad and our situation. I didn't even feel like getting off the bus and going to school, but knew I had to.

And, of course, the minute I walked into my first class, Gill hit me with, "Hey, did you forget to do something last night?"

I hadn't even reached my desk yet.

"What?"

"What do you mean, 'what'? You forgot to call Callie last night," she sniped, completely oblivious to my mood.

I stood there stunned. The last thing on my mind was calling Callie.

"Gill, not now, okay? Not now."

"What do you mean, 'not now'? She waited for your call."

"Look, I never said I was going to call her last night, okay? That was *your* idea, not *mine*. Something more important came up, okay?"

She pulled her chin back and placed her hands on her hips. "More important than calling Callie?"

*Man, she really isn't getting it, is she?*

"Yes, Gillian, more important than calling Callie. My dad *lost his job* yesterday, *okay? Happy now?*" I hissed, which caused her attitude to change in a split second.

"*Oh.* I'm...I didn't know. I'm *so* sorry."

"Professor Michaels, may I go to the restroom please?" I asked as I stormed out the door without waiting for a reply.

Once in the restroom, I punched one of the stall doors, causing a loud echo to reverberate throughout the bathroom. Fortunately, I was alone.

*Boom!*

"God!" I yelled.

I stood at the sink, staring down at my clenched fists, shaking my head. I felt tears coming, but I forced them back. Fortunately, a pair of eighth-graders came barreling into the restroom, bringing an end to my pity party.

I grabbed some toilet paper from one of the stalls, blew my nose, rinsed my face, and headed out. The two students were chatting away, laughing, never knowing what they'd interrupted.

I knew I should get back to class, but I just didn't feel up to it, so I found the nearest exit and walked to the deli. I needed time to think. Fortunately, my classroom didn't face the back of the building, or Professor Michaels would have busted me.

I spent the remainder of that period eating a sausage, egg, and cheese breakfast sandwich and drinking a regular coffee. And thinking.

*What am I going to do? What if we have to move? What if I have to go to a new school? What about Callie? We literally just started going out. This fucking sucks!*

As I wallowed in self-pity, I noticed the time and knew I had to get back to campus for my next class. I could get away with blowing off one class, but not two. I threw out my trash and ran back to school.

As I ran into the building and turned the corner, I damn-near slammed into Callie.

"*Oh my God!*" I said as I caught her in my arms.

"Hey, Captain. You're in a bit of a hurry. Are you okay?" she asked, not knowing how okay I wasn't.

I grimaced. "Sorry about that Callie. Yeah, no, I'm fine. I'm just running late for class." My emotions were all over the place. Fear for my family's situation, anxious about blowing off my first class, and guilt for not calling her last night.

"It's okay. Will I see you later?" she asked, looking up at me with those magnificent eyes.

The guilt-o-meter went further into the red zone. "Yeah, yeah, definitely," I said. "And, uh, sorry about not calling you last night. Something came up."

"Were you supposed to call me last night?" she asked with a knowing smile.

*Sigh. Thanks, Callie.*

"Well, maybe not *supposed to*, but I was going to."

"No problem. Is everything okay?" Her eyes searched my face for telltale answers. I knew my entire being was off-kilter, and I knew she could tell.

"No . . . not really," I finally admitted, downcast. "But I don't want to talk about it here, okay?"

She reached up and caressed my cheek. I just leaned into it, allowing myself to get lost in her warm caress.

"That's okay. Later. We'll talk about it later, okay?" she whispered.

I nodded and took in a deep breath. I then took her wrist and kissed the palm of her hand.

"Thanks, Callie."

"Hey, what are girlfriends for?" she whispered and smiled.

*She said "girlfriend."*

*Yes!*

# 17 - A New Plan

The rest of the day went off without a hitch. I didn't even get in trouble for blowing off class. Professor Michaels tracked me down at lunchtime and asked me what happened. I explained that I had an upset stomach.

"I think something is going around," he said with understanding.

"I'm feeling better now, though."

"Well, that's good. But if you're not feeling well, maybe you should go to the nurse and head home."

I shook my head. "No, no, I'm feeling better."

"Okay. You can get with Gillian for the homework assignment, yes?"

I said I would, and he patted me on the back before he walked away.

*Sigh. Homework.*

After lunch, Callie came into the kitchen—no more waiting for me in the dining room, it seemed. She entered my work area like she owned the place.

"Oh, hey," I said, surprised to see her.

"Hey, Captain. It's okay that I'm back here, right?"

"Yeah, no problem. Just be careful. The floor can be slippery. I wouldn't want you to fall and hurt yourself."

"And who's this?" Sharon asked as she approached us.

"Hey, Sharon. This is Calista Christos, my, *um* . . . girlfriend."

"Oh. *Oh!* Well, it's nice to meet you, young lady. I don't recall seeing you around. Is this your first year at our school?" Sharon asked as she shook Callie's hand.

"Yes, ma'am. It's nice to meet you, too. *This guy* has *many* nice things to say about you." Callie replied with a big smile that showed off her pearly whites.

"*Really?* Isn't that sweet? Well, why don't you two kids head to class? You don't want to be late." She affectionately patted my shoulder.

"Thanks, Sharon. Everything's pretty much done. We had to leave a few of the pots soaking in the—"

She stopped me with a wave of her hand. "Yes, yes, we'll figure it out. We've been doing this long before you got here and will be long after you graduate. Now, scoot."

So, we left.

"She's sweet," Callie said.

"Yeah, she's the best. I think I'll miss her the most when I leave here," I said as we stepped outside into the bright fall-afternoon sunshine.

"So, I had lunch with Gillian."

*Uh-oh. Here we go.*

"And?" I said quietly, not ready to have this conversation.

"And she told me what happened. I'm really sorry about your dad."

*Friggin' Gillian. You're worse than the* Enquirer.

"Thanks."

"Are you doing okay?"

"To be honest, I don't know. I mean, I guess so. I don't know."

She took my hand and held it, allowing me a moment to compose myself, pulling me to the side, out of the way of students walking by on their way to class.

Then she asked the burning question. "Do you think you'll have to leave school?"

"I have no idea. God, I hope not."

"Well, whatever happens, I'm here for you, okay?"

She hugged me, and I returned the hug, not wanting to let her go.

"Thanks, Callie."

"Hey, what are girlfriends for?" She gently pushed some strands of hair from my forehead.

"C'mon, I'll walk you to class. I have a free period," I said.

***

After dropping her off at class, I hit the library for some peace and quiet, grabbing the table near the librarian. That was when things took a left turn for me.

As I sat there, pretending to review my homework, Allyson Fredricks, the girl from Professor Michaels' class, entered the library. After circling the room for a few minutes, she finally asked the librarian for help.

"How can I help you, dear?" our elderly librarian asked with her crooked smile.

"I'm looking for *A Midsummer Night's Dream* by Shakespeare."

"Ah, let me guess. You're going to try out for the play?"

"Yes, how'd you know?"

"You're not the first student to come up here, looking for a copy, and I'll tell you what I told them. Please hunt down Mr. Doherty and have *him* give you a copy of the play."

"Oh, okay. Well, thanks. I will," Allyson said and left the library.

I overheard the whole conversation, which got me thinking about my situation, and what the headmaster had said a few weeks ago at the assembly.

*Get outside your comfort zone.*

*Try something new*

Stuff like that.

*Well, trying out for the play is indeed outside my comfort zone. That was probably the book Callie was carrying around. I guess she's trying out for the play. Who knew?*

*Hmm. I wonder . . . if I try out for the play and get a part, and Callie does, too, then that would mean we could spend more time together. I mean, rehearsals are after school, after all. Well, after practices. And because it's a school thing, I wouldn't get home too late. I mean, I'd be on campus, and they know we all have homework and stuff, right?*

*Plus, if I'm in the play, could my folks pull me out of school, right? I mean, they could, but they'd* have to *let me stay, even if it's until the play finishes, right? Plus, they'd probably let me start driving my car to school, since rehearsals got out after the buses left.*

*Of course, on the flipside, it also meant I'd have to wear makeup and tights and stuff. Mmm. I don't know. Plus, I'd have to memorize all those lines. And my memory sucks. I couldn't remember Psalm 23 for Bible class last year. How the hell am I going to learn lines from a play? And it's Shakespeare to boot, with all those thees and thous.*

*I can hear Matt now, "Hey, hotpants, want a ride?"*

*I don't know. I'll talk to Callie about it later. I wonder when tryouts are?*

# 18 - The Captain and the Queen

**"I** think that's a *great* idea!" Callie replied brightly when I told her my idea after school.

"You *really* think so?"

"*Yes-sah*! Fantastic. Tryouts are next week. C'mon—let's go get you a copy of the play." She grabbed my hand and immediately led me to the auditorium.

"Whoa, whoa, slow down. I need to ask my parents first."

She stopped and turned to look at me, disappointment evident in her expression.

"Oh. What do you think they're going to say?" she asked sheepishly.

"Honestly, I have no idea."

She perked up. "Well, why don't we get you a copy of the play, just in case?"

*I guess that's not a bad idea. I'll show them a copy of the play, show them I'm serious about it, maybe they'll say yes. What's the worst that could happen?*

I nodded. "Okay, let's go. But we better make it quick. We don't want to be late for practice," I said as we headed to the auditorium, where Aaron Doherty had his office.

I knocked on his door. "Hey, Aaron?"

"Hey, kiddo. How's it going? To what do I owe the pleasure?" he said affably, gesturing for us to enter his office.

So, how do I describe Aaron's inner sanctum? That's what it was, really—an inner sanctum. It wasn't an office. An office had a desk, chairs, a bookshelf, and maybe a poster or two at most.

Stepping into Aaron's office was like stepping onto a movie set. He had a director's chair with his name on the back. He had a mass of picture collages from previous years' performances. Kids my age, costumed and made up, their acting roles documented in black-and-white.

There were shelves and shelves full of plays and musicals. And speaking of musicals, he also had a record player with stacks of records gathering dust next to it, underneath it, and on shelves behind it.

He had Broadway play posters hung up all over his office, from King Lear to Glengarry Glen Ross.

This was the inner sanctum of an artist. A performer. A professional who loved his craft and, more importantly, enjoyed sharing it.

One of the many reasons everyone loved Aaron was because he could bring out the best in his performers. It was his department and his stage, but his performers were the stars, and he made them shine, ever since the early '70s. And this year would be no different. He had an eye for talent, even when people didn't know they had any.

Aaron was just shy of six-feet tall, about 180 pounds, with a bit of a paunch around his middle. He was in his late forties, with salt-and-pepper hair.  Unlike his contemporaries in other departments, Aaron usually wore a comfortable button-down Brooks Brothers shirt, a pair of khaki pants, and boat shoes. I never saw him in a blazer and necktie, except for on graduation night. And even then, they didn't stay on long.

His face was a bit weathered, suggesting that he'd lived a life before teaching, but it lit up when he smiled or, better yet, laughed. He had the greatest laugh. His voice was a rich baritone, and he carried himself in such a way that no one could deny the man belonged center stage. Yet, he shared the stage and his knowledge, which made him the consummate professional.

"So, I was thinking of, um . . ." I started.

"He's thinking of trying out for the play," Callie said, which caused Aaron's eyes to light up.

"Really? Wonderful. I was expecting someone else from the football team to try out, but he's gone radio silent on me," he said. "What part were you thinking about trying out for?"

*What part? I have no idea. I'm still not sure I can try out for the play, let alone which part I should try out for.*

"Um, I, uh, part?" I replied.

"Ah. You have no idea. Not a problem." He scratched his chin. "Hmmm. Let's see . . ."

He then stood and started circling me, sizing me up.

"Mm-hmm. Mm-hmm. Yep, you could play that role. Maybe even that one, too." He was talking more to himself as I stood there, feeling self-conscious.

Callie watched the entire process with amusement, holding a hand over her mouth, as if that could hide her smirk.

"Tell you what," he finally said, slapping his hands together. "I think you'd be perfect for Puck."

"Um, Puck?" I said. "As in, hockey? Is this play about hockey? I thought this was a Shakespeare play."

This made him laugh—actually, it was more like a roar, with his deep voice.

"*Ha!* That's fan*tastic!*" he said, laughing and starting to tear up. "I can't wait . . . to tell that one to Helen tonight!"

He then went to his desk, wiping his eyes—the laughter had died back to a chuckle now—and pulled open a creaky desk drawer. He shuffled through some folders, finally pulling out a copy of the play.

"Here you go. No, it's not . . . *ha* . . . a play about hockey." He then took a few minutes to explain exactly what the play was about.

He had my attention, as always. Just listening to him speak was such a pleasure. He became animated as he described the background, the various characters—from Theseus, the duke of Athens, to Hippolyta, the queen of the Amazons, who, incidentally, was also the mother of Wonder Woman from the comic books, although she wasn't in the play, but an interesting factoid, nonetheless. The play revolved around the marriage between Theseus and Hippolyta, and the various characters involved.

Puck, the part he wanted me to play, was a mischievous elf, which Shakespeare and Aaron described as a "shrewd and knavish sprite" and a "merry wanderer of the night."

"I *did* have someone else in mind for this role, but I think you'd be perfect for it," Aaron proclaimed with a wave of his arms, all flourish.

Callie clapped with excitement, "Yay!"

I just stood there, stunned, with the copy of the play in my hand.

Aaron turned his attention to Callie. "And what about you, young lady? Have you been reading Hippolyta, like I suggested?"

"Yes, sir." She saluted playfully.

"Oh, please, call me Aaron. Everyone does."

"Okay, Aaron. Yep, I have."

"Good! I'll see you both at tryouts."

*Okay, then. I guess I'm trying out for the school play. Now I have to tell my parents.*

"So, you're trying out for the queen, huh?" I asked as we left.

She cocked an eyebrow and grinned. "Yep."
*I guess that would make us the captain and the queen.*
*Cool.*

# 19 - The Other Shoe

After another grueling practice and a good-luck hug from Callie before I hopped on the bus, I finally arrived home. I shuffled past Mom's car in the driveway and entered the house through the garage, which was still open, which was unusual, but then again, everything at my home was strange lately.

As I entered the kitchen, I found a meal still warm on top of the stove. Utensils and three plates were next to it on the counter.

"Hey, I'm home," I announced as I walked through the dining room.

No one replied, which was odd. I heard the TV on in the family room, and after taking my jacket off and putting it on the back of a dining-room chair, like usual, I walked into the family room—to find my mother holding my father, rocking him in her arms.

I never really thought of my parents as a couple, you know? I mean, they were my parents. I knew they loved each other. They argued every now and again. Laughed a lot, too. But they weren't all *lovey-dovey.*

Yet, that night, I witnessed something I had never really noticed before. My mom lovingly taking care of my father. I could tell he was upset about something, probably his job situation.

But instead of just letting him wallow in self-pity or worse, she sat there on the couch with her arms wrapped around him. His head was on her shoulders. She soothingly rubbed his back and stroking his hair. Comforting him. Letting him know everything would be okay. Loving him, selflessly.

She was assuring him that he wasn't alone in this.

It was the first time I recalled witnessing this in my house. And it shocked me, for some reason. It was so, I don't know . . . intimate. It set me back on my heels. I literally jerked backward and tried to slink out of the room, before either of them could see me.

My mother must have felt my presence, because she looked up and saw me standing there, with my mouth hanging open.

I didn't know what to do. I felt like a deer caught in a pair of headlights.

I started to mouth, *I'm sorry*, but before I could form the words, my mother tapped my father on the back and whispered something into his ear.

"Uh, hi," I said as I walked into the family room, feeling uncomfortable.

"Hey, hijo. How was school?" Mom asked.

"It was good. Am I *interrupting* something?" I asked cautiously.

Dad sat up straighter on the couch and adjusted his shirt. "No, buddy. Mom and I were just, um . . . talking. No, we're fine. How was practice?"

"Oh, okay. It was good," I said, still feeling like a heel for interrupting.

"Good, buddy, good. Why don't you go wash up? We're going to have dinner together tonight . . . as a family," Dad said.

"Okay," and I retreated to my room.

My parents went back to talking, whispering back and forth, as I walked up the stairs. After washing up, I met them at the dinner table, where my mother had already set the table. Next came Dad's famous roast beef and gravy, garlic mashed potatoes, and a side of broccoli with cheddar-cheese sauce again. I loved his cheese sauce.

"Tell me 'when,' sweetheart." my mother said as she served me.

"The usual," I said. I stood, took my glass to the fridge, and poured myself some milk. When I sat back down, my parents looked at each other.

*Uh-oh. This doesn't look good.*

"So, son . . ." my father started.

"Yeah?"

"I told you what happened."

I nodded.

My mother jumped in with, "Well, we want you to know that we've paid your tuition through the end of December."

While this news settled my nerves a little, I was still waiting for the other shoe to drop.

"That's . . . *good*," I replied cautiously.

"And I'm hoping to have a new job by then," my father continued.

"Yeah, I hope you do, too."

My mother placed her hand on my father's wrist and smiled at him, showing her support. "We all do, sweetheart."

Dad coughed lightly into his fist. "Thanks, babe. Anyway, we just want to prepare you, that if I don't have a job by January, we may . . . *may* . . . need to pull you out of that school and send you to public school to finish out the year."

*And there it was.*

*The other shoe.*

*Fuck!*

The news hit me like a kick to the nads. I pushed my plate away and sat back in the chair. I felt small and very alone.

"Look, son, I know this isn't good news, and your mom and I are going to do everything we can to make sure that doesn't happen. But you're old enough to understand the reality of our situation, and we want you to be prepared," he said as my mother nodded in agreement.

"So, what does that mean for college? Am I going to have to go to Suffolk Community?" I asked.

Dad shook his head. "Son, we're not there yet. Again, I may have a new job by then. We just want you to be prepared, that's all. Now, tomorrow, I scheduled a meeting with the finance director at your school, to discuss options."

"Okay," I said, as my appetite dissipated further.

"So, you'll have to keep your grades up and stay out of trouble, okay? And look, in today's world, we aren't the first family to go through this. I'm sure your school will have options."

"Yeah, okay, Dad." I took in a deep breath. "Can I be excused? I not hungry."

"Yes, sweetheart," my mother said, wearing a concerned expression. They both were, actually.

I just stood and left the table, taking my glass of milk with me. The moment I reach my room, I turned my radio on and plopped into my desk chair.

*Shit! This totally sucks! So, I spend all these years going to this school, just to wind up graduating from public school? I mean, sure, if I did something stupid and got kicked out, that'd be one thing. But I didn't. This entirely isn't my fault. Should I even bother trying out for the play?*

I sat there and sulked for a solid half hour, listening to *WBAB* when I heard a gentle knock on my bedroom door.

"Yeah?"

My mom walked in with my dinner plate in her hands. She placed it on my desk and sat down on my bed. She patted the bed, indicating I should sit next to her.

I shuffled to the bed and sat.

"How're you doing, honey?" she asked, reading my mood like a dime store detective novel.

I just sighed, shook my head, and folded my arms, downcast.

"I know. You think this is the end of the world, but trust me, okay? Just like I told your father earlier, it's not."

I looked up at her like she was crazy.

"I know, I know. You think I'm crazy," she replied. "But things have a way of working out."

"Uh-huh."

"For every door that closes, another opens."

I just rolled my eyes, shook my head, and stared at the plate of food on my desk, as my mother's fortune-cookie logic played in my ears.

"Honey, it's true. I can't tell you how many patients I've treated over the years, who've received horrible news, only to find out that the news actually saved their lives."

"If you say so, Mom." I sighed.

"Look, even though we're not an overly religious family, I do have faith that things happen for a reason. Your father is a good man. Strike that—he's a *great* man. And he's smart, too. Not everyone has his abilities. It's Grumman's loss. And before we know it, someone's going to snatch him up."

"Yeah, I guess."

"So, you're reading Shakespeare this term, huh?" Mom asked, pointing to the book sitting on my desk.

"Huh? Oh yeah, that. No. it's the play we're doing this fall."

"*Really*? Are you thinking about trying out for the play?"

She actually sounded excited about it. Maybe this wouldn't be so bad, after all.

"Well, I *was*, but now, I don't know. Why?"

"Well, I think it's a *wonderful* idea." She clasped her hands together as she looked at me with proud eyes.

That brought a smile to my face.

"*Really*, Mom?"

"Yes. With your good looks and personality? Hijo, you belong on the stage. So, what brought all this on?"

"Uh, well . . . um . . ." I couldn't get the damn words out.

My mom gave me a funny look. "Yes?"

"Well, there's this girl." There. That was a start.

Mom was already grinning, nodding her head. "Oh. I bet she's pretty, huh?" She nudged me playfully.

*Pretty? Yeah, you could say that. In fact, she's gorgeous!*

"Yeah, Mom. She's *really* pretty."

"What's her name? What's she like?"

"Her name's Calista Christos, but we all call her Callie."

"Christos, huh? Is she Greek?"

"Yeah, she is."

"And you like her?"

"I like her *a lot*."

I spent the next few minutes telling my mom all about Callie. It felt good sharing this news with her.

"Well, she sounds nice. When do we get to meet her?" she asked.

*Insert the sound of a needle scratching across a record . . . Um, meet her?*

"Uh, um . . . well, she's a boarder, so it's not like she can come over during the week. And I work on the weekends, so . . ." I shrugged.

She patted my hand and stood. I looked up at her and saw that she was still smiling.

"Well, I'm sure you'll both figure something out. Still, I'd love to meet her. And, please, regarding school and your dad . . . things will work out, okay? I promise. Now, eat your dinner while it's still warm. I heated it up in the microwave. And finish your homework."

She kissed my forehead, tousled my hair, and left my room. The moment the door closed, my stomach grumbled, so I sat at my desk and started eating Dad's amazing meal.

As I sat and ate, the only thought that played over in my head was . . .

*She'd* love *to meet her.*

*Oh, man.*

# 20 - Dad, Meet Callie

The following morning started out just like any other, until I got to the kitchen to grab some breakfast before hopping on the bus.

Lying on my wallet and house keys was a handwritten note from my mom:

Sweetheart,

If you're serious about the play, then please start taking your car to school. This way you won't have to worry about missing the bus at night. Please remember to register your car with the school today. We'll figure everything else out.

Love,

Mom


*Whoa! Are you kidding me? No friggin' way! This is mint!*

It was like angels had come down from heaven. The clouds parted, and this mighty weight was lifted off my shoulders. So, instead of running out the door to catch the bus, I strutted around the kitchen, high-fiving myself.

*Who's the man? I'm the man!*

I grabbed my things and walked out the front door, taking in a deep breath, like a man without a care in the world. I tossed my backpack into the passenger seat of my car and then moved over to the driver's side, opened the door, and rolled down the window.

I then leaned against the driver's side door, waiting for my bus to pass my house, like it did every morning for the past four years. My bus stop was at the corner of my block.

But not today. Not anymore.

As the bus passed, I reached inside the window, honked my horn, and waved, catching the bus driver's attention. I pointed at my car, dangled my keys, and gave her a thumbs-up.

She returned my thumbs-up with a smile and knowing head-nod. Instead of waiting for me at the corner, she stopped at the stop sign, signaled left, and went on her merry way to pick up her next passenger: LeShawn Moore, a sophomore who lived a few blocks over.

I started up my car, turned the radio to WXRK, and listened to Howard, Robin, Fred, and Jackie (*FU, Jackie!*) tease Baba Booey about his teeth.

*Yep, Mom's right. This is* all *going to work out. Thanks, Mom.*

I pulled into the student parking lot, parked next to Emilio's car, and walked right into the Finance Office. Fifteen minutes later, my parking passing was proudly displayed on my interior windshield.

As I walked to class, I ran into Callie, who apparently noticed my strut.

"Hey, handsome. You look happy." She gave me a quick hug.

"Yeah, you could say that. Check it out." I took the keys out of my pocket and twirled them around my index finger.

"Does that mean what I think it means?" she asked with big eyes and a grin.

"Yup, I got my car full-time now."

*Or at least until after the play.*

"Whoa, dude, was that your car I saw in the parking lot this morning?" Matt asked as he and Gill walked up to meet us.

I puffed out my chest—just a little. "Yup! My folks said I could start taking it to school."

"Thanks to the play," Callie added.

"I'm sorry . . . *play*? *You're* going to try out for the *play*?" Matt asked. He burst out laughing.

*Here we go.*

Gill smacked his chest and chastised her beau. "Shut up, Matthew. I think that's a great idea. You should do it, too."

"Yeah, that's not gonna happen," he scoffed.

I twirled the keys a couple more times before placing them back into my pocket. "Whatever, dude. I've got my car. That's all I care about."

"Really? *That's* all you care about?" Callie asked as she raised her shapely right eyebrow.

"Uh, no. I mean, um . . . well, you know . . ."

She shook her head and reached for my hand. "C'mon, Captain. Let's get you to class before you get yourself in trouble."

*Phew. Got out of that one.*

***

Around noon, as I was walking to lunch, I noticed my father's car parked in the quadrangle. In all my excitement, our personal situation had completely slipped my mind.

*Shit, I forgot he was coming to school today. I wonder how his meeting is going. God, I hope they don't kick me out because we can't pay.*

Seeing his car put me in an immediate funk. It was like the black cloud of doom had suddenly formed over my head and threatened to downpour.

As I continued toward the dining hall, I heard a familiar voice calling my name.

It was my dad, waving at me, with an unusually large smile on his face. I flipped around and headed in his direction. We gave each other a quick hug, and he told me he'd just finished his meetings with the headmaster and the finance people.

Under his left arm was a stack of paperwork tucked inside a manila folder. Lots of forms to fill out and instructions to be read, I guessed.

He looked really sharp. He was clean-shaven and wearing a suit, as if he were heading to a business meeting. Actually, in this case, he *was*, and the business was *me*.

"So, how's your day going, champ?" he asked with an unusually happy smile on his face.

"It's going okay. So, um, how'd your meeting go?" I gestured with a head nod toward the manila folder.

"It went really well. I've got to tell you . . . this place is amazing. It really is." He took in a big breath, which caused his chest to puff out, like he was king of the mountain. I hadn't seen this look on him in a long, long time.

"They totally understood our situation. They said I wasn't the first family to go through this and, unfortunately, probably wouldn't be the last."

I nodded, waited for him to continue. I realized I was holding my breath, but I couldn't help it.

"They told me they had contingency plans for families like ours, and all we needed to do was fill out some paperwork. They'd take care of the rest. I told them we could pay through the end of the calendar year, but they said to fill out the paperwork first, and then we'll see what they could do creatively while I look for another job and get us back on our feet."

I let loose a long sigh of relief and grinned.

Dad smacked my chest with the manila folder. "I know, right? I was surprised, too."

I could feel the black cloud dissipating from over my head as rays of sunshine peeked through the canopy of trees.

"Wow, Dad, that really *is* great news."

"So, where you headed?"

"Oh, I've got my work job."

"Got it. Okay, well, I don't want you to be late. I've got to get home and start on this paperwork." He was almost too cheerful about it. Who was ever happy to fill out forms? He was clearly experiencing the same sense of relief that I was.

"Okay, I'll see you later. Oh, I'll probably be a little late tonight."

"Oh yeah, that's right. Mom said something about you trying out for the play. I think that's a great idea. I can't wait to see you on stage."

*A great idea? He can't wait to see me? Really? Who is this guy?*

"Really?" I said.

"Sure, son. Heck, it's your last year of high school. You should get out of your comfort zone, sprout your wings, and try new things while you still can."

*While I still can? What does that mean?*

My expression changed from one of happiness to one of panic at his last comment. Fortunately, he caught it.

"Oh, no. No, no. I wasn't talking about that. I didn't mean . . . I just meant . . ." He stopped and swept his fingers through his hair. "Look, all I'm saying is, I think it's a great idea. Before you know it, you'll be off to college and then entering the workforce. So, enjoy your teenage years while you still have them. *That's* what I meant."

My heartbeat immediately slowed. "*Ohhh.* Okay, gotcha."

We stood there grinning at each other as another familiar voice called out, "Hey, aren't you going to be late for your work job?"

"Hey. Yeah, I was just heading in."

Seconds later, Callie was beside me, wrapping her arm around mine.

"Hi, I'm Calista," she said, extending her hand to my father.

My dad took her hand and bowed slightly. "Well, hello, Calista. It's a pleasure to meet you."

"Yeah, Dad, this is Callie. I mean, Calista. She's my, uh . . ." I stammered.

"Callie's fine. And I'm his *girlfriend*," she said with a smile that could take your breath away.

It was like God himself was shining His grace on her and lighting up her face, with His angels singing in the background. I could tell her smile had affected my father as well, the way he took a step backward.

*Like father, like son, I suppose.*

"Well, it's very nice to meet you, young lady."

"Me, too. I can see where *Captain* gets his good looks from."

This caused my dad to blush, and now *he* was stammering, "Captain? Oh . . . well, yes . . . thank you. Well, uh, listen . . . we'll have to have you over soon."

*Have her over soon?*

"I'd like that so much." She squeezed my arm.

*She'd like that? Oh, no. What's happening?*

"Well, I've got to run. It was a pleasure meeting you . . . Callie, right?" my dad said.

"Right."

"Right. Have a great rest of the day, you two. And good luck with your play tryouts." He gave me a quick hug and kiss on the cheek before heading to his car—a man with a purpose.

*Go get 'em, Dad.*

# 21 - Pizza Margherita

"He's so sweet," Callie commented as we started walking toward the dining hall.

"Yeah, he's a great guy. Thanks, Callie."

"Thanks for what?"

"For . . ." I suddenly was at a loss for words. "Just thanks."

Actually, I wasn't at a loss for words. I just wasn't ready to say them all just yet. Not in this setting, on the way to lunch.

*What I want to tell her is, "Thanks for being so sweet to my dad. Thanks for being so sweet to me. Thanks for your hug this morning, and all the other ones you've given me since we've started going out.*

*"Thanks for the hint of perfume you're wearing, which is still lingering on my clothes from your hug this morning.*

*"Thanks for your smile, which seems to part the clouds every time you do it, causing the sun to shine a bit brighter.*

*"Thanks for the way your hair bounces and sways as you walk, and the way it seems to reflect all the colors of fall.*

*"Thanks for cheering me up and making me laugh. Thanks for the way your eyes and nose crinkle a bit when you smile.*

*"Most of all, thanks for caring about me, even though we hardly know each other.*

*"Thanks for being my girlfriend.*

The rest of the day went off without a hitch. I ate a quick lunch, ran my work-job crew, and went back to class. Football practice was, well, practice. We had our first game coming up Friday night, so we worked through drills and plays, and we'd continue to do so the remainder of the week.

We were still rough around the edges, but so was every team we'd face, even though, to listen to our coaches, you'd think we were headed to war and were the sorriest excuses for men.

*Ah, glory days!*

Play tryouts were that evening. After grabbing a quick shower in the locker room, I packed up and headed out, happy to find Callie waiting for me outside the locker room, also freshly showered, wearing her blue and white track sweats, with her damp hair in a ponytail.

"Hey, Captain. Ready for tryouts, tonight?" she asked as she hugged me.

"Yeah, I guess so. I'm as ready as I'm going to be." I tried to sound brave but knew I was failing miserably.

*So much for my acting career.*

"Look, Aaron knows you haven't had time to memorize your lines, so don't worry about it. You'll do fine, okay?" she said, trying to reassure me.

I forced a grin. "Yep."

"Well, good."

"Yep, good."

After a beat of silence, she said, "So, because of tryouts tonight, I don't have to go to dinner at the dining room."

"Really? So, what are you going to do about dinner?"

"I don't know. What are *we* going to do about dinner tonight?" she asked, with a sly smile and raised an eyebrow.

"Pizza?" I suggested, already knowing the answer.

"Perfect. Let me just drop my stuff off in my room and change first, okay?" she asked.

"Sure, absolutely."

*Good thing I got paid this weekend and have some extra cash on me.*

I waited in the dorm lounge area for about fifteen minutes while Callie got ready. The lounge was a comfortable, inviting place with plenty of couches and armchairs for people to hang out.

I removed the play from my backpack and began to review my lines for the tryout. It was Puck's monologue, from Act II, Scene 1. The one that started with:

*Thou speak'st aright;*
*I am that merry wanderer of the night.*
*I jest to Oberon and make him smile*
*When I a fat and bean-fed horse beguile,*
*Neighing in likeness of a filly foal.*

Needless to say, I was nervous. I had no idea what I was talking about. Fortunately, Callie knew Shakespeare and would explain it to me over dinner. Otherwise, I would have flubbed my way through the tryout and failed miserably.

"Ready?" she asked as she entered the lounge area.

*Hmmm? Whoa!*

When she said she was changing, I didn't realize she was *changing*. I thought she was going back to her room to throw on her school clothes. Instead, *Callie the vision* came out.

She had slipped into a pair of Guess jeans, a white tee, a multi-colored sweater vest, penny loafers, and a pageboy hat. She wore a bit of makeup, too—some eyeliner, giving her eyes that Egyptian look, and a light shade of red lipstick.

She looked like a model in a L'Oréal commercial or something, and it blew me away. She was totally worth it.

"Wow . . . uh, yeah. I'm ready." I couldn't pull my eyes away from her.

"You like?" she whispered as she hugged me.

"Uh huh." I felt a familiar sensation occurring in my pants while butterflies buzzed about in my stomach.

"Good. C'mon, let's go grab some pizza."

I snapped out of my reverie. "You bet. Do you want me to drive, or do you feel like walking?"

"Well, it's only 6:15, and tryouts start at 7:45, so we have plenty of time to eat and walk around if you want."

"Walk it is," I said, holding the door open for her, allowing her to exit the building and me to take in her perfect backside.

*Sweet!*

Like before, we walked down the parkway, crossed the bank parking lot, walked past the deli, and past the Bench. The Bench was open, but it was a weeknight and still early, so they didn't have many patrons yet. Their bouncers weren't even on duty at this time.

As we walked, I caught another whiff of her scent, and it turned me on—even more than I already was. As we turned the corner to head toward the pizzeria, I pulled her close to me, wrapping my arms around her, and stared intensely into her blue eyes.

*Man, she's pretty.*

She just looked up at me and smiled, apparently knowing what I wanted. She leaned in close and tilted her head slightly. Our lips met.

We were standing there in public, making a very public display of ourselves, and I didn't have a care in the world. Soon, her soft lips parted, and the tip of her tongue entered my mouth, playfully flicking my own. As she did this, she pressed herself into me, feeling the effect she was having on me.

At that moment, I wished I'd driven my car instead of walked. Then again, we may not have made it to dinner, let alone to tryouts.

"Mmm. We better eat while we still have the time," she said, pulling away.

"Okay." My voice was barely there, but my smile was wide.

She reached up and wiped my lips softly with her thumb, which I kissed. I then wrapped my arm around her waist, and we walked to the nearby pizzeria, grabbing an empty table near the front.

A waiter approached, and we placed our drink orders. I looked at Callie and asked, "Does pepperoni work for you?"

Instead of responding to me, she looked up at the waiter. "Do you have Pizza Margherita?"

*What the hell is Pizza Margherita?*

"Absolutely. The best in the state."

*Of course it is.*

Callie playfully batted her lashes at me. "Would you mind getting that instead?"

*How the hell can I say no to that face?*

"It doesn't have anchovies, does it?"

She just laughed, "No. No, anchovies."

"Okay, I guess we're getting the Pizza Margherita."

"You got it. I'll be right back with your Cokes." The waiter actually clicked his heels together before turning and walking away.

"I haven't had Pizza Margherita in forever," she said.

*I have no idea what we just ordered, but if it makes her this happy, I'll order it every night.*

"It's that good, huh?"

She closed her eyes for a moment. "Mm-hmm. When it's done right, it's perfect."

*You're perfect.*

"I had it for the first time in Verona, Italy, when I was younger."

"Wow, Verona, huh? That sounds nice."

"It's the home of Romeo and Juliet. Have you ever been?"

I almost laughed. My family was not the world-traveler type.

"Nope. I've never been out of the country."

Her doe eyes got even bigger. "Oh, wow, really?"

"Never even been on a plane."

"Wow, *never*? I don't think I've ever met anyone who's never been on a plane before. So where do you go on holiday?"

*On holiday?*

"You mean on *vacation*?" I asked.

"Yes, sorry, on vacation."

"Oh, well, we go camping mostly. We'll go upstate or to Pennsylvania. We've also been to DC, and down to the Blue Ridge Mountains one summer, too. That was a lot of fun. We went with another family, friends of my parents."

I proceeded to tell her about our adventures in the mountains, hiking, swinging from a rope, swimming in the coldest of streams, and fly-fishing. As I regaled her with my adventure stories, our drinks came, along with a mushroom-shaped metal pizza stand and utensils. I supposed there was something about Callie that said we would be needing utensils with the pizza.

Moments later, the Pizza Margherita arrived.

Like other NY-style pizzas, this was thin crust. It had a perfect layer of red marinara sauce, topped with large bubbling chunks of mozzarella cheese perfectly positioned across the top. Between the mozzarella and marinara were fresh basil leaves and sliced plum tomatoes.

As the waiter placed it on the table, my mouth became an ocean of saliva. Between the sight and smell of this pizza perfection, I could barely contain myself.

"Here you go. Do you need refills?" the waiter asked, as he cut into the pizza with the spatula, and served the first bubbling slice to Callie.

"Yes, please," she said.

"Yeah, same here," I replied, never taking my eyes off the pizza . . . or the spatula.

*Dude, hook me up already!*

Before taking our cups, he placed a slice on my plate as well, and I became one with the aroma, as I shut my eyes, and inhaled.

*Mmm . . .*

"Is this how you remember it?" I asked as she lifted her slice like an old pro, folding it in half, and taking her first bite.

I don't know what turned me on more, the pizza or watching her take a bite.

"Oh my God, yes. This is *so good*," she moaned. It was incredibly sexy.

*Gulp! Check, please!*

"Well, don't just sit there staring. Take a bite, already. Tell me what you think."

I took my first bite and couldn't help but moan as well. Usually, I was a pure pepperoni-pizza guy. Periodically, I'd venture out and add sausage or meatballs to it, but this was something different. This wasn't pizza. This was *pizza*.

The waiter came back with our refills, as we devoured our first slices.

"So, what'd you think? Best in the state, right?" he asked.

Our mouths full, we both just grinned and nodded, which made him smile with pride as he walked away.

Callie then gave me the history of Pizza Margherita. It originated in Italy and was named after the queen of Italy, back in the 1800s. The recipe was simple, and the colors represented the Italian flag: red, green and white.

I was impressed. Who knew this much about pizza? I thought it started in the New York. I mean, I knew it was Italian, but I thought it was New York Italian. Not *Italy* Italian.

That weekend, I introduced my parents to Pizza Margherita, and it remained a staple in my house ever since.

*Thank you for your excellent creation, your Majesty!*

# 22 - Tryouts

It was close to 7:15 by the time we finished our meal. We grabbed one more refill, and I paid the bill. We boxed up the remaining slices, which Callie gave to Aaron when we made it to tryouts. It never hurts to get on the good side of the director, I learned. And there was no better way to do it than with food.

As we sat in the auditorium, a clipboard was passed around with all the parts listed and empty spaces next to the parts. We were told to fill in our names, indicating which part we were trying out for. I noticed Aaron scanning the crowd, as if he were looking for someone specifically. Then a look of disappointment crossed his face. I guessed that whomever he was looking for hadn't shown up.

I briefly wondered who was missing but then lost interest as the reality of my being there began to hit me. I felt every ounce of moisture leave my body and got the worst case of cottonmouth when Aaron took the clipboard and started calling people up to the stage.

First up, Sarah Lockebridge, a junior, was trying out for the role of Titania, queen of the Fairies. Sarah was pretty, in an unassuming way with short, curly black hair, pale skin, and pouty lips. At five three, she would make a perfect fairy queen, I thought.

She delivered her monologue without her book, received a bit of instruction from Aaron, tried it again, and nailed it. That was pretty much how the rest of tryouts went. The student went on stage—some with scripts, some without—received some critique, and were thanked.

Aaron had informed us that he would not make any announcements as to who got what role, if any, until everyone had tried out, whether they were new to acting or not. Every now and again, someone surprised him, he said, so he asked for patience.

When he called Callie up to the stage, I got nervous for her. I squeezed her hand just before she stood. She handed me her hat, brushing back her hair, and made her way to center stage with the confidence and presence of a seasoned professional, not some arbitrary twelfth-grader. I wasn't the only one to notice, either.

Most of the students there were used to performing in our theater program. Rarely did someone new join the little cavalcade of gypsies. As she took center stage, people behind me started whispering.

"Who's that?"

"It's that *new* girl."

"Who does she think she is, *Meryl Streep*?"

I glanced back and cleared my throat, receiving blank stares for my troubles.

*Oh, go screw yourselves, and shut the fuck up.*

Callie was trying out for Hippolyta, queen of the Amazons.

"Whenever you're ready," Aaron said.

With a confident nod, Callie transformed on stage. It was a very subtle transformation, but it captivated everyone. Students literally stopped what they were doing and watched as Callie delivered her monologue, as Hamlet said, "trippingly on the tongue."

When she finished, she morphed back into the usual Callie. Her performance was nothing short of perfect, at least in my eyes. Admittedly, I didn't know all the ins and outs of acting, but this was crystal-clear brilliance. She stood there bright-eyed, bouncing slightly on the balls of her feet, waiting for her critique.

"Thank you, Callie. Nice job. Okay, who's next?" Aaron said.

*I'm sorry, but what do you mean, thank you, Callie, nice job, okay, who's next? How about—holy shit, that was the best performance of the evening so far. How about—you can have whatever role you want. How about—a star is born!*

Unlike me, who sat there with my mouth agape, Callie seemed to take it all in stride.

"Thank you," she said. She smiled and exited the stage, returning to her seat next to mine.

"So, what'd you think?" she whispered.

"Callie, you were *awesome*. You nailed it."

A few of the other students came up and started patting her on the back, telling her how good she was.

Again, she took it all in stride, never being prideful.

I was basking in her glory, so to speak, when I heard Aaron call my name. *Huh?*

I flushed with nervousness. I wasn't ready.

*Maybe this was all a mistake. C'mon, I'm not an actor. This is crazy. What was I thinking?*

I stood and received encouragement from Callie and the others who had gathered around their new queen.

"You'll do great," Callie whispered.

*Uh-huh. Why do I feel like throwing up?*

The space between the stage and my seat was approximately twenty feet, give or take. It felt like a mile. As I walked, I developed tunnel vision. Everything else around me collapsed, and all I could see was the center of the stage.

"Ready?" Aaron asked as I stood center stage.

"Uh-huh." So eloquent. In my right hand was the script. In my left was Callie's pageboy cap.

I'd forgotten to hand it back to her.

I quickly tucked the cap into the back of my pants, which earned me a few giggles from the audience. But I wasn't there for comedy. I thought I'd melt right into the floor.

"All right, settle down back there," Aaron shouted, and then he turned back to me. "Okay, whenever you're ready."

In other words, *any time now, spaz.*

I cleared my throat and said a quick prayer to whatever theater god would listen. I then looked over Aaron's shoulder and saw her. My personal muse. Sitting there, smiling at me. Encouraging me. Telling me everything would be okay, to relax and breathe.

Having her there felt like someone had gently placed me in a warm bath.

She gave me a thumbs-up and then blew me a kiss.

*Man, she's pretty.*

She then gave me the hand gesture to get rolling, and just like that, I looked down at my script book for a moment, looked back up, and delivered my lines from memory, as if I'd been doing it forever. Like it was no big deal.

It was nothing short of a miracle.

I nailed it.

# 23 - Reality Check

At the end of tryouts, as promised, Aaron handed out all the roles. I earned Puck, and Callie earned Hippolyta, which surprised no one. Only a moron wouldn't give her that role, and Aaron might be many things, but he wasn't a moron.

Then we got the rehearsal schedule. For the following two months, we'd be busy . . . *very* busy. We'd be rehearsing each Monday through Thursday night, and the closer we got to opening night, we'd rehearse on Friday, Saturday, and Sunday as well.

"So, get your rest. We can't afford to have any of you sick for opening night," he said, then he excused us, reminding us of practice the next evening. And to keep up with our studies, of course.

***

Surprisingly, Dad was waiting up for me when I got home.

"So, how'd you do? Did you get a part?"

I grinned. "Yeah, I did."

"Nice job, champ! I'm proud of you!" he said, giving me an enthusiastic high-five.

"Thanks, Dad."

"Hey, I came home and filled out all the paperwork. All I need you to do is deliver it to the financial office tomorrow morning when you get to school, okay?" He handed me the thick manila folder.

"Sure thing. As soon as I get to school, I'll turn it in."

"Good. Thanks, buddy. Did you eat?"

"Yeah. Callie and I grabbed some pizza before tryouts."

Dad grinned and popped an eyebrow. "Callie, huh? She's a real pretty one, son. Polite, too."

"Yeah, she's great." I felt like my cheeks were burning. Thankfully, he quickly moved on.

"Okay, well, I imagine you have some homework to do, so I won't keep you. I'm going to watch the news and turn in soon myself. I have a phone interview tomorrow with a recruiter. Wish me luck."

"That's awesome, Dad. Good luck."

"Thanks. We'll see."

I tucked the folder into my backpack, grabbed a tall glass of milk, and went to my room to do my homework. I got little sleep that night. Between Callie, the tryouts, the paperwork I had to deliver in the morning, and Dad's interview, my head was spinning.

It had been a great night, though. A *really* great night.

***

The subsequent weeks flew by. Between Callie, school, football, play rehearsals every night, plus washing dishes on the weekends, which sucked but I needed the cash, it felt like I was burning the candle at both ends. Before I knew it, mid-September became mid-October.

Throughout it all though, my one constant was Callie. She was great. My North Star. She kept me sane and focused in the right direction.

Some nights, I would bring a change of nicer clothes with me and eat in the dining room with the rest of the students, sitting with Callie at her table, which made Gill laugh and Matt jealous, for some reason.

The more I did it, the harder time he'd give me. It was like he couldn't be happy for me or something. It just didn't make any sense, but I ignored it. He was my best friend, and sometimes even your best friend can act like a jerk.

After dinners, Callie and I would gather our things and go to rehearsal. Sometimes, we'd take a quick detour and hop into my car to sneak in a little make-out session or two . . . or *three* before heading to rehearsal.

A few times, things got hot and heavy. We really steamed up the windows, if you know what I mean. We almost blew off rehearsal but decided against it.

I never expected us to get this close, this fast. I didn't even know it was possible. Of course, I didn't really have a point of reference. I guess it's what happens when you spend most of your waking hours with someone.

Yep, those weeks were, indeed, a happy haze. Of course, they weren't all full of wine and roses. We had our teenage moments as well. It was during this time when we had our first fight.

Whose fault was it?

Well, I'll give you a hint.

He stands about five feet, ten inches tall and is brown-skinned with brown eyes and curly black hair. He has two brown thumbs and looks just like this guy, your humble narrator!

Yep, it was totally my fault.

# 24 - Our First Fight

According to some, I'm a bit moody when I lose, and with our football team's record of 2-4, I was moody quite a bit. Okay, I admit it. I wasn't moody. I was a jerk.

"You need to get over it. So you lost. Big deal," Callie said after our latest loss.

"Cal, you just don't understand. You guys never lose. We lose all the friggin' time."

"That's not true. Sure, we have a winning cross-country team, and yes, some of us are going to State, but that doesn't mean I don't know what it's like to lose at something."

I just shook my head and sat there sulking on the bleachers overlooking our football field.

"Are you going to be like this all night? This is our first free night in a while," she said, clearly tired of my attitude.

"Like what?" I snarked back.

"*Seriously?*" Her eyebrows shot up and a look of exasperation crossed on her face.

I just turned my head and didn't reply. Okay, maybe my communication skills were a bit rusty. Maybe they didn't really exist. Who knows for sure? But I was a stubborn cuss.

Plus, this was my first relationship, and I clearly was still in the learning stages. The only other examples I had were my parents, who clearly loved and cared for each other. And Matt and Gill, who argued periodically, especially when Matt got all . . . *handsy*.

Neither my mother nor Gill ever got fed up and walked away, so I thought Callie would sit there and deal with me as well. I figured if I had a black cloud sitting over my head, she'd stay and endure it with me.

Yeah, I figured wrong.

She stood suddenly, slinging her purse over her shoulder. "Well, listen.

When you want to grow up and act like an adult, instead of pouting like a two-year-old, and actually *want* to spend time with your girlfriend, then come and find me."

*Wait . . . what?*

"I'm going to my room."

And off she went.

"Callie! *CALLIE!*"

But she just ignored me, throwing her hands up in the air, and kept walking, grumbling something in Greek to herself as she walked away. At least, I think it was Greek.

*Great! Just fucking great!*

Through my scowl, I watched her stride away with serious purpose. And she was dressed for fun, too. Since it was our first free night in a while, we decided we would go out after the game and have some fun.

I had a full tank of gas and a pocket full of cash. I was going to surprise her and take her to Adventureland, the amusement park in Farmingdale, because they stayed open later on Friday and Saturday nights.

I'd mentioned it briefly one night, and she told me she loved amusement parks—her favorite had been Rockaways' Playland in Queens—but that she'd never gone to Adventureland before.

Even though the weather was cooler now, I figured we could still walk around, hit some of the rides, eat some junk food, play some games, and then find someplace to park for a while.

Again, I figured wrong.

*You jerk!*

Instead of spending the evening with my girlfriend, who wanted nothing to do with me that night, I went home.

"Hey, you're home early. I thought you and Callie were going out tonight," my Dad said as I walked in the front door in full-on pout mode.

"Yeah. Me, too, but she got mad at me."

"What'd you do?"

"Nothing."

"Uh-huh. So, why's she mad?"

"Well . . . we lost again today."

"I know. I was there, remember?"

"Oh, right."

"So, why is she upset?"

"Apparently, I'm moody when I lose."

This comment caused him to swallow his lips, trying to prevent himself from smiling.

"You don't say?" he said, and a chuckle escaped.

*Oh, shut up!*

I shook my head and stuffed my hands in my pockets. "Yeah, yeah . . . I know, I know."

"So, what'd you do?"

"Nothing. I just sat there and sulked, which apparently pissed her off."

"Listen, son. No one likes to lose," he said. "And, yes, I understand you probably wish Callie felt the same way about it as you do, but she doesn't."

"Clearly." I rolled my eyes.

"Look. You didn't ask, but let me offer you a bit of advice I wish my old man had given me when I was your age."

I tried to imagine him as a seventeen-year-old, sitting down and talking to Grandpa. I couldn't quite get there.

"What's the advice?" I asked.

"If this girl is as important to you as I think she is . . . She *is* important to you, right?"

I bobbed my head.

"Okay, good. That's what I thought. So, don't let this thing between the two of you fester for too long, you know what I mean?"

I shrugged. "I assume you're working tomorrow, correct?"

"Yeah. I go in around two."

"Okay. Well, I suggest you nip it in the bud, track her down tomorrow morning and apologize. Apologize for your poor attitude and ask for her forgiveness."

"But . . ." I started, which earned me a raised hand, indicating me to stop and listen.

"No. No *buts*, champ. Say you're sorry, and do something nice, like bring her flowers or something. Do you know what her favorite flowers are?"

"No."

"Okay, well, you can never go wrong with roses. *Red* roses. It doesn't have to be a million of them. One should do the trick." He slapped me on the back and gave me a wink.

"You think so?" I was actually starting to feel a little better. Dad's advice gave me hope.

"Trust me. I know so. Where do you think you get your attitude from?" He was smirking as he crossed his arms in front of him.

I just smiled back.

"In college, there were some nights I thought your mother would kill me," he said.

"Oh, yeah?"

"Oh, yeah. Fortunately, I was a quick learner, and she forgave me. So will Callie. Just tell her you're sorry."

"I will."

"And next time . . ."

"What makes you think there'll be a next time?"

"Because I watched you guys play tonight." He let loose another hearty chuckle.

*Ha, ha, very funny.*

"Anyway, next time just talk to her. At the end of the day, that's all she really wants."

"How do you know?"

"Because that's what they all want, son. They want us to talk to them. Share our feelings with them. Let them in."

*Share my feelings, huh? I guess I can do that.*

# 25 - I'm Sorry

The next day, I got up earlier than usual. On Saturday's, unless I had chores to do, like mowing the lawn, I got to sleep in late. But, today, I had a different mission. Today, I was going on my apology tour.

After wolfing down a bowl of cereal, I went to a local florist up in Setauket.

The moment I walked in the door, I heard, "Hi, can I help you?" The lady hadn't even given me a chance to breathe, but there was no doubt, the customer service was Johnny-on-the-spot.

They probably didn't see a lot of teenagers come into their store, especially at nine in the morning.

"No, thanks. I'm just looking," I replied as I walked over to their cooler full of a rainbow of roses.

I had no idea there were so many colors and varieties. Talk about confusing. I decided to ask for help after all.

"Um, actually, I *could* use some help." I gave her a sheepish smile.

"Sure thing. What's the occasion?"

*The occasion of "being an ass to my girlfriend."*

"Um, well . . . I sort of . . ."

"Let me guess," she said with a knowing nod. "You're looking for something that says . . . you're *sorry*?"

Clearly, I wasn't the first person to walk in looking for an apology flower. I shuffled my feet and murmured, "Yes, ma'am," which earned me a chuckle.

"How much are you looking to spend?"

*How much? I have no idea.*

And my expression must have shown it because she jumped in with another save.

"Here, why don't you buy one of these? Nothing says, 'I'm sorry and I love you' like a single red rose."

*Whoa, whoa . . . slow down there, sister! I never said I loved her. I mean,*

*I like her. I like her a lot, but . . .*

Once again, she picked up on my panicked expression.

"Or . . . if you're not quite there yet, a simple pink rose will also do the trick."

*Phew! A pink rose it is!*

Ten minutes later, I was driving up the school parkway with a pink rose, baby's breath, and greens wrapped in pretty paper and a handwritten note, which simply read, "I'm sorry."

I parked my car in the quad, inhaled a deep breath, and took the long walk to Callie's dorm, hoping she'd be there and was in a forgiving mood.

Even though it was the weekend, because it was a boarding school, there was a bit of activity on campus. People were milling about, and some took notice of me making my way to the dorm carrying a flower, which embarrassed me a little. It's not that I was ashamed of giving Callie flowers. I was ashamed of the reason behind it.

As I walked up the steps to the front door, I noticed girls looking out their dorm-room windows, which faced the front of the building. Some were pointing excitedly, while a few others, once they saw me, left their room, presumably to find out who was getting flowers and, more importantly, why.

I ignored them, taking another deep breath, before entering the dorm. The bright morning light cascaded in behind me as I opened the door to the lounge, slightly blinding some of the girls sitting on the couches.

"Hey, is Callie around?" I asked the first girl I saw, Diana McNamara, a sophomore.

She eyeballed the floral arrangement, smirked, and said, "I'll go check."

As she left the room, I felt like an animal on display at the zoo. The entire room seemed to be staring at me. Some of the girls smiled, some giggled, and some whispered between themselves.

*Yeah, yeah, take it all in. Me in all my apologetic glory.*

Moments later, Diana returned and said, "She wants to know what you want."

*Seriously? C'mon, Callie, you're killing me.*

"Can you just tell her I need to talk to her, please?"

"Fine. I'll be right back," she said, rolling her eyes and shaking her head, causing more giggles around the lounge.

*Ha, ha. Laugh it up, fuzz balls. Laugh it up.*

Moments later, the door leading to the dorm rooms opened, and out stepped Callie, arms folded, with a stone-cold look on her face. And of course, she wasn't alone. The rest of the "Amazons," including Gill, came to back up their "mighty queen."

*Seriously? You brought backup?*

"What do you want?" she asked pointedly from across the room.

*Okay. I'm standing here on a Saturday morning with a flower in my hand, and you want to know what I want?*

*Seriously?*

"Um, can I, uh . . . talk to you?" I asked, gesturing her to come closer to me.

She huffed out, "Fine."

"We'll be right here," Gill said as Callie nodded and walked toward me.

I just shot her the stink eye.

*Et tu, Gill? I guess it's chicks before dicks, huh?*

"So, what do you want?" Callie asked, her chin lifted, arms folded defiantly.

To be honest, her defiance and body language turned me on a little. There was something sexy about the way she stood there, all *what do you want?*

"I just wanted to apologize for yesterday," I mumbled.

"I'm sorry, but I didn't hear you."

"I said, *ahem*, I, uh, wanted to *apologize* for being a *jerk* yesterday."

I then handed her the flower, which she accepted. She smelled the rose and smiled. It's funny the things you notice at moments like this one. Her expression immediately changed the moment she held the rose.

Then she read the note. I noticed that the pink color of the rose matched the pink in her cheeks.

"Do you mean this?" she asked, holding the card up.

"Yeah. I'm sorry, Callie. Really. I mean it." I tried to look as pathetic as possible. "Forgive me?"

She chewed on her pouty lower lip for a minute, leaving me hanging for what felt like hours.

Finally, she hugged me and said, "Yeah. I forgive you. Just don't do it again."

"Awwwww!" was the response from the crowd.

"Can we get out of here?" I whispered.

"Yeah, definitely. Wait here. I'll go grab my purse."

"Okay. I'll wait for you here."

A few of the girls followed her through the doors, giggling. Gill stayed behind.

She walked up and patted my shoulder. "So, you messed up, huh?"

"Yeah, you can say that."

"She was pretty upset last night."

"Yeah, I know. I was a jerk. It's just that we lost *again* yesterday, and it pissed me off."

"I hear you. Why do you think I left Matt alone last night? He's worse than you are."

I shrugged. It was true. He threw stuff around the locker room all the time. Definitely worse than me; still, we were a pair of hotheaded Latinos who needed to chill out. Knowing it and doing it, however, were two completely different things.

Gill said, "And he better watch his temper before it gets him in trouble."

"Yeah, I've told him that, too."

I looked up to see Callie coming through the door, a brown leather purse over her shoulder. She took my hand, as we left the building, leaving the gossipmongers behind us. I was just happy the "show" was over, and that Callie had forgiven me.

*Thanks for the advice, Dad.*

# 26 - Raking Leaves

The October weather seemed to change on a dime. One night, we went to bed at the end of another "Indian Summer" day and woke up the following morning to the chilly fall Long Island air.

It was like God had picked up His remote control and simply changed the channel. We went from the blues and greens of summer, to the burnt oranges, yellows and browns of fall in no time at all. You could smell it in the air, too, as leaves slowly transformed and fell to the ground, blanketing our campus.

This, of course, meant only one thing at our school.

It was time for the annual Raking of the Leaves! It was a decade's old, time-honored tradition, when the school's first set of students had gathered along with the faculty and staff to rake up the plethora of fallen leaves. Then, the leaves would be gathered up for a controlled burn. Every year, it was the same. And it actually was pretty fun.

Even though I was scheduled to work that night, I was granted the time off. I didn't want to miss my last *raking-of-the-leaves* event, especially since my girlfriend would be there, too, working alongside me.

*Girlfriend. That still sounds funny to me. I . . . have a girlfriend.*

Callie came dressed to work, but somehow managed to even make *that* look like a something from out of a magazine or catalog. She wore a white turtleneck under a gray school sweatshirt, an old pair of blue jeans, which accentuated her curves, and a pair of work boots.

Her hair was pulled back into a ponytail, which stuck out the back of a school baseball cap. A pair of work gloves completed the look. She was simply adorable.

For the next couple of hours, students and faculty alike hit the campus like a group of well-trained soldiers on a battlefield. As we raked, a pack of faculty kids or *fac-brats*, as we called them, ranging in ages seven to ten, would roam the campus, looking for large piles of leaves to attack and romp in, like a pack of wolves.

As the kids walked around, hitting the various piles, their parents would eventually chase them off. They were kids, and this large property was their playground. You really couldn't blame them.

When they came by our area, they spotted a large pile Matt, Callie, Gill, and I were just finishing. It was about six feet in diameter and about four feet high.

Who could resist it? Certainly not these kids. We heard them snickering behind a few trees, just yards away.

Before we knew it, the pack was stampeding our way, eyes focused on the colorful pile in front of them, giggling as they pounced on their prey.

*Boof!*

Leaves seemed to explode in all directions. After making their typical mess, they were chased off by the faculty members supervising our crew to look for their next victim, leaving us there to clean up the mess.

"*Greeeeeat!*" Matt said, shaking his head as we surveyed the mess.

Gill giggled at us. "Oh, it's not that bad."

"Yeah, it's not like it'll take us that long to fix it," Callie said. "Besides, it looked like fun."

Callie then dropped her rake, turned around, and fell backward into what was left of the pile.

*Boof!*

Another explosion of oranges, yellows, reds, and browns hit the air. Callie lay amongst the scattered leaves, giggling like one of the frac-brats.

"*Oh, Perfect!* That's just *perfect!*" Matt scoffed as he threw his hands in the air.

Not to be outdone, Gill followed Callie's lead, finding her own pile of leaves not too far away.

*Boof!*

While the girls laughed and started making leaf angels, Matt and I stood over them—me smiling, shaking my head, and laughing to myself, and grumpy Matt mumbling to himself.

*Lighten up, dude. They're just having fun!*

As Callie looked up at me with her beautiful smile, the world around us seemed to melt away. Suddenly, I was very turned on. All the colors mixed with her beauty and playfulness . . .

*What are you waiting for, idiot?*

I dropped my rake and leapt in next to her.

*Boof!*

I began tickling her sides, causing leaves to scatter around us. At that moment, though, we didn't care one bit about the mess. We were a pair of teenagers in love—*love?*—playing in the leaves.

"Ha, ha . . . stop! Ha, ha . . . *STOP!*" she squealed with delight.

When I finally did, I stared down at her, my heart about to burst with . . . *love?* She reached out and brushed leaves out of my wavy, dark hair, gently tossing them to the side.

I did the same for her.

And then I leaned in for the kiss, witnesses be damned.

Just as we were about to get our game on, Matt shouted, "Dude . . . *dude!* Mr. Ford's coming! Mr. Ford's..."

Mr. Ford was headed our way in his pickup, ready for us to fill the truck bed with leaves.

The rumbling sound of the diesel engine and Matt's warning immediately got our attention. Callie and I quickly parted and hopped out of the leaf pile.

"Okay, what the *heck* happened *here?*" Mr. Ford yelled as he stepped out of his truck.

"Uh, well, uh . . ." Matt started.

"*Uh, well, uh . . .*" Mr. Ford mimicked. "Save it, Salvatore. I saw what happened."

"Oh," was all Matt could say at that point.

"Yeah, *oh*. And you," he pointed at me, "*you* should know better."

*Why should I know better?*

"I mean I've come to expect *this* from Salvatore, but not from *you*." He bent over and picked up a mass of leaves, shaking his head in disgust.

"Sorry, Mr. Ford," I replied, my cheeks coloring.

Callie stepped up. "Yeah, sorry."

Gill said the same.

"Pfft." He waved a dismissive hand and started to walk away, but stopped and added, "Pick up your rakes and clean this up. I *was* coming over to tell you, you could go, but now . . ."

We all groaned, realizing we had nearly been finished for the day and could be joining others in the dining hall for fresh-baked cookies and warm spiced apple cider.

Mr. Ford then pointed at Matt. "And Salvatore?"

"Yeah?"

"Based on your performance this week on the football field, it's no wonder this is taking you forever."

"*Hey!*" Matt said, spinning to face Mr. Ford.

As he spun, his face was met with the pile of leaves, courtesy of Mr. Ford. *Boof!*

We all just stood there, stunned, wanting to laugh, yet understanding that we probably shouldn't.

"*That's* how you toss something!" he shouted at Matt before bursting out in laughter.

*Oh . . . he was kidding! Leaf War!*

Suddenly, piles of leaves flew back and forth. We chased each other around like a pack of wildlings. The war lasted a solid five minutes until Mr. Ford finally threw up his hand.

"Okay! Ha, ha . . . okay . . ." he managed to say between heavy breathing. "Okay, let's rake up this mess and grab some cookies and cider."

Callie and I shared a look. She was beaming. I was beaming.

*It doesn't get any better than this!*

# 27 - Baklava and Baseball

Weeks passed since the leaf war, but the battle continued. What battle? The battle for the pennant, of course!

From the middle of October to the last week of the month, a fever swept throughout Long Island and the entire tri-state area.

*Mets Fever!*

The New York Mets, perennial underdogs of New York baseball, made it through the playoffs and into the World Series against New York's arch nemesis, the Boston Red Sox.

The Red Sox had the series lead going into game six. All they had to do was win the game, and they'd take home the trophy, and end "the curse of the Bambino." Even though they were playing in New York, Boston had the momentum, having beaten the Mets two days prior, 4-2.

I took Saturday night off from work so I could watch the game at home with my folks and Callie, whom I'd invited over. And she'd accepted!

I was just about to leave to pick up Callie when Mom pulled in the driveway.

"She's not here, yet is she?" Mom asked, seeming nervous.

"No, I'm just leaving to go pick her up. Why?"

"Oh, okay, good. So, I have time to shower up, and make myself presentable then."

She kissed me before heading inside as I just rolled my eyes and left to pick up Callie at school.

Callie was waiting for me outside her dorm building. Even though she was a Yankees fan, she knew that I was a lifelong Mets fan, so she had gone to the local mall with some girlfriends and bought herself some gear—a blue vintage Mets t-shirt over a white turtleneck, blue jeans, brown boots, and a Mets cap.

And she was a nervous wreck.

Just like my mom, she was anxious about their first meeting.

Mom was Dad's problem. I had to deal with Callie.

"Do I look okay?" she asked.

I held the door open for her. "Yeah, babe, you look great."

"Should I bring something? I should bring something, right? We should stop so I can pick something up."

"*What*? No. Seriously, my dad's putting out a spread. We don't need to stop for anything."

She was biting her thumbnail now as she slid into the passenger seat. "But what about your mother? I should bring her something, shouldn't I?"

I got behind the wheel and twisted around to look at her. "Would it make you feel better if we stopped at the supermarket to get something?"

This put a smile on her face, and the nail-biting stopped. "Yes, it really would. You don't mind, do you?"

"No, not at all." I couldn't help but chuckle.

She smacked my shoulder. "It's not funny. This is important. I'm meeting your mother for the first time. This is a big deal."

"Okay, okay, I'm sorry, don't hit me. I'll stop. I'll stop."

I got a kiss on the cheek for that one.

The game didn't start until the evening, giving us plenty of time to stop off at Waldbaum's, the local supermarket, for something.

"What should I get? What do your parents like?" Callie asked as we walked into the store.

"I don't know, babe. Anything."

"That's not helping. How about dessert?"

"That sounds great. Let's pick up some dessert." I started walking toward the frozen-food aisle, but she jerked me in the other direction.

"I'm thinking more of a cake or something."

*But I want ice cream.*

"I guess that'll work."

We perused the bakery selections . . . all of them. Cakes, pies, muffins, donuts. Nothing struck her fancy.

This went on for a solid ten minutes, which felt like hours.

Finally, she asked, "Do you know of any bakeries in the area?"

"Only one, and it's in Smithtown."

"How are is that from here?"

"About ten minutes away, in the *wrong* direction. Why?"

She looked at her watch and bit her lower lip.

*Man, I'd like to bite that lip.*

"Would you mind if we went there?" she asked sheepishly.

"Callie, c'mon. Let's just pick up some ice cream."

"Please? For me?" She nuzzled her face against my neck, throwing in a few kisses. My personal Kryptonite.

"Okay, fine, fine. You win. Let's go," I said.

She cheered, "Yay! Thank you. I'll make it up to you. I promise."

"Yeah, yeah, promises, promises."

Ten minutes later, we entered the local bakery in Smithtown to search for the *perfect dessert*. For a Saturday night, it was busier than I'd thought it would be. I grabbed a spot in line, while Callie searched each display case for that elusive ideal dessert.

Then I heard it. The sound of success.

*"Yes!* They have baklava!" Callie shouted as she stood in front of a display case that housed the sweet Greek dessert.

*Ladies and gentlemen, we have a winner!*

Two cookie samples and twenty-five minutes later, we were pulling into my driveway.

"Okay, we're here. Ready?"

She adjusted my rearview mirror and started fidgeting with her hair and clothes.

"Um, yeah, I guess so. How do I look?"

*Oh my God, not this again.*

"Callie, you look fine. Seriously. C'mon, let's go inside. I don't want to miss the first pitch."

"I look just *'fine'*?"

*Oh, dear Lord.*

"No, no, you look great. Seriously, you couldn't look any better. Let's go inside, okay?"

She took another moment—to my immeasurable frustration—to stare at her reflection in the mirror. She removed her cap, brushed her hair back and forth with her hand, and then put her cap back on.

She grabbed some lipstick from her purse, applying a thin layer of red color to her full lips. She then practiced her smile, in the mirror and then at me.

I rolled my eyes and burst out laughing.

"Shut up. This is important. I have to make a good first impression."

I'd had enough. I was getting hungry and wanted to watch the game. I had to get this girl out of the car and inside the house before Sunday morning came.

"Callie? She's going to love you, 'kay?" I said softly.

"Really?"

"Really."

"Okay. Let's go inside."

*Oh, thank you, God!*

*Let's go, Mets!*

# 28 - Dinner Guests

The meeting between Mom and Callie went off, as I knew it would, without a hitch. Dad was happy for the baklava, and I was damn happy to see what he'd prepared for our meal. The whole house was filled with the heady aroma of slow-cooked, herb-crusted roast beef with homemade gravy.

He was my hero.

I high-fived my dad, who was putting the finishing touches on the food—or whatever wizardry he did in the kitchen—and grabbed two glasses of Coke for Callie and me.

I walked into the family room to find my mother and Callie sitting face to face on the couch, laughing as they chatted. The moment, I stepped in, they turned and looked at me and then started laughing.

"Oh my God, you're right. I can't believe I never noticed it before," Callie said, a hand over her mouth.

"See? I told you," Mom said as Callie nodded.

"Told you what? What's so funny?"

"It's nothing. It's nothing." Callie stood and walked over to me.

"Uh-huh." I handed her the glass of Coke. "I bet."

"Your mom is so funny . . . and sweet, too," she whispered as she took her glass.

I eyeballed my mom and raised an eyebrow. "Yeah, I bet."

My mother sat there with her hands in her lap, all innocence, except for the sly grin that gave her away.

*Mm-hmm.*

"Oh, stop. She is. C'mon, let's sit down," Callie said, taking my hand and guiding me to the couch.

"Oh, Dad said to tell you ten minutes till dinner."

Mom said, "Okay. Good. I'm starving. Listen, I'm going to go set the table."

"Would you like us to help you?" Callie asked.

"Oh, no, sweetheart. It's okay." Mom waved her hand in the air as she walked to the kitchen.

"So, what was so funny?" I asked.

"It was nothing. Your mother is very sweet."

"I told you things would be okay."

We put our drinks on the coffee table and snuggled up closer together. She had her head on my chest, her feet tucked under her bottom. I was stretched out across the couch. When I gently rubbed Callie's back, I could feel her body relax and noticed that her breathing pattern had slowed.

I half expected her to start purring. She reciprocated by slowly rubbing my chest with her manicured fingernails. We were in heaven.

"This feels nice," she whispered, as I made believe I was watching TV.

"*You* feel nice."

She kissed and patted my chest as I lay there smiling, taking in the pheromones. Had Mom not come in moments later, Callie and I might have fallen asleep right there on the couch, we were so comfortable.

"Dinner's ready," Mom announced as she walked back into the room. Just then, the phone rang.

We reluctantly parted ourselves from one another and headed to the dinner table. Dad was holding out the phone to me. "It's Matt."

I grabbed the phone. "Hey, dude, what's going on?"

"Not much. Are you watching the game?"

"Does a bear shit in the woods?"

"Want to watch it over here?"

"Nah, Dad made dinner, and Callie's over." I smiled at Callie who was settling into her chair at the table. She gave me a cute finger-wave.

"*Ohhh*, your *dad* made dinner, huh?" Matt said.

I could hear him salivating over the phone. Matt knew all about my father's skills in the kitchen.

I couldn't leave the poor guy hanging. "Would you like to come over?"

"Well, I wouldn't want to put you guys out or anything."

"Is it okay if Matt comes over to eat?" I asked my parents.

Dad gave me a thumbs-up. "Sure, champ. We have plenty." Mom nodded, and Callie was still smiling, so we were good.

"I heard him. Cool, Gill and I will be right over."

*Um, I never said anything about Gill.*

"Yeah, okay. See you soon. We're not waiting for you, though." I hung up and announced, "He's coming over, and he's bringing Gill. Meanwhile, let's eat!"

Halfway into our meal, I saw headlights pull into our driveway, announcing Matt and Gill's arrival. Callie and I excused ourselves from the table and waited for them by the front door.

I opened the door. Matt and Gill were walking up to the front porch, and they weren't alone. Walking behind them were Matt's hot sister, Kate, followed by some guy I did not know, who was carrying a case of Budweiser on his shoulder, like a boom-box radio.

*I guess we're having a party. Damn, I was hoping for some leftovers.*

# 29 - Let's Go, Mets

Matt slapped me on the back. "Hey, bro, thanks for the invite. We're starving."

*What the fuck, dude? First you, then you add Gill, and now hot Kate, and . . . who's this guy with the beer?*

"Yeah, sure, not a problem. Hey, guys."

We did the introduction routine, and I learned that Beer Guy was named Spencer—"Spence" to his friends.

"Hey, nice to meet you guys. Where do you want me to put this?" Spence asked, gesturing to the case of beer.

"Uh, follow me to the garage. We have a fridge out there."

"Before you ask, he's *just* a friend," Hot Kate added as she walked by.

Dad and Mom were standing in the doorway of the dining room, smiling and greeting everyone as they piled into the house. More introductions. My parents assured them they were all welcome to partake in the feast in the kitchen.

"Excellent. We're starving." Matt said.

Soon, everyone was seated at the table, and digging into this amazing meal Dad prepared.

"Anyone else want a beer?" Spence asked as he pushed away from the table.

Matt, Kate, and even my dad asked for one.

Dinner wrapped up just as the game was starting. Callie, Kate, and Gill insisted that my parents relaxed while the six of us cleaned up.

*So much for me having tonight off.*

Ten minutes later, I was yanking a full trash bag from the garbage can.

"I'm gonna take this out. Back in a minute."

"I'll come with you," Callie said.

She followed me through the laundry room, out to the garage, and out the side door leading to the metal garbage cans on the side of the house. After tossing the bag into the can and replacing the lid, Callie attacked.

She spun me around and pushed me up against the side of my house.

*Thud!*

*Ow, my head!*

She placed both arms on either side of me and leaned in, smiling and raising her eyebrow. I was trapped, not that I was complaining, aside from my head hurting a bit. She then bit her lower lip and gave me a quick hungry-looking once-over.

*Dessert time!*

I pulled her in and kissed her, savoring the taste of her lips, tongue, and a little leftover gravy.

Heaven.

Things were just starting to get hot, when Gill called out to us.

"Hey, you two. Did you get lost?"

I sighed loudly, and Callie giggled.

"Damn, I was having fun, too," she whispered in my ear.

"Yeah, me, too."

"I noticed," she said, doing that arched-eyebrow thing again.

*Damn!*

I blushed, causing her to giggle, as we walked back inside to join everyone in the family room.

The game started slowly, with Boston taking the lead in the first two innings, scoring one run in each inning. Things didn't look too good for the home team. The black cloud that sat over my house with Dad's lack of work seemed to extend to Queens and Shea Stadium, and over the entire Mets dugout.

By the end of the fourth inning, half of Spencer's case of beer was gone, and the mood in the room was a bit sour.

"Hey, who wants dessert?" my mom asked, trying to cheer up the room.

That seemed to perk everyone up.

Sure enough, the baklava and my dad's double-chocolate brownies were a huge hit. The Mets, on the other hand, not so much. The announcers were pretty much calling the game in favor of the Red Sox.

But as the great Yogi Berra once said, "It ain't over till it's over." To everyone's surprise, the Mets never gave up, and we were soon watching a game heading into extra innings.

The Red Sox took the lead in the top of the tenth inning, bringing home two runs.

Talk about sucking the oxygen out of the room.

Matt: "Oh, c'*mon*!"

Dad: "Un*believable*!"

Me: "Are they *trying* to lose?"

Mom: "Hey, hey, the game's not over, ye of little faith."

Callie: "Yeah, we still have the bottom of the tenth."

Gill: "Yeah."

*Damn cheerleaders.*

With Callie sitting comfortably in my lap, we watched as Boston retired our first two batters. I didn't feel like watching the end of the game. I knew what was about to happen.

"You ready to go?" I whispered to Callie.

"Are you sure? They still have one out to go."

I snickered. "Are you kidding me? It's the Mets, babe. There's no way they're going to pull this one off."

"Okay, I'll go get my sneakers," Callie said, just as Kevin Mitchell came up to bat and hit a pinch-hit single, causing everyone in the room to cheer.

I immediately grabbed Callie, who was still standing in front of me and pulled her back down into my lap.

"You know what? Let's see what happens."

She leaned back and kissed my neck, whispering, "Okay, Captain."

I don't know if it was her whisper, her kiss, the change in atmosphere, but the crowd wasn't the only thing stirring in the room at that moment. And I wasn't the only one to notice, either, as Callie adjusted herself and skooched further down into my lap.

I stared at the TV, afraid to move, not knowing what to do. My focus was on just one thing right then, and it wasn't baseball. Callie, on the other hand, seemed to enjoy my predicament, making it worse with every "adjustment" of her body.

*Did she just purr?*

Fortunately, Ray Knight came to my rescue and hit a single, scoring Gary Carter, advancing Kevin Mitchell, the tying run, to third base. The tension in our family room was palpable. Even Callie stopped messing with me, as Mookie Wilson came to the plate.

*C'mon, Mookie. C'mon!*

With the count, two balls and two strikes, Bob Stanley, Boston's relief pitcher, threw a wild pitch, allowing Kevin Mitchell to run home, and score the tying run. This also allowed Ray Knight to advance to second base, putting him in a potential scoring position.

At that moment, it became "standing room only" in my family room. A hopeful hush came over all of us, as we dutifully stared at the 25" color screen, watching Mookie Wilson prepare for the next pitch. You could feel the momentum shifting. The crowd in the stadium was louder than I'd ever heard them.

"C'mon, Mookie. *C'mon,*" Matt shouted.

Dad clasped his hands together and shook them in the air. "Let's go, Mook. Make it happen!"

The announcers gave us the count, "Three and two to Mookie Wilson."

The next pitch not only shifted momentum, but seemed to put the nail in Boston's coffin, as Mookie Wilson hit a routine ground ball to first base, one that any little leaguer could have fielded, and forced the game into the next innings.

The gods must have heard Dad's comment—and all of our prayers, as Vin Scully gave us the play by play:

"So, the winning run is at second base, with two outs, three and two to Mookie Wilson. A little roller up along first . . . behind the bag! *It gets through Buckner! Here comes Knight, and the Mets win it!*"

The stadium exploded with cheers, and you could feel any hope Boston had of removing "the curse of the great Bambino" wither away on a vine.

Our family room exploded with cheers as well. Spencer sprayed everyone in his immediate area with beer, as Callie and I jumped up and down into each other's arms, shouting and yelling.

In his excitement, Dad grabbed my mom and planted one right on her lips! I shrugged my shoulders and did the same with Callie.

Matt turned and smooched Gill.

However, when Spencer tried to plant one on hot Kate, she stretched out her arms and held him at bay.

*Poor Spence. I guess we can add another victim to the pile. Kate's hotness strikes again. Well, she* did *say he was just a friend.*

# 30 - Get the Pom-Poms

Friday, October 31, 1986. Yep, that year, the stars aligned, and our Halloween dance happened on Halloween night, the same week the Mets won the World Series. Now, you should understand something. At our school, for religious reasons, not every teacher celebrated or participated in Halloween.

These same teachers also had a say in how we *celebrated* Halloween on campus. Apparently, a few years prior, some students chose to celebrate in a racy way, wearing lingerie from some place called *Victoria's Secret* to class. From what I heard, students in that class learned her secret.

Now, I don't know if they would have allowed that in public school, but at a Christian private school?

Yeah, that's not happening!

Anyway, this year, since Callie and I and Matt and Gill were all going out, we decided to double date in matching costumes. The girls borrowed our football uniforms, and went as football players, while Matt and I went as cheerleaders.

There was just one element to the cheerleading costumes that we had to create. And that would involve bras for each of us. Easy for Matt—he had hot Kate to borrow from. I had to ask my mom.

*Good times, good times.*

She was in her bedroom, folding clothes. I cleared my throat and said, "Mom, I, uh, need to borrow something from you."

"How much?"

*Let's see. How much does my dignity cost?*

"No, it's not money. Tomorrow's the Halloween dance at school, and the girls are dressing as football players."

"Oh, that sounds like fun. What are you and Matt going as, cheerleaders?"

My head jerked back in surprise. "Yeah, how'd you know?"

"*Really?* Ha! I didn't know until you just told me. How funny," and she giggled, of course. "So, what are you going to wear?"

*Here we go.*

"I'll be right back." I retrieved the costume from my room and returned, holding it up for her to see.

"Oh, wow! You're going all out, huh?"

My face couldn't have been redder. "Yeah, you could say that."

"So, let me guess, you need to borrow a *bra*, am I right?"

I sighed and nodded. She tried to hide another giggle behind her hand but failed miserably, as she snorted and then broke out into a fit of laughter.

She managed to say between gasps, "Okay, but I get to see the outfit on, and I mean all of it, bra and all!"

That sent her into another fit.

*Oh my God, seriously?*

"Mom-*ah*!" I protested.

She waggled her finger. "Ah-ah . . . no outfit, *no bra*. Oh, and let me get your father. He needs something to improve his mood. Here, you can borrow this one. I just took it out of the laundry. I'll be right back." She tossed me her bra and headed off to fetch Dad for the "show."

*Are you friggin' kidding me? Mom, you're killing me!*

I took her bra, along with the rest of my costume, and went to my room to change.

*I can't believe I'm doing this. This is ridiculous. Callie better appreciate how humiliating this is. What was I thinking? This is so wrong.*

I stripped down to my underwear and socks and proceeded to put "the outfit" on. First, the bra.

The hard part was the clasps in the back. After contorting my body this way and that, I finally gave up and left it dangling from my shoulders. I figured Mom—or worse, Dad—could help me with it on Halloween night. At that point, I would stuff it with socks or something.

I then slipped on the skirt, which was easier than I expected. Like the bra, I left the side zipper mostly open.

Instead of wearing the uniform blue bottoms, I kept my underwear on underneath. Tomorrow, I'd put on a pair of gym shorts as well. The last thing I needed was this skirt slipping off and to be standing in the middle of the dance floor in nothing but my underwear.

I'd had nightmares like that when I was younger. I didn't need to make it a reality.

Next, I slipped on the cheerleading top, which came down as a V-neck. I turned and checked myself out in the bedroom mirror, shaking my head at my reflection. You could tell that my bra wasn't fastened, as it rested just above my stomach.

*Maybe I'll skip wearing the bra tomorrow.*

*I can't believe I'm doing this.*

"Hey, kiddo, are you finished yet?" my Mom called from her room.

*There's way too much joy in her voice.*

"Yeah, yeah...I'm coming."

I slowly turned the knob and opened my door.

*FLASH!*

"What the . . . ? *Mom! No!*" I yelled as she snapped another picture.

She and my dad were standing in the hall—with Mom behind the camera and Dad with a shit-eating grin on his face. Yep, this definitely made him feel better.

"Looking good there, champ."

I was *this close* to flipping him the finger. In fact, I wanted to give them both the double cannon. Of course, I didn't. I was embarrassed, not stupid.

Instead, I said, "Ha, ha, very funny."

"Oh, honey, you look adorable. Come here. Let me fix your bra," Mom said, handing the camera to my father, who started snapping away as she fixed my bra.

"Seriously, Dad?" I groaned.

"Ha! You look great, there, champ! Real great!"

After clasping the back, my mom adjusted the bra, so it sat better across my chest. "There, how does that feel?"

"It feels ridiculous."

"Oh, stop. You look fine. So, um, are you going to . . . you know?" she asked, mimicking someone stuffing their bra, which made me go from caramel brown to bright red. My ears were on fire. I wanted to hide in a hole.

*Oh, shoot me now!*

"Oh my God. Yes, Mom. I'm going to stuff my . . . I mean, *your* bra."

"Hold on. I'll go grab him some socks. I'll be right back," my dad said.

Mr. Helpful, in no time, returned with two socks bunched up into balls.

"Here you go. Put these in there."

I reluctantly complied, and soon I went from flat-chested to a nice pair.

"Ooo-la-la! Looking nice there, champ!" he howled with laughter, as he snapped another picture. "How about an action shot? Do you have pom-poms?"

"Yes, I have pom-poms, and no, I'm not getting them."

"Oh, c'mon. Go get the pom-poms. It'll be fun. You'll look cute," my mom said.

I had to admit—I did like the fact that this was causing them so much joy. But it sure seemed like a helluva sacrifice on my part. As they stared at me, waiting for my answer, I grunted, rolled my eyes, and got the damn pom-poms.

*I can't believe I'm doing this.*

"Okay, hold them up and smile!" Dad instructed.

I complied with every command. I had lost my mind.

"Okay, shake 'em this way."

"Do this."

"Do that."

"Can you do a split?"

They were having a grand ol' time at my expense. After a solid ten minutes, which felt like an eternity, we concluded the fashion show.

Dad said, "Oh my God, that was fantastic. Son, you're a really good sport. I wouldn't have ever done that for my father."

*Now you tell me.*

***

"The night" was upon us.

We put on our costumes in the locker rooms after having a quick bite at McDonald's. Of course, the girls had to add some serious makeup to the cheerleading getups, and Matt and I allowed it . . . I mean, why not, at this point?

After the shock of hearing catcalls and whistles from my classmates had worn off, I actually had a great time at the dance. I even stood long enough for someone to take a picture of Callie and me, which actually made it into the yearbook.

Callie and I danced the night away, as did Matt and Gill. Who knew dressing up as a cheerleader would have been so much fun?

# 31 - A Surprise Visit

We had four weeks left until opening night for the play, and everyone was on edge. Between midterms, rehearsals, sports, and the everyday life of a hormonal teenager, things were stressful.

While some waited for early acceptance letters from colleges, others worried about their latest SAT scores. We started rehearsing on Saturdays now, which meant I had to adjust my work schedule. Fortunately, Mr. Anagnos at the diner understood and allowed me to come in to work later than usual.

Between rehearsing scenes on that Saturday, we were fitted for our costumes, which felt *weird*. The cheerleading outfit a few weeks prior was one thing. A fairy costume was something else entirely. My fairy costume included me wearing green tights and a matching green sparkling top with wings.

Granted, I had the body for it, but I was still a self-conscious teenage boy. The last thing I needed was someone busting my balls for wearing a pair of green tights and matching wings.

During my fitting session, Callie stood in the doorway watching, thumbnail between her front teeth, smiling from ear to ear.

"What's so funny?" I asked her.

"Nothing. You look so cute."

"Uh huh."

"Please hold still." Corrine Gregory, the costume designer, was turning me this way and that.

How could I hold still? I felt like a side of beef, getting manhandled.

"Ow!"

"Well, if you don't hold still, I won't stick you with another pin." Corrine chastised.

"There. You're done," Corrine said, stepping aside to allow me to check myself out in the full-length mirror.

That's when we overheard Aaron saying, "Oh, Callie's in the back. Follow me."

As I admired my reflection in the mirror, I noticed Callie's expression change when she turned to see who Aaron was talking to. It was like she saw a ghost. I then adjusted my view to see what was going on.

Standing in the doorway, was a frowning man with a pencil-thin mustache and wearing impeccable attire—a navy-blue, pinstriped, three-piece suit, a crisp white shirt, a red power tie, matching handkerchief, and shiny black wingtips. His salt-and-pepper hair was flawlessly slicked back.

Grumpy-puss himself . . . her father.

"Uh, *Father*, what are you doing here? Is everything okay?" she asked, transforming from the confident, self-confident girl I knew to a delicate flower.

"Calista, what's going on? What are you doing here? Explain."

Her eyes became downcast the moment he barked at her. It was as if the very oxygen in the room had escaped. You could hear a pin drop as his command echoed.

"I asked you a question, *young lady*," he said in his thick Greek accent. "Explain yourself."

"Well, Father, I . . . uh . . ."

*Since when does she stutter?*

"She's one of the leads in the play," I chimed in, standing there in my green tights and frilly costume.

Her father shot me a flat look, as if I were an insignificant bug about to get smashed under his shoe.

"Come with me, *now*," he barked at his daughter and then turned on his heels and walked away.

"Okay."

Aaron, Corinne, and I looked at each other as Callie dutifully followed her father. An uncomfortable moment of silence passed. I wanted to say something, but I wasn't even sure I'd really seen what had just happened. I was dumbfounded.

Finally, Aaron broke the ice by asking Corinne to leave the room so he could talk to me. She quickly shuffled out.

"What was that all about?" he asked.

By now, everyone on campus knew Callie and I were going out. The downside of attending a small school. Everyone, including the faculty, knew your business.

"I have no idea."

"Didn't her father know she'd tried out for the play?"

"I don't know. We never . . . I mean, I thought . . . uh, *my* parents know." Like that explained everything.

You could see the wheels spinning in Aaron's head. We were four weeks away from opening night, and one of his lead actors might get yanked from the play. And not only was she one of his leads, she was his star.

The moment she hit the stage, she shined, brighter than any previous actor he'd worked with in a really long time—he'd said so often. Aaron took pride in working with her, too. You could see it when they were together. Teaching her the nuances of Shakespeare. The subtleties of movement. How the rolling of your fingers or making a graceful entrance made all the difference in a scene.

Callie, for her part, seemed to pick it up like fish to water. Everything seemed to come naturally to her.

Aaron had found his muse.

And now, her father was threatening to take it all away from him—from all of us, really. From me! I'd signed up for this play because of her. If it hadn't been for Callie, I wouldn't have gone forward with it at all. Would never be standing in a room, being questioned, in a pair of green tights and matching wings.

"Let me go see what's going on."

"You *may* want to change first," Aaron wisely reminded me.

"Yeah, good call."

After carefully removing my costume and changing back into my jeans, I went searching for Callie and her father. Aaron, for his part, went back to rehearsals, while Corinne's next victim, Ron Park, the guy playing Theseus, came in for his fitting.

I stepped outside to a cool November late-morning. The sun was shining, and squirrels jumped from tree to tree, preparing for the upcoming winter. It would have been almost magical save for the shiny black Mercedes Benz parked in the quadrangle.

The car was a black four-door with tinted windows. Ominous. The driver, dressed in black with matching black sunglasses and what appeared to be an earpiece in his left ear, stood guard, surveying the grounds as if waiting for an attack that would never come.

*This is Long Island, for God's sake, not Beirut, dude. Settle down.*

I stood at the top of the stairs in front of the auditorium, searching for

Callie and her father. The driver briefly glanced my way. He must not have considered me much of a threat because his gaze didn't linger.

*Who* is *this guy? What the hell does her father* do *for a living?*

Then I noticed the car began to shake a bit and I could hear shouting from inside.

*Aha. Found them.*

Moments later, the rear passenger door opened, and Callie stormed out of the car, slamming the door behind her, clearly upset.

The driver's side rear door immediately opened, and her father stormed out. As he did, the driver ran to hold the door open for him. If I weren't witnessing something horrible, I would have laughed at the way he fumbled for the door. But this was no laughing matter.

My girlfriend was clearly shaken and upset. And her father was about to bear down on her like a lion pouncing on its prey.

"Young lady, don't you slam the door on me when I'm talking to you!" he yelled in his deep voice. He reached her, taking her shoulder and spinning her around to face him.

"Father, I'm *not* quitting the play. You *can't* make me!" She was crying, and her shoulders dropped. She seemed defeated, despite what she was saying.

"Young lady, I did not spend all this money to send you to this school, so you could waste your time performing in a *play*. Had I known, I would have sent you back to Greece, like I originally wanted to do, and still may do."

Suddenly, Callie bowed up again. "*Mana* would have allowed me! She would have *wanted* me to do it!"

That seemed to hit a nerve. Her father took a step backward, placing his hand over his heart, as if he'd been shot.

"How *dare* you. You know very well that—"

"No, Father, no! You know *I'm right*!" she insisted. "I'm *not* leaving school, and I'm *not* quitting the play!"

"Young lady, you will do as *I ask*!" he roared.

*That's asking? I'd hate to hear what demanding looked like.*

"*No!*" she shouted and then tearfully ran off toward her dorm.

The Benz driver attempted to go after her, but her father raised his hand and waved him off.

*Down, boy. Stay. Woof!*

Her father took out a white handkerchief from his pocket and wiped his face. That's when he noticed he wasn't alone. I'd witnessed the whole thing.

This seemed to annoy him, some *boy* was watching his family drama, the dirty laundry, unfold itself for my viewing pleasure.

Although I took no pleasure in it whatsoever.

He then gestured with his head from his driver to me, as if to say, *get rid of him.* The Man in Black started walking my way, which I took that as my cue to leave. I pulled my keys from my pocket, jangling them as I did so, gestured at my car, also parked in the quad, and walked past the driver, who let me pass without saying a word.

I had to go home anyway to get ready for work, so I hopped into my car, my heart racing and sinking at the same time, not knowing what would happen next. Was Callie going to quit the play? Was her dad going to pull her from school?

*Was this the last time I would see Callie?*

# 32 - Washing Dishes

I popped in my *AC/DC* tape, *Who Made Who,* and as I started my car, church bells rang out from my speakers, followed by the sound of electric guitar. I put my sunglasses on and stared out the windshield at Callie's father, wondering what he'd do.

As he scratched his chin and looked up at the sky, he seemed to be weighing his options. He then snapped his fingers, and his driver immediately came to the back-passenger door, opening it, allowing him to seat himself. After taking care of his *master,* the driver straightened out his already immaculate black outfit, and went to the driver's side, hopped in, and left the quad.

I looked at the clock on my dashboard, wondering if I had time to hop out, hunt down Callie, and find out what was going on. Unfortunately, I didn't have the time. I barely had enough time to get home and change into my work clothes.

Around 7:30, after the dinner rush at the diner, we had a lull, so I took my break. Like most weekends, I ordered up a burger and fries and grabbed a Coke from the dispenser.

Instead of eating in the kitchen, I grabbed a spot in a corner booth, away from the paying customers. As I took my first bite, three familiar figures entered the diner, one smirking, and two smiling widely.

Matt, Gill, and Callie.

Mr. Anagnos greeted them warmly. "'Ello, 'ello. Welcome, welcome. Are you here to see *our* friend?" he asked, nodding in my direction. He handed them each a menu as they walked by.

"Hi, Mr. Anagnos. Yeah, if that's okay? I know he's on duty, but—" Matt said.

"Of course, of course, come this way. Follow me. Oh look, there he is. Hey, your friends are here to see you," he hollered to me as he brought them to my booth. "Someone will be right with you. Stella! You have customers."

Then he leaned over to me and whispered, "Not too long, eh?"

*Uh-huh. Sure. To them you're all Mister Smiles, but to me you're all "Get back to work!"*

"So, how're things this evening, kids?" Stella asked as she came to the booth.

Everyone did the small-talk thing and ordered drinks and fries. Then Callie leaned over and gave me a quick hug and kiss, even though I was a sweaty, stinky mess.

"Hey, Captain." Her tone lacked its usual spark.

*But she was smiling when she came in. So, that's a good sign, right?*

"Babe, are you okay?"

"Yeah. No. I don't know." She sighed, melting into me.

I took her hand, and we excused ourselves. I found a quiet corner in the rear of the diner. We sat down.

"So, that was your dad, huh?"

Tears immediately built up in her eyes, and she shook her head, holding her hand to her mouth.

As grimy as I was, I held her close to me, allowing her to cry in my arms. A few minutes passed, and, in the distance, I noticed people started to come into the restaurant, which meant my dinner break was almost over. Mr. Anagnos would soon be hovering.

I lifted her chin so I could get a long look at her. "God, you're beautiful."

"No, I'm not. I'm a mess." She turned her eyes away from mine, blushing.

I did the chin thing again. We were once again staring . . . *into* each other, it felt like. "No, you're not. In my eyes, Callie, you're beautiful."

"That's because you need glasses," she joked, sniffing back her tears and wiping her face with some napkins I handed her.

She gently blew her nose and giggled to herself, like she'd just heard a joke.

"What's so funny?"

"Nothing. You. This." She lifted the tear-soaked napkins and shrugged.

"*This* is funny? And you say *I* have a strange sense of humor."

I then noticed Mr. Anagnos working his way toward us, giving me the high sign that my break was over.

"Looks like you have to get back to work, huh?"

"Yeah, looks like it. I hate that, though."

"I don't want to get you in trouble. I'm fine."

"Callie?" I whispered in her ear.

"Yeah?"

"I love you."

Her blue eyes lit up as she gasped in response.

I was a little surprised, too, to be honest. I'd been planning on saying it at some point soon, but not this evening. Not this moment. Not smelling like I'd fought and lost a battle in the kitchen.

It just . . . *happened*. The words just slipped out.

"I love you, too." She took my face in her hands and planted a wet kiss on my lips.

The kiss stopped Mr. Anagnos in his tracks, and he did an immediate about-face.

*I guess he can give me a few more minutes.*

As we parted, Callie caressed my face with her right hand. We stared longingly into each other's eyes. The power of love was real. Suddenly, the background noise of the restaurant seemed to vanish. At that moment, I had tunnel vision, and all I could see was this beautiful girl sitting next to me.

And it wasn't just any girl. She was *my* girl. My blue-eyed, brown-haired, olive-skinned, pouty-lipped Greek goddess from heaven. A girl who I didn't even know just months ago. Who in a short period of time had changed my life. Who, based on what I'd witnessed today, may be taken away from me.

Maybe forever.

I didn't even want to think about it.

In the distance, I heard someone clearing his throat. It was Mr. Anagnos. He was out of patience. Time to get back to work.

I wanted to quit right there and then. I wanted to take off my sweaty, grease-stained apron and toss it right in his face. Walk out. But I didn't. I couldn't. I needed the job. Besides, it wasn't his fault.

If I were in his shoes, I'd do the same thing. He had a restaurant to run, and the dishes weren't going to wash themselves.

After another gentle kiss, we stood and held hands as Mr. Anagnos approached us.

"Mr. Anagnos, I'd like to introduce you to my girlfriend, Calista."

"Calista? Is that Greek?" he asked.

Of course, this was a common question he asked everyone with olive skin. To him, *everyone* was Greek. In this case, though, he was correct.

"*Yes. My last name is Christos,*" she responded—*in Greek*, much to our surprise.

Both my and Mr. Anagnos's eyebrows shot up in surprise. Mine, because

I never heard her speak Greek. His for a different reason, I was about to learn.

"*Christos, as in Stelios Christos?*" he asked, also in Greek.

Callie just smiled and sighed, nodding her head.

Of course, all I could make out were the names. Everything else to me sounded like gibberish. But I was gathering that Callie was used to this back-and-forth. Had heard it before, and maybe even often.

Mr. Anagnos immediately raised his hands, like he'd won the lottery, and gave her a familial hug, like she was his long-lost daughter or something. He then walked her around the restaurant, showing off his various Greek décor and furnishings.

He then called for his wife to come out from the back office to meet her. When she came out and found out who Callie was—clearly someone notable—she immediately brushed her hair back, straightened her clothes, and gave her a hug, giggling as she did so.

*What the hell is going on?*

As the Anagnos's were fawning all over Callie, Matt and Gill came over.

"What the hell's going on?" Matt asked as the three of us stared at the spectacle.

"I have no idea. One second I'm introducing Callie to Mr. Anagnos, and the next thing you know, *this* happens."

Soon Mr. Anagnos was introducing Callie to some of his regulars, who greeted her and shook her hand, some clearly recognizing her last name. It was repeated often during this impromptu meet-and-greet.

Then he held up a finger and said, "Wait," to no one in particular, it seemed. He went into the kitchen and returned with a jug of olive oil in hand, pointing at it. "*Christos*, see?" he said proudly to everyone who was watching.

Callie smiled and bowed her head graciously.

Then it hit me.

*Ohhhh . . .* her dad was the Olive Oil Man.

"What's going on? Who's the girl?" Stella asked as she sidled up next to us, handing Matt his check for the Cokes and fries he and Gill had ordered.

"That's my girlfriend," I said proudly.

*And she loves me.*

# 33 - Good Grief

As the hullaballoo died down, Callie walked back to our small group and rolled her eyes.

"Uh," was all I could think to say.

"Yeah, sorry about that."

"How do they know you?" Gill asked.

"That's . . . well, a long story."

I turned my head toward the door, noticing more customers entering the restaurant.

*Shit! I've got to get back to work.*

Callie placed her hand on my chest. "Listen, you go do what you have to do. I just wanted to stop by and see you, to let you know that everything's okay."

I didn't want to let her go. Wanted to know more about who her dad was, about her.

"What are you doing tomorrow?" she asked.

"Nothing." The minute I said it I wondered how that could possibly be true, with my schedule. But it was.

"Can we have lunch tomorrow? I'll explain everything."

"Yeah, of course. What time do you want me to swing by and get you?"

"How about 12:30?"

"Done. I'll pick you tomorrow."

"I love you."

"I love you, too."

***

When my shift finally ended in the early hours of the morning, Mr. Aragnos thanked me for having Callie come in. He went on and on about what an honor it was to have the daughter of the great Stelios Christos in his restaurant.

He never called it a "diner." To him, it was a restaurant, just like any five-star place in New York City.

I just nodded. I wanted to ask him some questions but was just too damn tired.

He went on. "Stelios Christos's daughter in *my* restaurant. I can't wait to tell people back home. They won't believe me."

He was waving his hands in the air as he left the kitchen.

*Uh-huh. The great Stelios Christos. Yeah, well, I wonder what you'd think of the* great *Stelios if you saw the way he treated his daughter.*

***

After a fitful sleep—in fact, what amounted to just a couple of hours, really—I finally gave in to my stomach and padded down the stairs to the kitchen. I grabbed a bowl of Life cereal and some OJ, and sat on the couch to watch some TV.

*Flintstones* reruns, to be specific.

*Yeah, I know. I'm seventeen years old, and I'm watching cartoons. Sue me. Who doesn't love Fred and Barney?* And it kept my mind off my upcoming lunch with Callie.

I had a million questions to ask her. Plus, we had said *it* last night. Twice. In front of Gill and Matt.

*I can hear it now.*

*"Ohhh . . . you're in love." Followed by kissing noises.*

Dad came down in his bathrobe and slippers, heading to the kitchen for a cup of coffee. "Hey, buddy," he said in a low voice.

I just gave him the head-nod. I was still too tired for conversation.

Like me, Mom worked the late shift and, presumably, was still in bed sleeping, so we kept the noise to a minimum, out of courtesy.

Shortly thereafter, Dad settled next to me with a cup of coffee and the thick Sunday edition of *Newsday*, our local paper.

"You're up early. How was work last night?" he asked as he read the latest box scores.

"You know, the usual."

"That's good. Here, want the comics?"

"Thanks."

*Why not?*

I started with *The Peanuts*.

It was the classic scene with Lucy holding the football for Charlie Brown, promising not to pull it away. Sure enough, by the last panel, Charlie Brown is flying through the air.

*I know how you feel, Charlie Brown. Good grief!*

"You okay?" he asked, glancing at me from the corner of his eye.

"Huh? Yeah, yeah. I'm just tired."

"You should have slept in. Well, remember, the Giants game starts at 1. I'm making my world-famous chili."

*Shit, I forgot all about the Giants game. And Dad's making his chili, too? Damn, I really am losing it.*

Just like other families across America, Sunday was football day in our house.

Our team was the New York Giants.

And I was going to miss it. Because for the first time in my life, there was something more important to me than football. And her last name was Christos. The *mysterious* Calista Christos.

"Um, Dad? I, uh, sort of have a lunch date. With Callie."

He looked at me like I had three eyeballs.

"Oh." His tone was one of disappointment.

*Damn.*

"Yeah, sorry. I wasn't thinking."

"No, it's okay. Maybe you'll make it home in time for the second half."

I gave him a small smile. "Yeah, maybe. I'll try."

***

At 10:30, I went to the kitchen and dialed Matt's house. There had to have been some discussion after they'd left. He'd have the scoop.

"Hello?" answered the sultry voice of Miss Kate Salvatore.

"Hey, Kate. Is Matt around?"

"Hey there, sexy pants. How're you doing? Are you still *cheating* on me with that pretty girl?"

*Yeah, right. As if anyone with half a brain would ever cheat on you.*

"Sorry, babe, but as your brother always says, a man has needs," I joked.

"*Wow*! You really *have been* hanging out with that pig!" She laughed. "Okay, stud, I'll go get him for you. Hold on."

"Yo!" Matt replied, picking up another line, Kate hanging up as he answered.

"Yo! So, what happened after you guys left the diner? What'd Callie have to say? What's her deal?"

"Dude!" He laughed. "She's . . . wow. Listen, you need to hear this stuff from her, not me."

*Now he's being Mister Manners? Great. Just great.*

For Matt Salvatore to hold off on further commentary, it could only mean one thing:

*I'm screwed.*

"What do ya mean, I need to hear it from her? What did she say?"

"Dude, I'm telling you, you need to hear it from her. Trust me."

I couldn't believe what I was hearing. It actually pissed me off a little and worried a lot.

"*Fine.* I've got to go. Talk to you later."

I hung up without waiting for his response.

*Good grief!*

# 34 - Devil's Advocate

By 12:15, I was parking my car in the quad and heading to pick up Callie in her dorm. Even though I was a few minutes early, I didn't care. I wanted to get to the bottom of this mystery.

*So, her dad makes olive oil. Big deal. It's only olive oil, right? Is it some sort of magical olive oil or something? That doesn't make her royalty, does it?*

As I walked up the steps to the front door, images of famous princess entered my mind. Prince Diana. Princess Grace. Princess Leia from the Jabba scene.

I envisioned Callie dressed in a white lace and crystal-covered gown, a diamond necklace and tiara as accents. Her hair was pinned up, showing off her swan-like neck. She was breathtaking, and everyone bowed when she passed by. She allowed a hint of a smile behind her gloved hand, like she was hiding a secret.

*Jesus, I'm losing it.*

As I reached the door, it opened, and out poured a few girls I knew.

"Hey, are you here for Callie?" Cassidy Keane, a sophomore, asked me.

I smirked and said, "Yeah. Is it *safe* for me to enter?"

"Yeah, you can go in." She laughed and rolled her eyes dramatically, holding the door open for me.

A very comfortable-looking Gill was sitting on one of the couches, dressed in an oversized white Champion-brand sweatshirt, turned inside out. She wore a pair of navy sweatpants and socks rolled up over her sweatpants.

Surrounding her were textbooks and notebooks. She flitted a pen back and forth like a propeller as she read. The moment I walked in, she looked up with her cherub face and smiled.

"Hey! Here for your lunch date?"

"Yep. Some night, huh?"

"Oh my God, you have no idea. I'll go get her."

*Yeah, no kidding.*

I didn't have to wait long before she returned from the nether-regions of the dorm. "She'll be right out."

"Thanks."

I was hoping she'd spill the beans, but she just busied herself with her books. I couldn't stand it any longer.

"So, what the hell did she say last night?"

"Well, a lot, actually. She'll have to tell you the whole story, though."

*I can't believe this! The queen of gossip won't tell me? What the hell did Callie say?*

Fortunately, I didn't have to wait too long, as the door opened and out walked my princess. I'd half expected her to be wearing the gown and tiara from my vision. Instead, she was wearing a pair of form-fitting, black Guess jeans, white Keds, and a blue-jeans jacket over a white cropped top and page-boy cap. And just a tad of makeup—some mascara and lip gloss.

Yep, she was definitely my princess.

"Hey, Captain," she said, smiling.

"Ready for lunch?"

"Yes, I'm starving."

"Me, too. Come on, princess. Your chariot awaits."

"Princess, huh?" she giggled.

We said goodbye to Gill and walked to my car.

"So, where to?" Callie asked.

"I don't know. What do you feel like having?"

My question elicited a wicked smile on her face, followed by a giggle.

"Oh, sweet Lord," I replied, smiling as I brushed my hair back. "Want to go to Port Jeff?"

"Sure. I haven't been there yet, and I hear it's real pretty."

"It is. We'll grab a bite and walk around, cool?"

"Cool."

And it was cool, until we got into the car. Then things got . . . hot.

I'd barely put the key in the ignition before Callie jumped me right there in the quad. She gave me a long, sensuous kiss. One that I readily accepted and reciprocated.

"Wow, what was that for?"

Sitting back in her seat, she grinned and started playing with the radio dial.

"I missed you."

*Shit, if that's how she acts when she misses me for one night, I can't wait to find out what she does when she misses me over Thanksgiving break.*

We pulled out of the parking lot, heading eastbound on Route 25A toward Port Jeff. Callie found a song she liked and started singing and dancing along to it as I drove. I did my best to pay attention to both the road ahead and the girl to my right. The girl was definitely winning out. I had to slam on the brakes at the light, on the corner of Route 25A and Nicolls Road, to avoid colliding into the car ahead of me.

"Whoa, sorry about that," I said.

"It's okay, I'm okay. Are *you* okay?"

"Yeah, yeah. I was, um, distracted."

I felt adrenaline course through my veins, and my heart was beating like a jackhammer. Fortunately, neither of us were injured, just shaken up a little.

Ten minutes later, we were pulling into downtown Port Jefferson, a local town on the North Shore of Long Island known for its ferry to Connecticut, amongst other cool things. The town was already dressed up for Christmas, only a short seven weeks away.

It was my favorite holiday, so I didn't complain.

For lunch, we decided to go to a popular restaurant, The Devil's Advocate.

It was an American Bistro, in the style of a New England nautical printer's shop. It was also well known locally for its overpriced burgers and for serving alcohol to underage teens, especially on the weekends.

Callie and I didn't wait long for a table. We were seated next to a window overlooking Main Street. As we were seated across from one another, we were told the cocktail menu was on the table, perpetuating what I already knew—they indeed served minors.

"You want one?" Callie asked with a mischievous look on her face.

"I don't know. Do you?"

"Sure, why not? When in Rome, right?"

Our waiter approached wearing a white button-down shirt, black apron, and black pants. You know, penguin stuff.

"So, what'll you have to drink?" he asked.

"I'll have an Absolut Vodka Seabreeze, please," Callie said.

"And you sir?" he asked, without even asking for ID.

*Like she said, when in Rome . . .*

"I'll have a beer."

"Um, what *kind* of beer would you like?" he asked.

"Oh, uh . . . a Bud?" I said, as he rolled his eyes and nodded.

*Yeah, yeah, I know, dude. Rookie!*

We reviewed our food options until our drinks came, mine in the bottle without a mug, and hers in a tall, clear glass. We ordered cheeseburgers and fries, and when the waiter left, we raised our drinks in the air.

"To you," I whispered.

"To us," she replied.

# 35 - Who *Are* You?

As we settled in, I broached the elephant in the room. I had to know the answer.

"So, um, Callie?"

"Yes?" she replied, flirtatiously raising her shapely eyebrow.

"Okay, now stop that." I wagged my index finger at her, which she reached out for and . . . honked.

"*Honk!* Stop what?" she asked.

She then ran her foot up my leg, causing me to jump in my seat, and her to laugh.

*Whoa!*

"Okay, okay. You got me."

She giggled wickedly, causing some stares from the nearby patrons.

*Nothing to see over here . . . nothing to see.*

"Anyway, so . . . uh, about last night at the diner. And before that, at school with your dad. What was that all about?" I asked. "Who *are* you?"

"Your girlfriend."

"Cal-*lie*."

She smiled and then looked outside the windows for a moment, as if she were collecting her thoughts. She wasn't quite squirming in her seat but was clearly a bit uncomfortable.

"Hey, hey, it's me. You can tell me anything. You know that, right?" I asked.

"Yeah, yeah, I know. It's just—"

"It's just what? You said you'd explained everything today."

"It's a long story."

"Are you, like, a princess or something?"

She'd just taken a sip of her drink and, when I'd asked the question, she did a spit-take, showering my face with her Seabreeze.

"Oh my God! I'm so sorry!"

She couldn't help but giggle as she started patting at my face with her napkin. Naturally, our food arrived at precisely that moment, of course. The waiter set the food on the table, checked that it was to our satisfaction, which it was, then walked away. Callie started cleaning my face again.

"Callie, it's okay. I've got it. Seriously. Anyway, so, what's the deal? Who are you? And I already know you're my girlfriend, so…"

"Well, I'm not a princess. Trust me, you'd know if I were one, at *that* school."

She was preaching the truth. There was no way that secret would last a New York minute at our school. If royalty were attending, we'd all know it. They'd probably hold another assembly, just to prepare us.

"My family is sort of famous in Greece. That's why your boss knew who my dad was."

"How famous?"

"Very."

"Famous for what? Olive oil?"

"Famous for practically *everything*," she said with an eye roll. "Sorry, I'm just so tired of my father."

I just nodded in understanding. I was tired of him already, and I barely knew the guy.

"He's what you'd call an industrialist. He has his fingers in everything." She spread her fingers out like a spider.

"Everything, huh?"

"You have no idea. Supposedly, between him and his business partners, they practically saved the entire economy of Greece, back in the late '70s and early '80s, between his 'shipping and mining interests,' as he calls them."

"And don't forget his olive-oil business," I joked, earning me a laugh.

"Right. We can't forget that."

I listened to her explain more about her family history. Between bites of my burger and occasional nods, I pretended to understand what she was talking about. To be frank, I only understood a portion of it.

I mean, sure, anyone who grew up in a coastal town, like our quiet Three Village township, knew about shipping. But it wasn't really part of our local economy. Not the way she was describing it.

Shipping companies were located farther up and down the coast. As for mining, well . . . I've heard about mining towns in Pennsylvania and West Virginia, but I didn't know much about them, aside from Billy Joel's song,

"Allentown."

"Our last name is plastered on buildings all over the country, from olive groves to shipping yards to mines. Almost everyone in the country either works for, or has worked for, one of my father's companies."

*Whoa. How rich is this guy?*

"There was even talk of him running for office and replacing Apollo with my father's face on the 1000 drachmae when I was younger. Thank God *that* never happened."

*Jesus. No wonder he walks around like his shit doesn't stink.*

"His business is the reason we've traveled so much. It's also why he spends so much time in DC. People always assume he works for the government or something, and I never correct them."

"So that's why Mr. Anagnos was showing you off to everyone last night and waving around that olive oil."

She laughed. "Yeah. He wanted to show me that he used *our* brand of olive oil. It's worse in Greece. Whenever I go home, people go crazy at the sight of me. It's so embarrassing. People actually follow us around with cameras."

I could tell she was tired of the attention.

"It's one of the reasons I like going to school here in the States. No one knows me, aside from the occasional Greek immigrant I bump into . . ."

"Like last night," I finished.

"Yeah, like last night."

"And what about yesterday at school? What's your dad's problem?" I asked as she took another bite of her burger.

She rolled her eyes and wiped her mouth. "I guess you're not going to let this go. *Fine.*"

"Look, if you don't want to talk about it . . ."

"No, no. I said we could talk about it and that I'd tell you. It's just that he gets me so . . . *uuuughhhh!*" She shook her fists in the air.

"Parents, right?" I joked.

"Yeah, *exactly.*"

"So..."

"So, my father is . . . what's the expression?"

*An asshole?*

She snapped her fingers. "Old school. *Very* old school. Even though he expects me to get an education, he also expects me to get married and start a family when I turn twenty-one, like my older brother and sister did."

This information caused me to jerk my neck back and raise my eyebrows. *Whoa! Twenty-one?*

"Exactly," she said to my nonverbal reaction.

"Isn't that a bit, you know . . . young?" I asked. "What does your mother have to say about all this?"

She winced at the mention of her mother.

"I'm sorry, did I say something wrong?"

"No, it's . . . okay. It's okay," she whispered. "My mother . . ."

By her response, I knew what was coming. Her lip quivered.

"She passed away over the summer. From cancer."

*Cancer. Fuck, that sucks!*

"Callie, I'm so sorry. I had no idea. Why didn't you just tell me?"

I immediately pulled my chair next to hers and held her in my arms as she began crying. We stayed this way for a while. Like a leaf, she shook in my arms. I rocked her gently and kissed her head, telling her everything would be all right.

"I'm right here. I'm not going anywhere," I whispered.

After a few minutes, she stopped crying and began sniffing. I took her napkin from her lap, reached up, removed her cap, brushed her hair back, and wiped her eyes, as she fought back a smile. She took the napkin from me and wiped her nose. Her bottom lip continued to quiver a bit.

She looked so fragile.

I leaned in and kissed her lips lightly, tasting her salty tears.

"Better?" I asked.

"Yeah, I'm sorry about that."

"Don't apologize."

She leaned into my arms and rested her head against my chest. The folks around us were staring but trying not to stare. It didn't matter. The waiter soon came over to check on us, but I just shook my head at him slightly and waved him off. He gave me a knowing head-nod and walked away.

"I must look like a mess. I'll be right back. I'm going to the restroom to clean up."

"Yeah, okay."

And off she went.

I still didn't know the whole story, but at least I'd learned the gist of her situation. And in my opinion, it sucked.

*Callie, you may not be royalty, but you're a princess to me.*

# 36 - The Secret Ingredient

I paid the check, leaving our half-empty drinks on the table, and stepped outside with a plastic to-go bag in one hand and Callie's hand in my other.

"Hey, do you want to drop this off in my car and then walk around some?"

"I'd love that."

After dropping the to-go bag in my car, we started up one side of the block and then down the other, looking in the windows of the various stores in the small downtown area.

As we walked, I asked a few more questions.

"So, he really expects you to get married and start having kids right away, huh?"

"Yeah, can you believe that?"

"Wow. He's really old-fashioned."

"You have no idea," she muttered, stopping to stare at a crystal pony hanging in one of the windows.

"He already has someone picked out for me, too. Some guy from a *good Greek family,*" she said, mimicking her father.

"Ah, a good Greek family, huh? What would he think of this brown boy?"

She thought about it for a moment and then laughed, shaking her head.

"That bad, huh?"

"*Yeah*, that bad."

"Oh."

She stopped to look directly at me, realizing how hurt I felt by her comment.

"But . . . my mother would have loved you."

"Oh," I choked out.

"More importantly, I love you. So, screw him." She kissed me long and hard.

*Yeah, screw him!*

After another half-hour of sightseeing, we were loath to part, so I invited her to my house to watch the football game. My dad's "world-famous" chili helped sealed the deal.

Smart girl.

*** 

As we stood at the front door, I could see my father sitting on the couch, wearing his Giants jersey and drinking a beer. His eyes were glued to the TV—the one o'clock football game.

Callie was bouncing on her toes as I put the key into the door and turned it to open it, inviting her in. I found it very cute.

As we entered, we were met with the scrumptious aroma of Dad's chili cooking. The cinnamon-laden spices—Dad's secret ingredient—and the scent of homemade cornbread filled the house, making my mouth water the moment I stepped in.

Dad turned around and noticed I wasn't alone. He immediately got up from the couch, with a big smile.

"Hey, champ! You made it home in time for the Giants game! And I see you brought a special guest. C'mon in! How're you doing Callie?" he said as he greeted her with a hug and smile.

"Hi. I'm doing great. Ready for the game?"

"Yes, ma'am. Well, don't be shy. Come on in. This game is almost over. Can we get you something to drink?"

"Yes, please. Whatever you have will be fine."

"Sure thing. Hey Buddy, grab me another one, while you're in there please," he said as he escorted Callie to the sofa.

*Uh, Dad, she's here to hang out with . . . Oh, never mind.*

"Sure thing, Dad. Where's Mom?"

"Working. She'll be home later."

"Gotcha."

Even though I'd recently finished a cheeseburger and fries for lunch, the chili seemed to call to me. After entering the kitchen, I grabbed a wooden spoon, stirred the yummy chili, and made sure to sample some as well. It melted in my mouth. Another perfect batch.

I fetched our drinks and a bag of pretzels, and returned to the family room to find Callie and Dad chatting away. He was explaining to her the rules of the game.

She just sat there nodding, like a good pupil, even though she knew the rules. She was polite that way.

Before the game started, Callie excused herself, and went to the bathroom, leaving Dad and me alone.

"Listen, champ. I'll only stay downstairs for the first half of the game. I don't want to cramp your style, okay?"

*Yes!*

"Oh, okay. Thanks, Dad."

"But keep the hanky-panky to a minimum. She seems like a *nice girl*."

"She is, Dad. She really is."

As Callie came back, I excused myself and ran to my room to retrieve my Giants gear. I grabbed my *lucky* Lawrence Taylor jersey and then chose a blue, slightly faded Giants t-shirt for Callie.

"Here you go. This is for you."

"Aww. Thank you, babe. How do I look?" she asked, standing and twirling.

Dad and I gave her the once-over. Dad quickly gave her a thumbs-up and returned his attention to the game, but my focus stayed on the gorgeous creature standing before me.

*God, I want you.*

She looked amazing, standing there dressed in my oversized Giants t-shirt. I guess the lustful smile on my face spoke volumes, because she playfully stuck her tongue out at me, and giggled, before sitting in my lap, to watch the game.

She curled up, laying her head on my chest, and we watched the game. It was so awesome—watching football and playing with my girl's hair. As far as I was concerned, it didn't get any better than that, and all was right in the world.

***

As half time approached, the Giants were up 10-0. At the two-minute warning, Dad went to the kitchen to check on his chili and cornbread.

He made it back to the family room to see the end of the first half.

"So, who's hungry?"

Callie jumped up from my lap. "I am!"

"Ditto!" I said.

"Well, all right! Let's get our chili on!" Dad shouted.

Callie goosed me as we walked into the kitchen and started cackling at my spastic reaction. I immediately turned and started tickling her, forgetting that we had an audience.

"Ha-ha-ha! Okay, stop it! *Stop it!* You win. *You win!*"

"Okay, you two. Come get your chili," Dad said, smirking and shaking his head.

"Mmm, this smells really good," Callie said as Dad handed her a hot bowl of his latest delectable masterpiece.

"Thanks, Callie. I hope you like it."

Instead of eating at the dining room table, we took our chili and cornbread back to the family room to watch the football highlights of the day, waiting for our game to continue.

Callie and I sat next to each other on the floor, placing our bowls on the table in front of the couch, while Dad sat in his armchair.

*Oh . . . oh . . . hot, hot! Damn, it's good, though. Dad outdid himself!*

"Mmm, Dad. . ." I said, giving him a thumbs-up.

"I agree . . . mmmm," Callie said, giving him a double thumbs-up, which put a broad smile on his face.

"I'm glad you both like it. Callie, want to know the secret ingredient?" He had a twinkle in his eyes. One I know all too well.

*Oh, no. Dad, please don't . . .*

"Sure," Callie said.

"Spit." No buildup. No warning. Just "spit," which caused Callie to spit out some of her chili.

"Oh my God, Dad! Callie, he's kidding. I swear. *Dad-ah!*"

Dad was near tears he was laughing so hard. "Oh, that was . . . so . . . so . . . bwaaahhahhaa! Oh, Callie. I'm sorry. It really was a joke."

She blushed and smirked. "Very funny."

Dad clapped his hands and said, "Well, listen, you two. I'm going to go watch . . ." he chuckled some more, ". . . the rest of the game upstairs. Oh, Callie. You're so funny."

"Oh my God, I'm *so* embarrassed. When he said 'spit,' I just . . ."

"I know, I know. I'm *so* sorry. It's an old family joke. I should have warned you."

"It's okay. It *was* funny, though."

"Yeah, that's my dad. He's a regular Eddie Murphy."

After cleaning up Callie's projectile reaction and finishing our meal, we snuggled up on the couch to watch the second half of the game, periodically *enjoying one another* during the commercials, if you get my drift.

*Yep, all is indeed right in the world.*

# 37 - Callie's Mom

Ever since the Giant's game, Callie and I were practically inseparable. Now that I was mobile with my blue-mobile and had to stay after school because of the play, we rarely spent time apart.

You'd think that we would drive each other crazy, but we didn't. We grew closer, and even found ourselves finishing each other's sentences, like we'd been together for decades.

It's like God had put us together for a reason. And who were we to argue with God? She completed me, and vice versa.

My dad had a few interviews but still hadn't received an offer yet, which was slowly driving him mad. To make matter worse, he was beginning to take it out on Mom and me.

He started getting on me for not working over the weekend—football, the play, and my girlfriend were filling my schedule. I explained to him that Mr. Anagnos understood, and was okay with it, but Dad wouldn't listen.

"You made a commitment to Mr. Anagnos," he'd said.

"But, Dad, he said it was fine and that I could make it up to him over Thanksgiving break. He's even coming to the play."

"And that's another thing. Just because you're in a play and have a girlfriend now, doesn't mean you get to shirk your responsibilities around here."

And then he'd stormed off to track down his next victim: Mom.

Almost every weekend, it was the same thing. Wash, rinse, repeat.

Deep down, I knew that even though he was yelling at us, he also was beating himself up more. Fortunately, with Thanksgiving around the corner, he would keep himself busy preparing the menu, even with our limited funds.

"How're things at home?" Callie asked one Saturday after rehearsal.

"'Bout the same. How're things with your dad?"

"'Bout the same."

Callie wrapped her arms around me. She knew just what I needed that crisp November afternoon. Comfort and support.

"You want to go take a walk?" Callie asked.

"Yeah, 'kay."

We left the dorm lounge and headed to the local SUNY college campus across 25A, on the other side of the train station. Winter was right around the corner. Before we knew it, snow would blanket the ground, and Callie and I would bundle up in our winter gear. Me in my leather jacket, and Callie in some expensive designer coat that probably cost more than my car.

The funny thing was, ever since I'd found out about her wealth, she never lorded it over me. The fact that she came from a wealthy family and had a lot of money was never an issue between us.

Another thing I loved about her.

That afternoon, the sky was a mix of hazy gray and blue. Even though it was cloudy, the sun shone brightly. Comfort weather.

"I've never been to the university campus before, have you?" Callie asked, stepping over the train tracks.

"Sure, a bunch of times. Over the summer, they did some cool fireworks on the Fourth of July."

"July," she whispered, and her whole demeanor changed from perky to sad.

I knew immediately what was going on. Her mother had passed over the summer, but I'd not been sure of when exactly. Must have been around that time.

"Callie, I'm sorry. I didn't mean to . . ."

"It's okay. You didn't know."

"Want to talk about it?"

She sighed but didn't say "no."

It seemed like she was ready to talk but having a hard time getting started. I guided her to a large patch of grass on campus, and we sat down.

"So, what was she like?" I asked.

"My mana was the best."

*There was that word again: Mana. I wonder what it means?*

"Mana?"

"Yeah, it's what I called her. It's Greek for 'mother' or 'mom.'"

I didn't respond, just nodded. I didn't know any Greek terms, other than a few curse words, "baklava" and "Opa!" because of the diner.

*Learn something new every day.*

"She was beautiful. She had thick, gorgeous hair. Long and dark brown.

Big sweet eyes. The prettiest smile and the best lap to lay your head in, you know?"

As she said these words, she allowed herself a whisper of a grin.

I just nodded. My mom had a great lap, too.

"She was so full of love. And no one messed with her mora, Greek for 'babies.' Not even my father."

I chuckled at the mention of her dad, picturing her mana ruling the roost.

"Oh, yeah?"

"Oh, yeah. No one messed with her kids. I remember this one time: some kid was bullying my older brother. Apparently, this kid was jealous of all the money my father made and began picking on my brother, Nick."

"Nick, huh?"

"Yeah, that's my older brother's name. My sister's name is Cassandra."

"So, what'd your mother do?"

"When she found out, she stormed right out of our house and tracked this kid down." She swung her arms, elbows bent and fists clenched, imitating her mother.

*God, she's so cute.*

"We all followed behind her and watched as she grabbed him by his ear and dragged him to his own house, right to his mother. She then warned the child and the mother to leave her son alone or *they'd* regret it."

"Whoa, really? Then what happened?"

"I guess the lady knew my mother and was definitely mortified. She immediately started apologizing like crazy to my mana, and then she slapped the boy right across his face, right in front of us. We'd never seen anyone do that to their child before. That reaction surprised all of us, but especially my mother. "

"Wow, I bet."

"Yeah. My mother felt horrible. She immediately knelt down and took this kid into her arms, as he stood there crying."

"She sounds like a special lady."

"She is . . . I mean, she was."

I grabbed hold of her hands, and we took a moment to absorb the memory.

"After that, the kid, Gianni, became my older brother's best friend. He was even his best man at his wedding."

That caught me off-guard.

"Really?"

"Yeah. Since that day, he spent almost every day at our house. He even called my mother 'Mana.' And when she got sick . . ."

Her words died out, and she shook her head, holding back tears.

I waited, squeezing her hands.

She sniffled. "I'm sorry."

"It's okay, babe. No need to apologize."

We just stayed in that spot for a while. I pulled her close to me as she worked through her grief. Images of my parents went through my mind. I tried to imagine what it would be like to lose my mom. I tried to imagine the impact it would have on my dad and me. I imagined we'd pack up the house and move to something smaller.

Callie broke the silence. "Anyway, when she got sick, we moved to New York City."

"When was that exactly?"

"Last year, just before my old school started, actually. We moved to an apartment overlooking Central Park. Even though there were specialists in Greece, my father wanted only the best for my mother, which meant relocating to New York."

I stayed quiet, not wanting to interrupt. I knew I was about to hear more of the truth, and it seemed like she was prepared to continue this path.

"They diagnosed her with breast cancer. Unfortunately, when they caught it, it had already spread to her lymph nodes."

*Lymph nodes?*

"They tried everything. Chemo, mastectomy, you name it. Every time she went into the hospital, she only came out weaker. Eventually, she lost all her beautiful hair and had to wear a wig. And she lost so much weight."

She spent the next forty-five minutes telling me about her mother's struggle. She told me her father used to be so loving, but the moment his wife became sick, he became cold and distant, like her mother had become damaged goods.

His behavior had a chilling effect on the family. Since she was the youngest and lived at home with her parents, she saw it most. When they moved to New York, her sister and two-year-old nephew came to stay with them for a few months.

But after a few months, the sister had to go back home—being away from her own family was putting a strain on her marriage. During the day, when Callie was in school and her mother was at home, a private nurse would care for her mother, but the moment Callie got home, she took over, and her grades suffered. But she didn't care.

"I was surprised that our school even accepted me, to be honest." Then she shrugged. "I guess money talks."

I had just been thinking the same thing—*money talks*—but didn't dare say it. Her father would have used all his power to get her into whatever school he wanted.

"Yeah, I guess."

My thoughts immediately went to my family's struggles with finances and how close I'd come to not being able to stay at the school. Hell, I still wasn't sure we'd make it past December. I sure hope so.

Callie continued with her story, describing when her mom had taken a turn for the worse, and they had to get hospice involved. When that happened, both Callie's siblings, along with their families, came to New York. Her father got them both apartments in the same building as Callie's.

"We all took shifts being with Mana, even my brother- and sister-in-law," she said. "It helped that everyone worked for the family business."

I wondered if she was expected to follow suit.

"We were all there . . . when she . . ." Callie bit her lip, again fighting back the tears.

"It's okay, Cal. I've got you. I'm here," I whispered as I rocked her gently in my arms.

"I'm sorry."

I kissed the top of her head.

"No need to apologize. I love you, Callie."

She whispered, "I love you, too."

And then she went on to tell about her mother's passing, how they'd flown the body back to Greece, where she was buried in a family mausoleum. She said people from all over Greece came to the funeral, including their president, Christos Sartzetakis.

*Wow.* That *was* impressive.

"After the funeral, my father decided it'd be best if I remained in the States to complete my education." There was a touch of disdain in her voice. "He said, that since he'd be spending most of his time there, it'd be best for everyone. Of course, I never got a vote." She shrugged. "So, we flew back to New York, and he enrolled me at our school."

I turned her around to get a better look at her face.

"I remember seeing you move in, your first day."

"Yeah, I remember seeing you, too."

Her blue eyes were rimmed in red but as beautiful as ever. We held each other's gaze for a long moment, then I wiped the tears from her face and kissed her softly, which earned me a smile.

"You have no idea how much you've helped me these past months," she said as a tear ran down her cheek. "You have no idea . . . how much I love you."

The love in her eyes penetrated the depths of my soul.

"I might have some idea . . . because I feel the same way about you, Callie."

*More than you'll ever know.*

# 38 - Cracks in the Armor

Football season was over. We ended with another losing record, 3-7, which surprised no one. Our last game had been two weeks before Thanksgiving break. Fortunately, it was an away game, so we weren't defeated in front of the home crowd.

To be honest, I actually had a good game.

I caught two touchdown passes from Matt and did well on defense. Matt, on the other hand, was sacked a few times, and threw three interceptions, including one that our opponent ran back for a touchdown.

Matt got pretty banged up out there. The other team simply out-muscled us and outplayed us. They were a bigger and better team.

Callie and Gill didn't have a meet, so they hopped a ride with Dad to the game.

After the game, Dad, Callie, and Gill tracked down Matt and me.

My dad said to me, "You gave it your all out there today, kiddo. You really left it all on the field. I'm proud of you."

"Thanks, Dad."

"I'm proud of you, too, Captain," Callie chimed in, hugging me.

Even though I still hated losing, I made sure not to pout. I'd learned my lesson. If I wanted to pout, I had to do it in private.

"Thanks, babe."

As she snuggled me, Gill was trying to do the same with Matt, but he wanted no part of it. He was still upset with his final performance and loss.

"Gill, you don't understand. This was my last football game ever, and I *sucked*!"

"Matt, it'll be okay," she said, trying to soothe his ego.

"No, Gill, it won't. Just leave me alone. I'm going to hop on the bus. Hey, you are coming?"

"No, I'm going to grab a ride home with my Dad."

"Fine, whatever. I'll see you later."

And just like that, he walked away, leaving Gill standing there in shock. No hug. No kiss. Nothing.

*What a dick.*

***

As Thanksgiving neared, Callie became a bit antsy. Her father, the ever-pleasant man that he was, told her to just head into the city and stay there over break . . . *by herself.*

Hired help would be there to cater to her every need, while he was out of town, busy with work. Doing what exactly? Who knew? Even his American clients would be breaking for the holiday. I thought it was an excuse to blow her off, but I never said anything.

I wanted to ask her to stay with us, but I knew my parents wouldn't allow it. Luckily, Gill came to the rescue. The moment she heard Callie was going to spend her break by herself, she called her parents in Connecticut and asked if Callie could join them for Thanksgiving.

Of course, they said yes.

And to everyone's astonishment, her father agreed to the new plans.

So, instead of staying home alone in New York, Callie packed up and went to Connecticut, spending the week with Gill and her family.

The night before the girls left, we double-dated and hit a movie at the triplex in Stony Brook. Our choices were as follows. First, we could go see *An American Tail*, the animated movie about a young mouse named Fievel Mousekewitzan and his journey immigrating to America from Russia.

*Pass.*

Choice two was a sappy love story, starring Tom Hanks, called *Every Time We Say Goodbye.* It was a movie set in WWII about a Protestant pilot, who falls in love with a girl from Jerusalem.

*Hard pass!*

The last movie was *Hoosiers*, the classic tale of a small-town high-school basketball coach, who transforms his team into champions. For Matt and me, there really was no choice. We're talking Gene Hackman, Dennis Hopper, sports, high school, everything a teen boy wanted in a movie, aside from sex and violence.

*We have ourselves a winner!*

So what movie did we see?

Yep, the sappy one with Tom Hanks.

For a Friday night, the theater was practically empty. We essentially had our choice of seating, so we found four center seats in a row, right in the middle of the theater. After buying our prerequisite bucket of popcorn and sodas, we settled in for the movie.

Throughout the movie, especially during the romantic scenes, Callie and I would kiss. We didn't dry hump each other or anything like that—just a sweet kiss or two.

For some reason, this seemed to bother Matt. Whenever we kissed, he would shoot us a look, and either roll his eyes or clear his throat, like we were disturbing him from enjoying this movie.

*Dude, what's your problem?*

To make matter worse, whenever he tried to do the same with Gill, she would either give him a quick peck or wave him off.

Once, Gill even said, "Matt, honey, c'mon. Knock it off. I'm trying to watch the movie."

*Oh, shot . . . blocked!*

This put him, understandably, in a sour mood, which lasted the rest of the evening, including our trip to Friendly's for dessert.

It was there, in that restaurant, that I witnessed for the first time the chink in Matt's armor.

He'd been my best friend since we started school. We played sports together, hung out together. To be frank, I looked up to him. I didn't have a brother of my own, and he was the closest thing to it.

Was he moody? Sure, what teenager wasn't? I knew I had my moments that he put up with. But this was different. This was a guy I didn't recognize. He wasn't usually like this when it was just the three of us.

But now that I had a girlfriend, it was like *I* was cramping *his* style. Like we were in competition, but not in our usual friendly way.

Callie and I were our usual "fawning all over each other" selves. Nothing too crazy, just young love, true love. You know. Holding hands. A kiss or two, here and there.

And I noticed, just like at the movies, whenever Callie and I were affectionate to each other, Matt would try to do the same to Gill.

Gill would either begrudgingly consent to his advances—and that's how it felt from an outsider's perspective, *begrudging consent*—or she would just tell him to stop, which didn't sit well with Matt and his enormous ego.

"Matt, c'mon, you're embarrassing me," Gill said.

"Jesus, Gill, give me a break." There was an edge to his voice, and then, "You know what? *Fine!*"

It caught all of us by surprise and made for an awkward date night, which sucked because this was my last night with Callie before break.

To make matters worse, Matt had driven that night, which meant I'd get dropped off first.

*Great. Now Callie's going to have to deal with his bullshit on the way back to school. Sorry, babe.*

While I was sorry, I didn't know how sorry I'd be.

# 39 - Broken Window

The ride home was as pleasant lying buck-naked, covered in honey, over a pit of pissed-off fire ants. Callie and I sat in the back seat, while Matt and Gill argued all the way to my house. Once, he took a corner hard, throwing Callie and me from one side of the car to the other.

"Dude! What the fuck! Slow down!" I yelled from the back seat.

"Sorry. See what you made me do?" he yelled at Gill.

"Me? I'm not the one driving like a maniac!"

"Hey, just slow down, okay? I want to get home in one piece," I interjected.

Matt waved a hand in the air dismissively. "Yeah, yeah, fine." Then he muttered something else I couldn't hear under his breath.

I turned and looked at Callie, mouthing, *I'm sorry.* She gave me a wink and a smile.

She was being a good sport about it, but I was not happy with Matt. At all.

Ten minutes later, we landed in my driveway. Matt barely missed blowing into the back end of my car as he came to a screeching halt.

*What an asshole! What's his problem?*

"Hey, Callie's going to walk me inside, okay?" I told them, not really caring if they minded or not.

Matt did the hand-wave thing again. "Yeah, fine, whatever. Take your time." Then he looked out his driver's-side window—another dismissal.

As we walked to my front door, I could hear Matt and Gill arguing from the car. I heard affectionate things like, "Why were you being such a bitch tonight?" and "Why are you being such an asshole?"

You know…love talk.

"Hey, do you want me to drive you back to school?" I asked Callie as we stepped inside.

"No, you better not. I'm afraid what he'll do if he's left alone with her tonight."

"Okay, well . . ." I said, bouncing on the balls of my feet.

Fortunately, it was late, and my parents were already in bed, so Callie and I were alone.

"I'm going to miss you," I whispered.

"I'm going to miss you, too."

"I love you, Callie."

"I love you, too."

She leaned her warm body into mine and kissed me long and hard in the front hall.

"Mmm . . . are you sure you don't want me to take you back? You *could* hang out here for a while."

*A man's gotta have hope.*

I gave her the puppy-dog eyes.

She giggled. "I *can't*. Not the way he's acting tonight. Rain check?"

"Anytime."

We agreed to talk in the morning before she headed out with Gill, and then I reluctantly let her go.

I stood in the doorway, watching Matt back out of my driveway, praying they'd make it there safely. It was past 9:30, the cut-off time for phone calls at my house, unless it was an emergency.

At 10:00 the following morning, the phone rang.

My father yelled up the stairs, "Champ, phone. It's Callie."

"Thanks, Dad. I'll take it up here, in your room."

I dashed into their room and grabbed the handset.

"Got it," I yelled.

"Got it?" Dad asked into the phone.

"Yep. Thanks, Dad."

"Have a great Thanksgiving, Callie," he said before hanging up.

"Thank you, sir. You, too." Once we were "alone," she added, "He's very sweet."

"Yeah, he's the best. So, how did it go last night?"

"Wow, you *don't* want to know."

I felt a chill run through my body. "That bad, huh?"

"You have *no* idea."

"What happened?"

Matt and Gill had argued the whole way back, not caring that Callie was in the backseat. In the parking lot at school, he came to a screeching halt, like he'd done in my driveway. This pissed me off, and Callie hadn't even gotten to the meat of the matter yet.

"Uh huh, then what?" I asked.

"Gill and I immediately jumped out of the car. She didn't even kiss him goodnight or say goodbye."

"Wow."

"Yeah. But . . . Matt refused to take the hint. He turned his car off and got out."

*Crap. This ain't good.*

"Go on," I said.

"Gill saw him, and she started running for the dorm. He chased after her."

"Oh, no."

"Yeah. He caught up to her outside the dorm, and the arguing started again. They were so loud that one of our dorm parents came out and asked Matt to leave."

"Oh, crap."

"Yeah. Then Matt started arguing with *her.* She told him if he didn't leave, he'd get a week's worth of detention when we got back from break."

"So, what did he do?"

"He left. Or at least we thought he did."

*Oh, no. Matt, what'd you do?*

"Don't tell me . . ."

"Yeah. He came back. Apparently, he left campus and parked his car in the bank parking lot, only to return and go behind the dorm . . . and started *throwing pebbles* at Gillian's window."

I just groaned.

"Yeah, only she wasn't in her room. She was in mine, crying. We had no idea he was out there."

"So, what happened?"

Why I asked, I did not know. Because I was already suspecting I knew the answer.

"Well, when she didn't come to the window, he got angry. Angrier, I should say. He thought she was ignoring him."

"Uh-huh. Makes sense. Then what?"

"He started throwing the pebbles harder and harder until he accidentally broke the window, which got *everyone's* attention. Then the campus security guard came. You know the one."

"The guy who walks around like he's Rambo?"

"Right. *Him.* Well, he tackled Matt to the ground and almost got him arrested."

"*What?* Are you *f-ing* kidding me?"

"Wait, it gets better."

I was pacing the floor at this point, incredulous. "*Better?*"

"They wound up calling the headmaster *and* his parents."

*Fuuuuck!*

"Oh, no."

"Oh, yeah. And the headmaster was already packed up and ready to head out of town for the holidays. *He was pissed.*"

"Oh my God. Matt's an *idiot*! Why didn't he just go home and cool off?"

"I have no idea."

"So, what happened to him? How much trouble is he in?"

"I'm not totally sure, to be honest. I know he has to pay to replace the window."

"That makes sense."

"I also think he was suspended," she said in a low voice.

My heart hit the floor.

*Dude, what were you thinking?*

# 40 - Surprise Call

Callie and I spent the next half hour proclaiming our love for each other, the way teenage lovebirds do. This was the first relationship for either of us, and we'd both fallen hard.

After hanging up with her, I thought about calling Matt but didn't. I didn't know what to say. I mean, I knew what I *wanted* to say, but wouldn't.

Didn't he know how good he had it? Didn't he know how awesome Gill was? Why was he acting like such an asshole? Why did he tear around and almost crash into the back of my car last night? Why did he come to a screeching halt at school, scaring Callie? We'd already lost one classmate this year in a car accident. Did we really need another loss?

I just shook my head as I stared at the handset before placing it back on the cradle. I was scheduled to work that evening at the diner, and I even took on some additional shifts to make up for lost wages and make my father happy. Plus, with Christmas around the corner, I wanted the extra cash.

The week was uneventful, and Mom and Dad worked together to create a magnificent array of dishes for Thanksgiving. It was nice to see them interacting in a loving way, despite the financial circumstances. They were smiling and flitting around like . . . teenagers in love.

Did my heart good.

Between turkey-day football games, I received a surprise phone call.

"Hey, handsome!"

My girl Callie.

"*Hey*! What are you doing calling me?" I asked, surprised to hear her voice.

I looked into the living room to make sure my parents were still watching TV. They were.

*Yes! Privacy!*

"What, you don't want me to call you?"

"I never said that. I'm just surprised, that's all. So, how're things going, so far?"

"I'm having a super nice time. Gillian's family is so nice. Her nine-year-old little brother's a sweetie."

"So, they're sitting right there, listening to your call, huh?" I joked.

"*What*? No! You jerk." She burst into laughter, which was contagious.

"Man, I miss that laugh. I miss you," I said.

"I miss you, too, Captain. That's sort of the reason why I called."

"Sort of, huh?"

"Well, Gill and I were talking . . ."

*Uh, oh. This can't be good.*

"You were huh? About what?"

"Well, since tomorrow is Black Friday, Gill's mom is planning on taking us to New York City tomorrow to go Christmas shopping."

"That's cool."

"Yeah, and Gill and I were wondering . . ." She didn't finish.

"Wondering . . .?"

"If maybe . . . you could . . . meet us there?"

I wasn't expecting that request. Such a great idea, too. "Wow, that would be so awesome, but there's no way my folk would let me drive all the way there."

"Let you what?" my mother chimed in as she walked into the kitchen.

"It's nothing, Mom, really."

"Ask her," Callie shouted, loud enough for my mother to hear her.

"Ask me what. Hi, Callie!"

"*Hiiiii!*" Callie yelled.

*Jesus! My ear!*

Mom looked at me with a raised an eyebrow, waiting for my question.

"Okay, well, Callie and Gill . . . you remember Gill, right? Matt's girlfriend."

"Yes, I remember her. Lovely girl. Very pretty."

"Yeah, her. Anyway, they want to know if I can meet them in the city tomorrow. Gill's mother is taking them Christmas shopping for Black Friday."

"Ohhhh. Well, I don't know, honey. I mean, how would you get there? Plus, the city, by yourself, on the busiest shopping day of the year, no less. I don't think so."

Her pouty face spoke volumes. While I appreciated her sympathy, I had been hoping for a different answer.

I went for broke and pressed on with pleading eyes.

"But I wouldn't be alone. I'd be with Callie, Gill, and Gill's mom. I could take the train in and meet them at the station in the city."

"Let me talk to your father about this." And she hustled to the living room.

"You heard?" I asked.

"Yeah, I heard. Fingers crossed."

"I don't see it happening. When are you coming back to school?"

"Sunday."

"Okay. Then I'll probably see you Sunday or Monday at school, depending on what time you make it back."

Just then, my mother stepped back into the kitchen. She held out her hand, gesturing for the phone receiver, and said, "Let me talk to Gill's mother."

"*Really* Mom? Sure, hold on."

Callie said, "I heard. Let me get Mrs. Thompson."

To my absolute astonishment, the two moms worked out a game plan, and suddenly, I was going to the city on Friday. Mrs. Thompson promised my mother that she'd pick me up at Penn Station and chaperone our little group the entire time.

I couldn't believe my eyes and ears.

"Really, Mom?"

She handed me the phone. "Really. Just be careful, okay?"

"I will, I will. Thank you, Mom. Thank you!"

My smile was humongous as I waited for Callie to come back to the phone.

Mom said, "Don't thank me. Thank your father." Then she rolled her eyes and walked away.

"Thanks, Dad!" I yelled.

# 41 - Food for Thought

I grabbed an old train schedule from our catch-all drawer and told Callie what time I'd make it to Penn Station. Before hanging up, I asked her about inviting Matt to join us.

"I don't think that's such a good idea," Callie said.

"How come?"

"Well, when Mr. and Mrs. Thompson heard what happened, they weren't too happy. They want Gill to break things off with Matt."

*Crap!*

"Oh. That sucks. How does Gill feel?"

Callie made a loud sighing sound. "She doesn't know. She said she loves him, but . . ."

And that about summed it up. Things weren't looking good for ol' Matt. I decided to give him a call. Turned out, he wasn't able to take my call because he was grounded. It made sense. God knows I would've been grounded or worse had I pulled that stunt

*As Dad always says, if you can't do the time, don't do the crime, you moron!*

As we sat and enjoy our holiday spread, the conversation turned to Callie.

"So, how is she doing? Enjoying her break?" Mom asked.

"Sounds like it."

I loved talking about Callie, but I was more focused on getting my plate set up. I poured gravy on my turkey, stuffing, and mashed potatoes, then added some cranberry sauce out of the can (*the way God intended it*), and sweet potatoes to my overflowing plate.

"Hmmm. I might need two plates," I muttered.

Dad had poured Mom some white wine, and she took a small sip before asking, "It's very nice of Gill's family to invite her over for Thanksgiving. What happened to her family?"

That was when I explained how Callie's mom passed away over the summer, from cancer. The moment I mentioned it, I saw a flash of pain cross my mother's face. She'd worked the oncology ward in the past and dealt with many cancer patients over the years.

My dad was equally saddened, his fork stopped in midair. "I didn't know her mom passed away."

"Yeah. She's still trying to, uh, get through it," I said, not knowing the right words to describe how Callie was managing her grief.

My parents nodded knowingly.

"Well, what about her father?" Mom asked, causing me to chuckle.

"That guy's a real assho— I mean, jerk, Mom. A *real* jerk."

I proceeded to tell them about his background, and how he doesn't celebrate most American holidays, including Thanksgiving. I told them how he was too busy to spend time with Callie over the break, and how he'd wanted Callie to go to their apartment in the city and spend the break by herself.

Mom shook her head when she heard this.

"That's horrible. Had I known this, we would have invited her to stay here with us. I'm sure we could have worked something out," she said.

*Oh,* now *she tells me.*

I also told them about how he'd treated her the first time I saw her on campus—like a dog who needed to obey him.

"Oh, come on, champ. I'm sure it wasn't that bad."

"It was worse, Dad. It was worse."

I then told them about how he treated her during rehearsal. About the driver/bodyguard standing outside the Mercedes as her dad yelled at her.

"He doesn't sound like a very nice man." Mom commented.

I couldn't have nodded more emphatically.

I concluded by telling them about his big business empire in Greece and how he supposedly has his name on everything over there—buildings, shipping yards, even olive oil.

"Oh and get this. After she graduates college, he expects her to marry some Greek guy, join the family business, and start having kids. Like, right after college, just like her older brother and sister did."

Dad's eyes went wide. "Wow."

"And how does he feel about his daughter dating a young Hispanic boy?" Mom asked.

"No idea. My guess is she hasn't told him. He'd probably chuck a fit."

Mom picked up her wine, but before taking a sip, she asked, "If that's the case, do you think it's a good idea to continue dating her?"

*What?*

"Um, yeah, Mom, I do. I mean, the heck with what her father thinks."

My parents looked at each other and then down at their plates.

"What?" I asked.

"Nothing, son, nothing. Just *be careful*, okay?" Mom said. "I know men like that. They're very controlling and can make life very *difficult* for people who . . . *cross him.*"

*Cross him? We're not crossing him. We're in love.*

"Mom's right, champ. Just, be careful, okay? Look, Mom and I both like Callie. We just don't want you to get hurt."

"I'm not going to get hurt." I countered, and my parents looked at one another again.

Dad held up his hands in defense. "Okay, champ, okay. It's just food for thought. Speaking of which, pass me the salt and pepper, please."

# 42 - Black Friday Begins

I got up early the next morning to a typical cool, gray Long Island November. I hopped out of bed, ready to hit the city to meet my girlfriend and Gill, along with her family. I threw on my favorite pair of Levi's, a button-down shirt, blue sweater, and sneakers. Next to my wallet on the counter, I found a slip of paper with some cash.

Mom left me one hundred dollars and a note to enjoy myself, which put a smile on my face. I sucked down my bowl of cereal, grabbed my brown bomber jacket, my tan Burberry scarf, and keys and said goodbye to Dad.

I drove myself to the train station and was pleased to see that the train was running on time. Business people shuffled back and forth, and I realized they all looked miserable. Oddly enough, they reminded me of my father when he'd been working at Grumman. He had the same pained expression when he left for work and when he returned. It was the first time I'd thought about that in a while.

As I grabbed my seat, my mom's words flashed through my mind.

"Remember to be careful, and don't talk to strangers. Also, if you get in trouble on the train, find a conductor. They'll help you. And keep your wallet in your front pocket, so you don't get pickpocketed."

I don't know how many warnings she had left to give, but I was happy not to hear any more than that.

I looked out the window and watched the Long Island landscape pass by. The closer we got to Penn Station, the dirtier and more urban the view became. The landscape transformed from warm, upper-middle-class homes to graffiti-strewn buildings.

As we pulled into Penn Station, nervous butterflies began dancing in my stomach. It had only been a few days since I'd seen Callie, but I missed her, something awful, as they say. I was excited to see her. Plus, this was the first time we'd been together in Manhattan, even though Gill's family would be there with us. It felt, I don't know . . . special.

"Next stop, Penn Station." The conductor announced as he walked through our compartment.

As instructed, I left the train, subconsciously patting my front pocket to make sure my wallet was still there, and walked up the steps to the main platform to patiently wait for Gill and her mom where we had agreed.

I'd never seen this many people in one place before, outside of a Mets game. It was controlled chaos, as people ran from one platform to the next or from one platform to an exit.

It was like being caught in the middle of a swarm of bees, and all you could do was get out of the way and lean up against the dirty wall; otherwise, you'd get stung, or worse. The cross-section of people at Penn Station amazed my seventeen-year-old eyes.

There were people dressed in upscale designer clothes, and people dressed in ripped-up rags, begging for change as they sat in their own urine. At least, I assumed it was their own. I never asked.

Fortunately, I didn't have to wait too long before hearing Callie's angelic voice over the cacophony of the station.

"There he is! Hey, *Captain!*" Callie shouted, waving and smiling ear to ear as she ran toward my open arms.

"Hey!" I said, catching her and giving her a big hug and kiss.

"Hey, *Captain*," Gill said with an elbow jab and sarcastic smirk. "Have you been waiting long?"

"Nope, I just got here. Man, this place is nuts. You'd think they were giving stuff away."

"You remember my mom, right?" Gill said.

I reached out and shook hands with Mrs. Thompson. "Sure. Nice to see you again. Thanks for letting me join you."

"Not a problem, sweetheart. Robbie could use a companion, while we ladies power shop. Right, ladies?"

*Uh, excuse me? Yeah, I'm not here to babysit Robbie! I'm here to hang out with my girlfriend.*

Mrs. Thompson must have picked up on my expression because she added, "But don't worry. You'll have plenty of time with Callie, too."

"Oh, uh, thanks, ma'am."

"Don't worry, *Cap*. My Mom's cool," Gill whispered. "Plus, I've got your back."

Apparently, they'd taken the train in from Hartford, Connecticut, to Penn Station, which is why it was convenient for them to meet me there. The moment we all stepped outside, a strong breeze blew past us. Winter was here.

We almost lost Robbie. Had Gill not been holding his hand, he would have blown away along with the small pile of trash that blew down the block of 34th Street.

"Okay, everybody. Stay close," Mrs. Thompson ordered. She turned right and directed us to our first stop, Macy's, just a few city blocks away.

It was like she was on speed, the way we made our way to the store. Like an old pro, she juked around people, jaywalking as she pleased, without a care in the world. We all just got in line behind her and followed suit. If this were a NASCAR race, her drag would have kept us close.

***

"I think she needs some help in there," Gill said, pointing to one of the changing rooms and giving me a knowing smirk. "Come on, Robbie. Let's go find mom."

*Some help?*

"Hey, Captain. Can you come in here a sec? I'm having trouble with this zipper," Callie called from the dressing-room area.

*Am I allowed in there?*

I looked around, shrugged my shoulders, and peeked my head inside the changing area. As busy as the store was, surprisingly, this space was relatively quiet. I walked in, feeling like I was walking behind enemy lines, and whispered for Callie.

"Callie! *Callie!* Which one are you in?"

Suddenly, I felt a hand grab the collar of my bomber jacket and drag me into a dressing room, closing the curtain behind me. Callie then spun me around, pressed her warm body against mine and pinned me to the wall, kissing me with her delicious lips.

When we came up for air, she said, "Mmm . . . I missed you."

I was completely lost in the moment, between her captivating blue eyes and smile.

"Same here."

I drew her close again for another kiss.

Things quickly got heated in the Macy's dressing room. I mean, she was in her lacy pink bra and panties, and her breasts were calling my name.

After a dangerously long amount of time had passed, Callie reluctantly pulled away from me.

"Mmm, you better get out of here, before we start something we can't finish. Can you hand me my bra, please?"

*Who said I couldn't finish? Oh, I'll finish, my friend. I'll finish.*

But she was right. This was getting a little risky. I honked her left boob, handed back her bra, and then poked my head around the curtain to make sure the coast was clear. It was. I darted out of the dressing room like a bat out of hell.

*Man, I love Macy's!*

# 43 - Tavern on the Green

After some impressive displays of power shopping by the three ladies, it was finally time to break and eat. I hated shopping, and other than the moment at Macy's with Callie, I had become bored enough to actually find myself enjoying spending time with little Robbie.

Yep, definitely time to eat.

As we drove through the city toward the restaurant, I noticed a look of sadness on Callie's face. She'd clearly had fun shopping, but she didn't seem happy. That's when it hit me. I remembered that her apartment overlooked Central Park, which meant we were near her home.

"You okay?" I whispered.

"Huh? Oh, yeah. I'm good. I'm good." She forced out a smile and took my hand.

"Your mom?"

Callie nodded and then turned to stare out the window.

I scooted closer and put my arm around her shoulders. I would have given anything in the world for her mom to still be alive. My heart ached for Callie.

The sun hadn't quite set yet, but the closer we got to the restaurant, the darker outside it became. As we came around a curve, from the back of the cab, I saw Tavern on the Green for the first time.

*Wow.*

I'd heard of Tavern on the Green from television and the movies, but I never expected it to look like this. The grandeur of the place was lost on no one that late Friday afternoon. Even Robbie was impressed. And that's saying something.

The moment you drove onto the circular driveway and saw the magnificent front archway, you knew you were at some place special. I felt like a kid at Disney World. I half expected Cinderella to roll up in her enchanted horse-drawn carriage.

The maître d escorted us through the lavishly decorated restaurant to a table almost in the center of the restaurant. Now, I don't care if you went there every day or if you were a tourist, like us, but if you didn't or couldn't appreciate the majesty of the place, there was something wrong with you.

From the twinkling chandeliers to the ornate candles to the lit Christmas trees and antique decorations, it was like we stepped onto the set of a Christmas movie. All that was missing was Santa Claus himself walking around and handing out candy canes.

We had a great time at lunch, laughing and chatting about the day. Periodically, Callie and I would hold hands under the table. She would make slow circles on the back of my hand with her French-manicured thumb, which sent sparks of love straight to my heart.

After lunch, our waiter came by and presented the dessert tray. It had everything you'd expect from a high-end New York City restaurant.

Three different types of homemade New York-style cheesecake, an assortment of seasonal berries, Crème Brule, a seven-layer carrot cake that was larger than my head, a death-by-chocolate cake and, of course, ice cream, made fresh on premise daily, as were all the desserts.

It all looked so good, but we were stuffed, and getting a little tired after the long day, so we declined the dessert, and Mrs. Thompson asked for the check.

When I reached for my wallet, which still contained the money my mom had given me, Mrs. Thompson merely winked and shook her head.

Without even looking at the bill, she handed her credit card to our waiter. I guess when you have money, you don't check the damages. Me? I would have checked to see if they'd charged us for the ice cubes in our water glasses.

As we waited for the waiter to return, Robbie asked to go to the bathroom, so I offered to escort him, which made Mrs. Thompson happy.

"So, how was your burger, buddy?" I asked as we entered the men's room.

"It was awesome. How was yours?" Robbie asked as we ponied up to the urinals.

"Awesome. And huge. How about them homemade potato chips, huh?"

"Yeah, those were really good, too."

After taking care of our business, we walked to the sinks to wash our hands. As we did, I overheard a familiar voice. My eyes immediately shot up to the mirror.

"Oh, excuse me."

I watched as he stepped aside, allowing some guy to enter the restroom before ponying up to the sink next to mine.

Washing his hands and checking his look in the mirror stood a well-dressed Mr. Christos. Even though he caught me staring at him, he didn't seem to recognize me. I must have been too insignificant to make it onto his radar.

"C'mon, Robbie. Let's go," I said quickly.

I suddenly felt the need to protect Callie from running into her father. I had a feeling if that happened, it wouldn't go over well. Especially after I saw who he was there with, after he left the men's room.

You remember those supermodels from back in the '80s? With their big hair, dressed to the hilt in their slinky dresses, high heels, and flashy jewelry? Yeah, that's what was hanging on Mr. Christos's arm. Some gorgeous brunette, about half his age, if not younger.

*So, let me get this straight. You don't have time for your daughter, but you have time for some bimbo? Real classy, dude. Real fucking classy.*

It would have destroyed Callie. I watched carefully as they were fortunately escorted to another section of the restaurant, and Callie was none the wiser.

"Are we ready to call it a day?" Mrs. Thompson asked as she signed the bill.

We all nodded in agreement.

"Mrs. Thompson, thank you so much for lunch. And for letting me come today," I said as we walked to the exit.

"Think nothing of it. I'm glad you came. Robbie certainly seemed to enjoy you."

"He's great. I enjoyed hanging out with him, too," I said and meant it, which put a smile on Robbie's face.

Callie and I had a cab to ourselves again as we battled the busy streets of New York, taking us back to Penn Station. Her dad was on my mind, and I tried hard to push the thought of him aside. I didn't want him spoiling any part of this day.

"Did you have a good day?" I asked Callie as I held her.

"Yeah, I did. Did you?"

"The best."

"Good, I'm glad."

As we kissed, and I noticed the cabbie watching us in his rearview mirror.

*Keep your eyes on the road, pal. There's nothing to see back here. Nothing at all.*

# 44 - Leave Her Alone

You ever get into a misunderstanding with your best friend? Over something you consider stupid? Yeah, that's what happened between Matt and me, the week school started back up.

I called him on Sunday, hoping he'd be un-grounded by then, and he was. But just for the phone. He was still grounded otherwise, until further notice.

"Dude, I'm sorry you're on restriction."

"Yeah, me, too. They even took my car away from me, and now I have to take the bus to school."

"Damn, that sucks."

"Tell me about it," he groaned.

"So, what happened, bro? What'd ya do?" I asked, pretending I didn't know the story.

He didn't have to know I'd talked to Callie about it. I really wanted to hear his side of the situation. Like my dad often said, there were usually two sides to every story.

"Dude, it was so stupid. I made a simple mistake, that's all."

"And that was . . .?"

"It was nothing. I accidentally broke a window. No big deal. It's not like I killed someone."

"You broke a window?" I replied with surprise in my voice.

"Yeah. Again, it was no big deal. I didn't mean to do it. I was trying to get Gill's attention, and I guess I hit the sweet spot on the window, and the glass broke."

I just whistled into the phone.

"Exactly. No big deal. It was Gill's fault, anyway. She was the one acting like a bitch all night. I mean, you saw her, right?"

*Wrong question, Matt.*

"Actually, dude, she was acting fine. You were the one who was acting . . . and I say this as your best friend, like a bit—*just a bit*—of an asshole."

"*What?* How can you say that? You saw her. How she was all, *knock it off Matt, get off me, Matt.*"

"Look I'm just . . ." And then I wasn't sure what else to say. I wanted to smack him upside the head.

"You what? All of a sudden, you're an expert in relationships because you have a girlfriend? If you ask me, *you* were the one acting like an asshole that night. You couldn't keep your hands off of Callie, and you kept throwing it in *my* face. You know how Gill is."

"Throwing it in your face? Are you nuts? We weren't throwing anything in your face. We were acting normal, in front of our best friends. I didn't realize it bothered you so much."

"Yeah, well, now you know, *Captain.*"

"You know what? Go screw yourself," I shouted and began to hang up the phone.

"Oh, yeah? You, too!" I heard him yell at the last minute, just before I slammed the handset back into place.

*What an asshole!*

***

Matt missed the first week back because of his suspension, and the gossipmongers ran wild with that one. You would have thought Matt had murdered someone, the way they were talking about it.

Even though I was mad at him, I still found myself defending him. He only broke a window. He didn't burn down the building.

Anyway, the following week, he returned to school, and of course, we shared our first class together. I got to class before him and grabbed a seat in the back row, where we normally sit. When he walked in though, he glared at me and found a seat in the front row.

*Seriously, dude? Whatever.*

I wasn't the only person to notice the glare or the fact that he didn't sit next to me. The school gossips stayed in overdrive that day. Last week, they were buzzing about him breaking the window. Today, he was clearly in a fight with his best friend. Oh, yeah, the tongues were wagging.

Like I predicted, the news spread fast. By lunchtime, Callie tracked me down in the kitchen to find out what was going on.

"Nothing. Matt's just being an asshole."

I didn't want to tell Callie his side of the story, since part of his issues had to do with us.

"What's going on now?"

"Nothing. He just doesn't like the fact that I didn't back him up when he told me about breaking the window."

A partial truth was better than nothing, I figured.

"Well, he was wrong. Doesn't he see that?"

"I don't know. Who knows? I guess not."

Callie rolled her eyes, incredulous. "Well, are you doing okay?"

"*Me*? Yeah, babe, I'm fine. It'll blow over. It's no big deal. It's not the first time he's been an asshole, and knowing him the way I do, it won't be the last time."

The rest of the day went by quickly, and our teachers didn't skip a beat in handing out homework. It felt like they'd missed torturing us or something.

Winter sports started up, which meant wrestling for Matt, who was captain of the wrestling team, and basketball for me. Similar to football, practically anyone who tried out made the basketball team. Depending on your skill level, you either played varsity or junior varsity. I was a starting forward for our varsity team.

Gill and Callie both tried out and made the swimming team. This didn't surprise me, because Callie certainly had the body for it. I hadn't seen her in action yet, but according to Gill, Callie swam like a fish.

When I asked Callie about her skills, she said she spent lots of time swimming in the Mediterranean.

"It was practically my backyard pool growing up."

*Must be nice.*

After practice, I entered the boy's locker room to shower and change out of my basketball gear and ran into Matt. I gave him the head-nod, but he just glared at me, so I steered clear.

*Jesus, dude. Get over it already.*

As became our norm, Callie was waiting for me outside the boy's locker room, after practice. Standing next to her was Gill, which surprised me. I didn't expect to see her waiting outside the locker room since "the incident."

"Oh, hey!" I said to Gill, my surprise obvious in my tone.

I threw an arm around Callie and gave her a squeeze.

Gill said, "Hey. Is, um, Matthew in there?"

I snorted out a laugh. "Oh, yeah. He's in there, all right."

"Could you please tell him that I'm waiting for him out here?"

*Please don't put me in the middle of this shit.*

Callie read my expression and quickly shot me *the look*.

*Fine!*

"I'll be right back," I said, reluctantly.

"Thank you," Gill said.

I just waved my hand as I walked back into the locker room. Tracking down Matt was easy. He'd used the same locker for the past three years.

"Hey. Gill's waiting for you outside."

"What does she want?" he barked.

"How the fuck should I know? She asked me to come in here and tell you that she's waiting for you, so I did. Later." I turned and walked away.

"Great, useful as ever," he mumbled to himself.

I flipped him the finger as I left the locker room.

I said to the girls, "He'll be right out."

"Do you want us to wait?" Callie asked Gill.

*What? C'mon, Callie! This is bullshit. It's none of our business. Let's leave them alone.*

The moment Gill responded with, "If you don't mind," I knew we were doomed.

Sure enough, Callie said, "No, not at all, right?"

She looked at me to confirm. What was going to say? No?

"Of course we'll stay," I said.

We heard the inner locker room door open, which meant someone was coming. Sure enough, it was Matt. His hair was wet and slicked back from his shower, and he was carrying his gym bag over his shoulder.

By the look on his face and the way his neck jerked back, like someone had yanked it with a hook, he was surprised to see Callie and me waiting with Gill.

"What are *they* doing here?" he asked, glaring at Callie and me.

Gill lifted her chin. "I asked them to wait, since I didn't know how long you'd be."

"I told you after lunch, that I'd meet you after practice. You didn't need to . . . you know what? Forget it. Come on. Let's go talk." He grabbed Gill's arm and practically dragged her up the hallway toward the exit.

Gill didn't like this one bit. And neither did Callie, based on her expression. They made it a few feet before Gill yanked free.

"See, this is what I'm talking about. You manhandle me like I'm your property or something," she barked at him.

"Gill, you're being ridiculous. C'mon, can we just go somewhere and talk about this before I miss my bus."

"You know what? Don't worry about it. Go catch your bus." She stormed back in our direction.

"Gill! C'mon. Don't be that way. Give me a chance." He caught up to her and grabbed her by the wrist.

That didn't sit well with neither Gill nor Callie.

"Hey! Leave her alone. You heard her. Go catch your bus," Callie yelled as Gill yanked free from Matt's grip.

In my mind's eye, I pictured her mother for some reason. I half expected her to wrap her arms around Gill to protect her from Matt.

"Mind your own business, Callie. This has *nothing* to do with *you*."

"Well, I'm *making it* my business," Callie replied, placing her body between Matt and Gill.

"Dude, tell your girlfriend to mind her own damn business before she says something she'll regret."

Now, *that* didn't sit well with me. No one, including my best friend, threatened my girlfriend.

"Dude, just go grab your bus," I told him.

Matt spun around and got in my face.

"And what if I don't, *huh?*" he asked, shoving me a little. "What're *you* gonna do about it?"

He continued to shove me, and I tried to maintain my composure, "Matt, knock it off. Go catch your bus and cool off."

"And if I don't? What the fuck are *you* gonna do about it, huh, *Captain?*" He shoved me again, harder.

"Matthew, leave him alone," Gill yelled, but he ignored her.

"Dude, I'm serious. Knock it *off.*"

I blocked his shove and got up on his grill in return.

Now remember, Matt was the captain of the wrestling team, and for good reason. He'd made it to the State finals the previous two years, and everyone expected him to do the same this year. He was an outstanding wrestler, who didn't appreciate anyone, even his best friend, getting up on his grill.

Matt just laughed at me, knowing I was outclassed and, more than likely, about to get hurt if I didn't back down. Usually, I would have. I've seen him in fights before and witnessed his skills.

But at this moment, none of that mattered. My heart rate skyrocketed, my veins filled with adrenaline, and my teenage testosterone levels went through the roof. I wasn't backing down.

He'd threatened the one person on the planet I cared about most. I didn't care if he could kick my ass and twist my body into a pretzel, I wasn't going to back down, regardless of the threat of an ass beating.

*And an ass beating I received.*

# 45 - My Beating

Matt shoved me hard into an innocent eighth-grader who made the mistake of trying to walk by us. The eighth-grader's backpack went flying in one direction while he flew in the other, landing hard like a ragdoll. The poor kid.

Fortunately for him, there was a girl exiting the girls' locker room at the time, who came to his rescue.

"Way to go, *asshole*," I said through gritted teeth, shoving Matt back.

*Mistake!*

He took hold of my wrist and twisted, shooting arcs of pain up my arm. He then moved his hip into mine, hooked his arm around my body and hip-tossed me.

Like that eighth-grader, I landed hard on the linoleum floor. The impact blew all the air from my body. My world was rocked, and not in a good way. I hurt all over, from the back of my head, which had bounced off the floor, to my lower back.

Before I knew it, he wrapped his legs around me, put me into a chokehold, and started punching me in the face.

*Bam, bam, bam!*

Both girls screamed as he whaled away at my head.

Callie jumped on his back and grabbed his hair to try to get him off me. All that did was piss him off more. Matt shoved her away, but not before Callie left three scratch marks across his left cheek, which added fuel to his fire. He continued to punch me—one punch after the other, in rapid succession.

*Bam, bam, bam!*

I tried to get him off me, but he wouldn't budge. He was bigger, stronger, and better trained than me. I was helpless, starting to see stars. I knew it, and so did he.

"What do you have to say now, big man? Not so tough now, are you?" he growled.

The girl's screams and our ruckus echoed down the hall. As he inflicted damage, students piled out of both locker rooms to witness my best friend beating the crap out of me. Blood poured from my ear and nose, and my eyes blurred from the punches. I tried my best to block the punches, but I couldn't even catch my breath, since he was choking me.

Fortunately for me, Coach Connor ran over and practically ripped Matt off me.

"Hey, knock it off, Salvatore! Get off of him!" he shouted.

Coach shoving him against the wall and got in his face. Matt, smartly, threw his hands up. As pissed off as Matt was, he knew better than to get into it with the man who trained him how to wrestle.

"You two. In my office. NOW!" he barked, jabbing a finger at Matt and me.

"But I'll miss my bus," Matt said.

"I don't care. Get in there."

He dragged Matt by the back of his collar, *escorting* him to his office.

As he did this, Callie and Gill were by my side, helping me up.

"Oh my God, are you okay?" Callie said through tears of anger.

"Oh my God, I'm so sorry about that," Gill said, horrified as she stared at me.

I didn't say a word. I just stood there, breathing hard, in and out, pissed off and embarrassed. I felt my right eye swelling up and blood dripping from my nose and right ear. Hot tears ran down my face. My vision was blurred, my ears were ringing, and my body ached all over.

"You! Get in here! Now!" Coach Connor yelled from his doorway, pointing in my direction.

I turned and glared at him. I was pissed. Very pissed. I stormed past Gill and Callie, pushed my way past Coach Connor, and came at Matt from behind. He was sitting in one of the folding chairs in front of the desk.

I grabbed him by the hair and threw him down to the floor, backward. I was able to punch him in the face twice and get in a good kick to the head, before Coach Connor grabbed me around the waist and carried me out of his office, shutting the door behind him.

I was fit to be tied.

"Let me go. Matt, *you motherfucker*. I'm going to *kill you*," I yelled as I tried to release Coach Connor's grip on me.

Fortunately, he had a strong grip. He literally lifted me over his shoulder and fireman-carried me to the boys' locker room.

"Put me down! Put me the fuck down! I'm going to kill him!"

"Calm down. You're not going to kill anyone," Coach said.

"I am too! Let me go!"

We were inside the locker room now, and Coach ordered everyone to clear out until instructed otherwise. Only after the last person had left the locker room did he finally put me down.

"You have two choices. You can calm down on your own, or I can drag you into the shower and calm you down myself. Your call," he said.

"Coach, I'm going to kill him," I said through hot tears and clenched teeth.

"No, you're not. Now calm down and tell me what happened."

"What *happened*? What happened is he's an *asshole—that's* what happened."

He rolled his eyes. "I will only ask you one more time. What happened?"

"He sucker-punched me, Coach. Then he flipped me to the floor, wrapped me up, put me in a chokehold, and started whaling on my face." I was still huffing and puffing and could hardly get the words out.

I pointed to my face. "Look at me!"

He blew out a breath and shook his head.

"Let's get you cleaned up." He placed his arm around my shoulder and escorted me to the sinks.

I reviewed the damage in the mirror. Sure enough, I had a swollen eye that would soon be black, and bloody ear, nose, and busted lip.

*You fucking asshole! I'm going to kill you for this! You motherfucker! I'm going to get you! You better stay the fuck away from me from now on. If I see you in the parking lot, I'm going to run you over with my car, like Christine, in that Stephen King book.*

Coach Connor did his best to calm me down and clean me up, but I had blood all over me. My shirt was ripped. My folks were going to kill me. But that was the least of my worries.

As I stood there staring at my reflection, I heard the locker-room door open, causing me to tense up. I half-expected it to be Matt, running to the sinks to continue my beating. Fortunately for me, it wasn't.

"Can I come in?" Callie asked from the doorway.

Coach Connor just sighed and nodded.

"Come on in, but make it quick," he said.

Callie made a beeline for me at the sink.

I didn't want to see her. I didn't want to see anyone. I was embarrassed. I felt humiliated. I had been *beaten up* . . . by my *best friend* . . . in front of my *girlfriend,* no less. As she touched my lower back, I winced. My breath became ragged, and I felt a new hot tear roll down my cheek.

"Callie, go. Leave me alone."

"No. Not until I know you're all right."

"I'm *fine*. Just leave me alone, please."

Of course, she didn't leave. She couldn't. It wasn't in her DNA. She was her mother's daughter. There was someone hurting in front of her. And not just any someone, but someone she loved.

She gently wrapped her arms around my whole aching body, and the gesture was so unbelievably comforting, I just let her do it, let myself cry out all the tears of anger and humiliation.

"Shhh. I'm right here. I'm not going anywhere. I've got you," she whispered.

"Why don't I leave you two alone for a few minutes?" I heard Coach Connor say, and he stepped out of the room.

"He's such an *asshole*, Callie. He's such an asshole."

"I know, I know," she soothed.

"I can't believe I let him sucker-punch me like that."

"It wasn't your fault. He's a bully and an asshole."

"I can't believe I've defended him over the years. I can't believe he was my best friend," I whispered, full of anger and betrayal.

"I know. I'm so sorry."

We stayed this way for a few minutes, her holding me by the sinks of our smelly boy's locker room. I wondered briefly what she thought of the place. Did it mirror her locker room? Did theirs stink like smelly sweat socks and disinfectant, too?

Minutes later, Coach Connor reentered the locker room. "Okay, you two. Let's wrap it up. We need to allow some of these boys back in here to finish changing, and I need to see *you* in my office."

"I'll wait for you," Callie said, wiping some tears from my face.

I leaned my head into her hand. "Thanks."

After she left, I took a few minutes to clean up. I splashed my face with water and blew my nose, then looked at my reflection one more time.

*You're a mess. Aaron's going to shit himself. Mom and Dad are going to shit themselves. I'm screwed!*

I went back to Coach Connor's office near the front of the building, expecting to find Matt inside as well. Fortunately for both of us, he wasn't there. I later found out that Coach had told him to go home and that he'd be calling his parents later that evening.

I plopped down in the same chair Matt had previously occupied.

"So, what happened again? This time, I want details," Coach said.

I gave him the entire rundown, leaving nothing out.

"I thought you two idiots were best friends?"

"We are. We were. He started it, Coach. Just like I told you. I don't care what he says. It was his fault."

"That's what I've gathered. Gill and Callie came to my office and told me the same thing, while you were cleaning yourself up. Listen, I know you didn't start it, but I am going to have to give you detention."

"*What*? But that's not fair. I was just defending Gill and Callie."

"I know, but we have a no-fighting policy here at school, as you well know, regardless of who started it."

I knew it, but I didn't like it.

"That sucks!"

"Yes, it does. Especially when the two who are fighting are best friends."

"*Were* best friends. *Were*!"

"Uh-huh. Well, I've seen things like this happen before. Believe it or not, it all blows over eventually."

"Whatever. Is that it? I have to get to play rehearsal," I replied with attitude.

"Yes, that's all. Come see me tomorrow for detention. You're going to have to serve three hours, starting tomorrow."

I stood, shaking my head in disbelief. "And what about Matt?"

"What about him?"

"Is he getting three hours, too?"

"Oh, no. He's getting suspended for a week."

That set me back on my heels. "Oh."

"Anything else you want to know?"

"Um . . . no."

"Okay, well, go on. Get out of here. Get to your play rehearsal. I still have calls to make. First to the Dean of Students, then to Matt's parents and then to yours."

"Mine? Why mine?"

"Because you got into a fight."

"That's not fair. My parents are going to kill me."

"No, they won't. I'll explain what happened. You'll be fine. And eventually, I'll make it home tonight, hopefully in time to put my kids to bed."

"Sorry, Coach." I lowered my head and shuffled out of the office.

# 46 - The Nurse's Office

Callie and I found a quiet bench on campus to sit and talk. Rehearsal was due to start in about fifteen minutes. The blood stopped flowing from my nose and ear. I could barely see out of my right eye, which was swollen and hurt like hell.

"So, what did Coach say?"

"That I was getting three hours detention for fighting, which totally sucks and isn't fair, and to track him down tomorrow for the detention assignment. And to make matters worse, he's also going to call my parents."

"Oh."

"Yeah, oh."

"Well, let's try not to think about that right now, okay?"

"Yeah, okay."

"I think we should get some ice on that eye," Callie said.

"I know. I can barely see out of it."

I was still shaken and upset. I couldn't believe what had happened. I was physically and emotionally in pain. I felt angry and guilty. Angry that my supposed best friend beat me up like that—*in front of* my girlfriend. And guilty that he got suspended for it.

I was having a hard time wrapping my head around it all. This was all new territory for me. I'd never been in a real fight before.

"C'mon, let's go to the nurse to see if she's still around and get you an ice pack," Callie said, standing and taking my hand.

"Look, I'm fine. Let's just head to rehearsal, okay?"

"No, not okay. We're going to the nurse's office."

"Yes, ma'am."

"And if the nurse tells you, 'No rehearsal,' then no rehearsal. Understood?"

I didn't respond because it was pretty much a rhetorical question. It even hurt to roll my eyes.

If this were a public school, walking to the nurse's office would be a waste of time at this time of night. It was after hours. The nurse would have already gone home.

But this was a private boarding school, which had a nurse on property twenty-four hours a day, and a physician on call, while school was in session. This meant the likelihood of us finding the nurse was fairly high.

Callie and I walked to the standalone building on campus, which functioned as the nurse's office, residence, and mini-hospital in case students needed to be supervised overnight.

We rang the after-hours doorbell. The interior lights came on, and soon after that, Nurse Lodge opened the door.

"Hi, kids. How can I help— Oh, my! Come in, come in. What happened?"

"Nothing. I got into a fight. I'm fine," I said as I sat on the examination table.

After a painful fifteen minutes of poking and prodding, Mrs. Lodge, a slender, gray-haired woman in her mid-fifties, gave me two Tylenol and an ice pack and sent us on our way.

"Have your parents call me if they have any questions."

At the mention of my parents, my body tensed again. In all the excitement, I'd forgotten all about them and what I'd be walking into when I got home.

*My parents, fuck! They're going to kill me. Matt, you asshole!*

Callie must have been reading my mind. The moment we stepped outside, she asked about my parents.

"What are your parents going to say?"

"I have no idea. They're going to be pissed."

"As they should be. I'm pissed."

"Callie, it was all a misunderstanding. You don't know him the way I do. He didn't mean to do it."

"Are you kidding me? You're defending him?"

"No, I'm not defending him. He's an asshole. He deserves to be suspended. I'm just saying . . ."

"No, you're not just saying. You're actually defending him."

"Well, I'm not, okay?"

"Yeah, okay."

"C'mon, let's get to rehearsal. I'll think about my parents later."

"You and rehearsal. Okay, let's get to rehearsal."

# 47 - Facing My Parents

The moment Aaron saw me, he dismissed me from rehearsal.

"Puck, head home. We're not rehearsing your part tonight anyway, okay?"

"Yeah, okay."

"I'm going to walk him to his car, okay?" Callie said.

Aaron nodded. "Okay. Don't be long."

At the car, Callie made me promise to take my time driving home.

"I will. I love you. I'll see you tomorrow."

"I love you, too. Be safe."

After a quick hug and kiss, I hopped into my car and drove home. Callie watched me drive away with a look of concern on her face.

*My parents are going to kill me.*

I never realized how much you needed both your eyes to drive. It took me almost a half hour to get home. The light outside my front door came on the moment I pulled into the driveway. It was like they'd been waiting for me.

I killed the engine and sat in my driveway for a minute, trying to figure out what I was going to say to my parents. How I was going to explain my face? I placed the melted ice pack over my eye, which wasn't hurting as much as before. The Tylenol had kicked in.

*Well, it's not like you can sit out here forever.*

I grabbed my things and walked slowly to the front door. I tried looking in the front window to see if anyone was sitting in the family room. Unfortunately, my father was sitting in his usual spot, while mom was waiting for me at the front door.

*Crap.*

The moment she saw me, her expression changed from anger to concern. I didn't make it inside before she started peppering me with comments and questions. Apparently, Coach was true to his word and had called my home.

"A *fight*! With Matthew, no less? What the hell were you thinking?"

"I'm fine, Mom. Thanks for asking," I smarted off.

"Don't you use that tone with me, coño."

*Oh crap. She's using Spanish curse words. Greaaat!*

"Mom, look. I— look. I…"

"Get into the kitchen and let me take a good look at you." She turned me around and pointed me toward the kitchen. Then she grabbed my hand and led me there.

*I guess I wasn't moving fast enough.*

Dad followed behind us. The moment he saw the damage, he whistled in disbelief and shook his head. "Please tell me you got in a few as well."

"Yeah, I got in a few."

"Good."

Mom looked at my dad with wild eyes. "No, not *good*. None of this is good." Back to me. "Tell me what happened."

I told the story for the umpteenth time, it seemed. This time, I included the part about Matt and the window.

"Matthew did all that?" Mom asked, surprised.

"Yeah, he did. So, what was I supposed to do? I wasn't going to let him threaten Callie."

"No, hijo, no. But, couldn't have you two worked it out? I mean, you two are best friends."

"I know, Mom. I know. I'd like to tell you 'yes,' but . . ." I pointed to my eye.

"Well, his parents called us, and they're equally upset."

*Great. Just great.*

"What'd they say?"

"That they want you two to apologize to each other and work it out. We want the same."

*Me apologize to him? Are they out of their fucking minds?*

"Apologize? But, Mom, I didn't do anything wrong! *He* hit *me*!"

She just gave me *the look*, and I knew the conversation was over. I looked at my father for support, but he clearly sided with my mother.

"Have you eaten yet?"

"No, and I'm starving."

"Well, your father made you a plate."

Before leaving the kitchen with my dinner, Mom handed me a fresh ice pack for my face and kissed my swollen cheek. Regardless of the lecture, I was still her one and only son, after all.

I spent the rest of the evening in my room, eating my dinner, doing homework, and pouting. I still couldn't believe I had to apologize to Matt.

Before turning in, my Dad stopped by to check on me, and give me the *friendship lecture.*

"Well, look. You and Matt have been friends for a long time. Again, I don't excuse what he did. As I understand it, he's feeling really bad about it."

"Well, good! He should!"

*The asshole!*

"I know. I know. You're right. He should. I'm just saying, if you think the friendship is worth saving, if you think he's worth it, then you're going to need to figure out how to forgive him."

"Uh-huh."

"Well, think about it. I'm turning in. I love you, champ."

"I love you, too, Dad. Good night."

*Forgive him, huh? Yeah, I don't see that happening anytime soon.*

# 48 - Detention

The next morning, the swelling in my eye and lips had gone down, but I had quite the black eye. At least I could see out of it well enough to drive. By the time I made it to campus, the story had already spread across the student population. It made me sick to my stomach. The stares were relentless.

*Yeah, I got into a fight and got a black eye. Get over it!*

Between classes, I tracked down Coach Connor as he'd requested.

"Reporting as ordered, Coach." I saluted.

He rolled his eyes and shook his head. "Uh-huh. Well, I had a long conversation last night with the Dean. He agreed with me about detention."

*Wait a minute. What do you mean he agreed with you? You mean, there was a choice here?*

"Coach, I still don't think it's fair."

"Son, life's not fair. The sooner you learn that, the better. Anyway, I understand your work job is in the kitchen, is that right?"

"Yeah, I'm one of the captain's in the kitchen, for lunch."

"Okay, good. Then this will be easy. I met with Mrs. Whitaker this morning, after breakfast."

*Great, now Sharon knows, too.*

"For the next three days, during lunch, you're going to report to Mrs. Whitaker in the kitchen. She will assign you your work."

"But I *already* work in the kitchen during lunch. How is this detention?"

He gave me a sly smile. "I never said your detention would be difficult, did I? I just said you were *getting* detention."

*Ohhhhh.*

"Hey, thanks, Coach."

"Go on and get to class before I change my mind, and have you report to the maintenance crew."

Between classes, I ran into Callie, or rather, she tracked me down like a bloodhound.

"I've been looking all over for you. What did Coach Connor say?"

I told her, and she let loose a sigh of relief. "Wow, you got lucky."

"Tell me about it."

"How're you feeling? How were your parents last night? I wanted to call you, but I got out of rehearsal late. Aaron wanted to find out how you were *really* doing. And then when I got back to the dorm, Gill tracked me down, and we spent half the night talking," she said without taking a breath.

*Whoa, slow down there, sister.*

"Sorry. Did I just throw up all over you? It's just that I was worried about you, and I know you were nervous about going home last night, and I wish I could have come with you to face your parents, and—"

I placed my index finger over her lips.

"Shhh. It's all okay. Come here," I said, taking her into my arms.

*To hell with public-displays-of-affection rules! What are they going to do, give me more detention?*

When she'd chilled out enough, I let her know what my parents had said, particularly the conversation I'd had with my dad alone.

"What are you going to do? *Can* you forgive him? I've got to be honest with you. I don't think I can."

"I don't know, babe. I just don't know."

And at that moment, I didn't. Fortunately, the bell rang, and it was time to move on to the next class, so I didn't need to think about it. I snuck her a quick kiss, and we parted ways.

***

The moment I hit the kitchen that afternoon, Sharon damn-near dogpiled me.

"Oh, my goodness, I heard what happened. Come here and let me see your beautiful face."

She gently grasped my chin and turned my head this way and that.

"Terrible, just terrible. I never liked that Salvatore boy. When I get my hands on him . . ."

Like I'd said earlier, Sharon was like a second mother to many, and she was very protective of her "babies," as she liked to call us.

"Well, listen, I'm not going to punish you for defending your girlfriend from that brute."

*I guess the story really did get around.*

"Just do your regular job, and I'll tell the Dean that I had you scrubbing pots for three days, okay?"

*Who am I to argue with such a good plan?*

I grinned. "You bet. Thanks, Sharon."

She bear-hugged me. "Oh, sweetheart, think nothing of it. No one messes with one of my babies."

***

Callie was waiting for me after lunch. But this time, she wasn't alone. Gill was with her. After the "how are you" and "oh my God, I feel horrible" stuff, I told Gill it wasn't her fault.

"Yeah, but if I hadn't asked you guys to wait . . ."

"Gill, listen," I said, taking her hand. "It wasn't your fault. You're one of my best friends. What happened last night was wrong, but it wasn't your fault. It was Matt's."

At the mention of Matt's name, Gill bristled. "Yeah, well, he can forget about getting back together after what he did last night."

"Sorry, Gill."

And I really was.

"That's because you're one of the good guys," she said.

"He sure is," Callie whispered with a smile.

# 49 - Dress Rehearsal

A week passed since the fight, and my black eye was pretty much gone. After committing the crime and serving his time, Matt returned to school. We essentially avoided one another. We didn't sit next to each other in class and didn't speak in the hallway or locker room.

He went his way, and I went mine. Gill, to her word, broke up with him for good, when he returned to school. Part of me felt bad for him. Not only was he suspended, but he lost his best friend and girlfriend in one fell swoop, and basically became a pariah.

Hardly anyone in school would speak with him. Part of me felt bad for him. No friends, no girl, and no car. All that was missing was a dead dog, and he would have been the living embodiment of a country-music record.

We were five days away from opening night, and we clearly weren't ready, despite our grueling rehearsals.

Of course, this didn't go over well with Aaron. He was fit to be tied. The whole week leading to opening night involved full-dress rehearsals. This meant everyone had to show up early, get into their makeup and costumes, know all their lines, and hit all their marks.

Except for a select few, Callie being one of them, no one seemed prepared, including yours truly. I was having a hard time memorizing the lines and relaxing on stage. I wasn't a trained thespian and was learning everything by the seat of my pants.

Aaron didn't want to hear excuses from anyone, me included. Whatever leniency I'd earned from the black eye was long gone.

"Listen, people. We're five days away from opening night," he yelled. "I can't *believe* none of you know your lines."

We sat there staring at him, terrified, not knowing what to say as he dressed us down.

"Look, this is *Shakespeare*. The *Bard*. We've been going over this material now for weeks. *Weeks*!" he shrieked. "Let's get it together, people."

We muttered our apologies and promises to get it together.

"Okay, let's start again from the beginning," he said. "Theseus, Hippolyta, and Philostrate, take your places. Okay, quiet, people. Quiet."

At this point, Aaron would only refer to us by our character names, even when he saw us on campus. He said it would help us with character development, or something.

We spent the next few painful hours rehearsing the play. We made it halfway through the play before Aaron had enough and dismissed us.

"As of tomorrow, we have four days, people. *Four Days*!"

We assured him we understood and apologized again.

"Don't be sorry. Be better. Now get out of here, and come back tomorrow, better prepared to run through the whole thing. Hippolyta, a moment of your time, please."

Callie followed Aaron to his office, while I took a seat on the stage, dangling my feet as I waited for Callie. Corrine walked by and reminded me to take care of my costume.

"I don't want have to fix any last-minute rips or tears. So, please be careful with it," she said.

"Yeah, yeah. I'll be careful."

*I'm not a child, Corrine.*

Ten minutes later, Callie and Aaron returned.

"Thanks, Aaron," Callie said.

"Just remember what I said. Natural."

"Got it. Natural." She glided toward me. "Ready to go?"

"Yep. So, what was that all about?"

"Oh, nothing. He was just giving me some last-minute tips, that's all."

Aaron must have thought a miracle occurred or the stars aligned, because two nights later, two days before opening night, we made it through the entire play. Yes, there were some *rough spots*, but we made it through without having to stop.

The day before opening night, Callie pulled me aside and asked me how I was doing.

"Are you nervous? Do you need help memorizing your lines?"

I shook my head. "Nope, I'm doing okay. I think I have most of them down."

"Okay, good. Just remember, when you're up there to breathe and relax."

"Breathe and relax. Got it."

"Pretend like I'm the only one out there. That it's just you and me, having a conversation."

"Yeah, in a strange language," I joked, causing her to laugh.

*Man, I love the way you laugh.*

It was that advice, and advice Aaron had given us early on in rehearsals—something about pretending everyone was sitting out there in their underwear—that helped me relax during the play. Of course, it didn't hurt to imagine Callie sitting out there in her lacy pink bra from Macy's.

Thursday night was our final night of dress rehearsals. Helen Doherty, Aaron's wife, walked around and took the pictures of everyone.

Rehearsals started sharply after last bell.

"If you're late, don't bother showing up," Aaron had told us the previous evening.

Fortunately, I was free last period, so I went to the library and finished most of my homework before meeting up with Callie after the last bell.

"Hey, Captain. I mean, Puck."

"Hey, Wonder Woman."

"Actually, she's my daughter," she corrected me.

"Whatever. In my opinion, you're Wonder Woman."

"Come on, Shakespeare. Let's get to rehearsal before Aaron has a coronary."

Our last night of rehearsals flew by. Before starting, Aaron gave us all a speech. He called everyone together—the stagehands, Corrine, Kevin in the booth—to take a seat.

"Okay, guys, this is it. Our last rehearsal. So, if you're going to mess up, fall, or break something, do it tonight."

Everyone laughed, grateful for the lightening of the mood.

"I want to thank all of you for your hard work. Listen, Shakespeare isn't easy. And I know this is going to be the first time for some of you on stage. I want to assure all of you . . . you're ready for this. You put in the work. Tomorrow evening, Saturday afternoon, and Saturday night will be a stroll in Central Park."

*A stroll in Central Park, huh? I just hope I don't get mugged.*

"For our three performances, I want you to leave it all on the stage. Do you know what I mean by that?" he asked. "I see by the look on your faces, that some of you have no idea what I'm talking about. Puck, you play football. Can you please explain it to everyone?"

*Nothing like putting me on the spot, Aaron.*

"Well, if you're talking about leaving it all on the field, then you want us to 'bring it.' Take everything we've learned in practice and deliver it during our performance."

"Exactly. I want you to *bring it*! I want everyone involved in this production to bring it, so that when we finish our final performance, we have nothing left to give. Because we'd left it all on stage."

Nods all around.

"Okay, now, let's get to work. I want to run through this twice tonight. No stopping. Even if you're bleeding or dying on stage, we're not going to stop. Understood?"

*So much for lightening the mood.*

# 50 - She Really Loves Me

Friday came sooner than I expected. Rehearsal the previous evening had gone well. We ran through the play twice, and we only stopped for dinner. More importantly, no one bled or died.

I was surprised how well I did. Even Callie complimented me on that.

Of course, I was no match for Callie. She looked absolutely stunning in her costume. Corrine had done a great job with the design. And the way Callie carried herself on stage and delivered her lines . . .

*Man, she's just awesome.*

All I thought about that day was the play. For every class, I sat in the back row and reviewed my script. I didn't pay attention in a single class. Fortunately, all my teachers seemed to give me a pass. I wasn't their first student performing in the school play for the first time.

Even Professor Michaels, who usually liked to bust people's balls for not paying attention in his class, wished me luck as I left.

"Good luck tonight, young man. I'm sure you're going to do great. My wife and I will be there tonight to support you."

My last class of the day was brutal. Between ignoring my teacher, who was lecturing on some Civil War battle, trying to concentrate on my lines, and staring at the clock as the minutes slowly ticked away, I felt like puking in my chair.

Let's just say, my nerves were getting the better of me. The minute the last bell blew, I practically flew out of class and ran to the bathroom to throw up. Yep, my nerves were *definitely* getting the better of me.

After rinsing my mouth out, I caught up with Callie who was heading to her dorm.

She smiled. "You ready for tonight?"

"As ready as I'm going to be. What about you?"

"I can't wait. I love opening night," she said.

*Of course, you do. If I had your talent, I'd be excited, too.*

"Well, that's good."

"Oh, sweetheart, are you nervous?"

"I don't know. Maybe a little."

"Oh, don't be nervous. You're going to do great! Trust me. You're ready for this." She gave me an encouraging hug.

"If you say so."

She cocked an eyebrow. "Well, I do."

There was no basketball or swim practice for us because of the play, which was scheduled to start at 7:30 p.m. Aaron wanted everyone there at 5:00. Since school let out at 3:15, Callie and I had plenty of time to walk around and relax, or at least *try* to relax, in my case.

"So, what do you feel like doing? We have a couple of hours till we have to report," Callie said as we walked to her dorm.

"I don't know. What do you feel like doing?"

Callie raised her shapely eyebrows and smiled a devilish grin, which made me laugh out loud.

*Are you sure you're not the guy in this relationship?*

"I heard something about a Hercules statue."

*Hercules statue? Nah.*

"Want to go to the beach?" I asked.

"It's kind of cold out, don't you think?"

"Meh, we can swing by my house and grab a blanket."

That worked for her, so after dropping her stuff off, we drove by my house, said hello to my father and grabbed a quick snack. I took the blanket off the back of our couch and drove to the West Meadow Beach, a local beach located in Stony Brook, overlooking the Long Island Sound.

On the way to the beach, we stopped at the deli and picked up a couple of hot chocolates. This was the first time she'd been to this particular beach. As I suspected, we were the only ones there. It was around forty-five degrees Fahrenheit outside.

We could feel the coolness of the crunchy sand through the blanket. It was a typical Long Island sky in December—gray with speckles of clouds. The sun reflected off the waves, and we could see Connecticut across the Sound.

We found a spot in the sand and settled onto the blanket, sipping our hot chocolates. Between her red nose and cheeks, the intensity of her blue eyes, which seemed to reflect the sky, and her incredible smile, she looked like someone in a fashion magazine. I couldn't believe how lucky I was.

We talked about everything, except the play, for which I was grateful.

As I finished the last of my hot chocolate, a cool breeze blew in from the water, sending a chill through my body.

"Are you getting cold?" Callie asked.

I chuckled. "You mean 'colder'?"

"Yes. And I am, too."

"Come on. Let's go. Aaron would kill me if I allowed his *Queen* to catch a cold."

I gathered up the blanket and escorted Callie back to the car, tossing our Styrofoam cups in the trash along the way. After shaking out the blanket, I threw it in the back seat.

Just as I put the key into the ignition, she took hold of my hand. I turned and stared into her sparkling blues.

"What's on your mind?" I asked.

She smiled, biting her lower lip, and raised her right eyebrow.

"Gotcha."

The blanket would come in handy once again.

Our hearts were racing as we became lost in the moment. Our pheromones quickly filled the car. Our love shined brighter than the winter sun slowly setting on the horizon. It may have been forty-five degrees outside, but it was around a hundred degrees inside my car.

Didn't need the blanket, after all.

I also didn't need to verbalize my love for her, nor did she for me. Her warm smile, fiery blue eyes, and tender touches spoke volumes.

*She loves me.*

*She really loves me.*

# 51 - The Cast Party

We sold out each performance, which made everyone, especially Aaron, proud. Opening night, I couldn't have been more relaxed, thanks to our rendezvous at the beach. I remembered all my lines, hit all my marks, and did so well that even Aaron said commented on it.

"I don't know what you did, but, Puck, you knocked it out of the park tonight."

*Ha, if you only knew. I'd definitely get suspended, if not kicked out of school and maybe thrown in jail.*

Our next two performances went very well, although our Saturday afternoon performance was a bit rougher than our final performance. The whole experience was interesting and fun. I'd never done anything like it before. Being at a Christian school, before each performance we gathered as a group, held hands and prayed.

While it felt strange at first, it also felt like the right thing to do. We do it before most of our sporting events, in the locker room, so why not before performing on stage. My parents came to both evening performances, and brought flowers for Callie each time, which she, and I, appreciated.

Teachers, friends, teammates, neighbors . . . everyone seemed to be there at one point or another. Of course, not Matt. Gill attended both opening night and Saturday afternoon, but she couldn't make the last show. Something about working on a special credit assignment for one of her classes.

Surprisingly, people from the diner came as well. Mr. and Mrs. Anagnos made sure they tracked Callie and me down to say what a wonderful job we had done. Of course, they made sure to take pictures with Callie in her regal attire so they could put it up on their "Wall of Fame."

If they only knew what an asshole her father was. What's that old expression?

*Never meet your heroes.*

Speaking of which, that jerk was notably missing from all of the performances. Apparently, Mr. Grumpy-puss couldn't be bothered. No one else from her family had come, either. I was sad for Callie. After each amazing performance, I'd watch her search the crowd and look for someone, *anyone*, from her family.

The look of disappointment on her face broke my heart. I wanted to track down Mister High-and-Mighty Businessman and savior to the people of Greece and give him a piece of my mind.

Of course, I didn't for a variety of reasons. First, clearly no one else's opinion would have mattered to this guy. Second, I suspected that he had no idea who I was or that I was dating his daughter. And third, he'd never listen to a *brown boy*.

That said, after our final performance, Callie did receive flowers from her dad, which at least confirmed that he'd *known* about the play. He just chose not to support his youngest child and attend her performance. Still, I tried to cheer her up that he'd sent flowers.

"Well, that was nice of him," I said encouragingly as she read the card.

"It's not from him. It's from his assistant. I recognize her handwriting. He couldn't even write his own note. He had to have his assistant do it for him." She sighed and shook her head.

"I'm sorry, babe. Hey, my parents brought you flowers. Plus, *I* love you. It's not much, but at least you have *that* going for you," I joked.

"Yes, they did. That's because they're sweet. And I love you, too. More than you know."

Callie then leaned in and kissed me for all the backstage world to see. As she did, we received cheers and wolf-whistles, but it didn't bother me. I just flipped them off and enjoyed the kiss, hearing the laughter echoing around us.

Then I heard a camera click and saw a flash go off.

"Mom-*ah!*" I whined as Callie giggled.

"What? It was cute," Mom said.

I rolled my eyes.

She proceeded to take an album's worth of pictures.

"Okay, now I want another one with you and Callie standing here."

*Click, click.*

"Okay, now one with just you."

*Click, click*

"Now, one with me, you, and Dad. Callie, sweetheart, can you take our picture?"

*Click, click*

You'd think we were putting together a spread for a major magazine or something.

"Okay, now one with all four of us." Mom snagged Aaron's hand as he was passing by. "Mr. Doherty, can you please take a picture for us?"

"Absolutely. I'd love to."

*Click, click*

"Okay, now one with you two and Mr. Doherty."

*Click, click*

"Now one with just you and Mr. Doherty."

"Moooom-*ah*! Come on. Enough with the pictures already. I've got to get changed and get to the cast party," I said.

"*Ai*, why are you complaining? You know you're going to love looking at these when I get them developed. Just a couple more."

Even though she was right, I still called for backup.

"Dad?" I gestured toward Mom.

"Okay, babe, come on. Let's wrap up the photoshoot. He has to change." He gently lowered her hand that held the camera.

As they walked away, Mom began rattling off people she'd have to send pictures to, in Puerto Rico and the Dominican Republic.

*Jeez, Mom, they're not going to care.*

But who was I to argue with a proud Latina mother?

***

Aaron and Helen held the cast party at their house after our final performance. Since it was being held at a faculty member's home, all the boarders got a free pass to stay out past their normal 11:00 p.m. curfew.

As a gift to Aaron, everyone chipped in some cash and got him and Helen a gift certificate for one of their favorite restaurants—the Good Steer, located in Lake Grove. It was a local staple and go-to restaurant for everyone in Suffolk County since the late 1950s. Hands down, one of the best burgers and fries in the state.

For the party, Aaron and Helen went all out. They had pizzas, sodas, chips, cupcakes, a cake—you name it, they had it. The entire cast and crew came, and we had a ball. Kevin Jenkins, our audio/video-lighting guy, played DJ for the evening.

My guess was, he'd spent so much time with Aaron over the years that he knew his record collection backward and forward. Kevin played everything from old Motown classics to '70s rock to current hits. I was surprised by how broad Aaron's collection was. Then again, when you run the dramatic-arts department at a high school, you needed to stay current with the kids' tastes.

Callie and I grabbed a few slices and cokes and sat together on one of many couches. Aaron made his way around and chatted with everyone.

"Well, Puck," he said when he approached us, "I've got to say, you did an exceptional job. Just exceptional."

"Thanks, Aaron. I appreciate it. But, I couldn't have done it without you and Callie."

"I was a bit worried about you at first. But, Hippolyta here convinced me she would work with you and get to you, you know . . . *relax*."

*Boy, did she ever.*

"Oh, yeah?" I looked at Callie, who had her lips closed but wearing a smile.

"Yeah, you were always so . . . tense," he added, mimicking me being all tense on stage.

"Oh, he wasn't that bad," Callie chimed in with a giggle.

"Well, whatever you did with him, it certainly paid off. You got him to relax and let the Bard simply flow trippingly off his tongue. Like I said, kiddo . . . exceptional." He gave me the okay sign.

*Ha, if you only knew what she did to relax me. Trippingly off the tongue, indeed.*

"He doesn't give out those types of compliments too often. So, he must really mean it," Helen said as she walked by, causing Aaron to laugh his great baritone laugh.

"She's right. I can be a tough SOB sometimes."

*No kidding.*

"So, listen . . . we're planning on doing *Guys and Dolls* in the spring. How's your singing and dancing?" Aaron asked me.

I damn near spit out my pizza.

Aaron rolled his eyes as Callie laughed hysterically. "We'll talk about it in January," he said before he and Helen moved on to their next victim.

After a couple of steps, Aaron shouted over his shoulder, "Callie, work on him again, would you? We need him for the next one."

I snickered and leaned in close to Callie. "You heard the man. *Work on me.*"

She actually blushed, which was a first.

"Oh, I'll work on you, all right," she said, elbowing me sharply in the ribs.

*Ow! Worth it!*

# 52 - Christmas Cookies

We were about two weeks away from Christmas break. As it approached, our lives returned to normal with school, basketball, and Callie's swimming. On the weekends, I'd spend time with Callie during the day and worked at the diner at night.

Callie's father had informed her that this year, she and he would spend Christmas together at their apartment in New York City instead of flying back to Greece, like previous years. This disappointed her because she was really looking forward to seeing her extended family and enjoy their holiday traditions.

On my end, Dad was still out of work with no apparent prospects in sight. Even though he was receiving both unemployment and severance, the latter would be ending soon, which added to his stress and the stress levels in our house. Mom did her best to assure him that things would work out, but he remained out of sorts most of the time.

Callie had pretty much become a fixture at our home. My parents liked her, especially my mom. She'd stay late on Friday nights and Saturday nights, and have dinner with us Sundays. The nights I worked, she'd stay and hang out with Mom, who would then drive her back to school.

Mom loved having her around. She said Callie reminded her of some of her old high-school girlfriends, which made me laugh, thinking about a high-school version of my mother.

After I told Mom about Callie's Christmas situation, her heart went out to Callie. Mom lost her own mother when she was in her early twenties, so she could relate to what Callie was going through. Add that experience to her few years working on the oncology ward, Mom was a good shoulder for Callie.

*Nurses truly are the unsung heroes of healthcare.*

They became two peas in a pod. Mom would even attend some of Callie's swim meets and cheer her on. If I didn't love Callie so much, I would have been jealous.

Callie participated in all our preparations for the holidays that year. On Saturday, she helped us pick out our six-foot tree from a local Boy Scout troop at a church lot near the house. She was so cute about it, too.

"What about this one?"

"Not bad, Callie, not bad. But let's keep looking, just in case," Dad said.

"Okay. How 'bout this one?"

I scrunched my nose and shook my head.

*Too skinny.*

Eventually, we found the perfect tree. A hardy Douglas fir. After getting home, we fully decorated the house and tree, lights and all.

"That was *so much* fun," Callie said as we sat on the couch, cuddling.

"You think so?"

"Yeah. Did you have fun?"

"Meh," I teased.

She just rolled her eyes and laughed at me.

Mom came in from the kitchen. "Callie, mija, what are you doing tomorrow?"

That's how Mom had started referring to Callie: *mija*, which is "my daughter" in Spanish.

"I don't know. What are we doing tomorrow?" Callie asked me.

"Watching football, what else? The Giants are on a roll."

"Would you like to help me make Christmas cookies while those two watch their football game?" Mom asked.

I thought Callie would cry. Her blue eyes grew wide, and her expression became a mix of sadness and glee.

"Really?"

"Sure, mija. It's the only thing his father allows me to do in the kitchen during the holidays," Mom said.

"I used to help my mother make cookies for Christmas. I miss that so much."

"Aw, mija. I'm sorry. I didn't mean to make you sad. Come here." Mom opened her loving arms.

Callie immediately left my side on the couch and embraced my mother, who wrapped her in *Latina love*, as I liked to call it.

Callie cried softly in my mother's arms. I felt so bad for her. It was her first Christmas without her mom. I didn't realize how hard it was for her. I didn't realize how much she missed her mother.

"Is there anything special you and your mother used to make for Christmas?" Mom asked as she wiped Callie's tears.

"We used to make all kinds of things. We'd make baklava, something called kourambiethes, and something else called melomakarona."

"They sound so *exotic*."

"My mom used to make a ton and hand them out as gifts."

"Well, if you know how to spell them, I'm sure we can find the recipes for them. Tell you what . . . tomorrow, while those two watch their football games, why don't you and I go to the library to see if we can find the recipes?"

Callie was thrilled, her sadness subsiding. "Really? You mean it?"

"Of course, mija," Mom said, caressing Callie's face.

"Thanks, Mrs.—"

"Mom. Just call me Mom, okay?"

***

The following day, I picked up Callie from school at noon. She was clearly excited with anticipation, because instead of waiting for me in her dorm, she waited for me in the quadrangle, wearing a big smile.

But she wasn't alone. Gill was standing with her. Apparently, she missed making cookies with her mother, too, even though she'd be seeing her in a couple of weeks.

She was probably just eager to get off campus, but I didn't care. Gill was one of my best friends, so if she wanted to hang out with Callie and my mom all day, making dessert, who was I to argue?

"You don't mind, do you?" Gill asked.

"Nope, hop in."

"Thanks, Captain," she replied.

Mom was happy to see Gill, too. She saw it as a girls' day out and by 3:00, they were walking through the front door with bags full of groceries.

"Hey, we're home. We need some help with groceries, please," Mom announced.

I got off the couch and helped retrieve the rest of the groceries. I couldn't tell who was the most excited—Mom, Gill, or Callie. They all had a holiday glow about them. Of course, it could have been the cold weather, too.

As they unloaded the groceries, Callie looked like a little girl, smiling from ear to ear. All she was missing were pigtails.

"Your mom is the *best*," Callie said, coming over and hugging me.

"Oh yeah?"

"We hit the library, found about a million different recipes, and then she took us to your diner for lunch. Mr. Anagnos seated us right away. Does he *ever* take a day off?"

I chuckled at that one. "No, never. He's always there."

Mom stepped in and said to me, "Well, you have a choice. You can either get in here and help or go back to your game."

"Bye," I quickly replied, kissing Callie before retreating back to the family room.

"Mm-hmm, I thought so," Mom said as I left, and Gill and Callie burst into laughter.

# 53 - Christmas Break

"**Y**esterday was so much fun," Callie said as we walked to class. "Mom said she had fun, too."

"You should have seen it when we made it back to the dorm, though."

"Oh, yeah? What happened?"

"The moment I walked in, they attacked."

"Who attacked?"

"Everyone. I guess word got out that Gill and I were going to your house to make cookies, and there was a group waiting for us to return to the dorm."

"No kidding?"

"No kidding. The moment I walked inside, they pounced," she said, miming a cat pouncing on a toy. "I think I have a few cookies left. I had to hide them in my desk."

We laughed, but . . . who could blame them? Who doesn't love homemade goodies? And the cookies they'd made were awesome.

Christmas break came before we knew it. I was secretly happy that Callie wasn't going off to Greece. At least she'd be in the States, somewhat nearby. The crappy part was she'd be spending that time in the proximity of her overbearing father, who clearly agitated her.

I'd almost asked if she could spend it with us, since she and Mom were so close. But I knew the answer, so I didn't bother asking the question. That said, Callie and I did make plans to see each other over the break.

According to her father's assistant, he would be in Washington for two days on the 22nd and the 23rd. Our last day of school fell on the 19th, and we weren't due back to school until January 6th, which gave us almost three weeks. So, we planned on seeing each other at least once during break.

With her father gone on December 22nd, we agreed that would be the perfect day to see each other. After checking the train schedule, we decided I'd take the 8:45 a.m. train into Penn Station, and we'd spend the day together—explore the city, grab some dinner, and then get me back on the 9:45 p.m. train home.

My parents didn't even blink an eye this time.

*Maybe I'm starting to wear them down.*

Callie and I had a tearful goodbye on our last day of school. I hung out on campus and waited in Callie's dorm lounge while she finished packing. As I sat there, her father's driver walked in.

*What the fuck is he doing here? I thought she was taking the train into the city?*

"Hello, I'm looking for Calista Christos?" he said in his broken English to one of the girls passing by.

"Oh, I'll go get her," she replied. He nodded and stood just inside the front doors, his hands clasped in front of him.

When Callie walked into the lounge, she said, "*Dimitri*? What are you doing here?"

"Your father sent me to pick you up."

Callie proceeded to speak with him in Greek, the words coming rapidly and her hands making all kinds of gestures. She did not look happy. Dimitri seemed to take it all in stride.

Based on how I had seen her father treat people, my guess was Dimitri was used to getting yelled at. After Callie finished dressing him down, he sighed and shrugged his shoulders.

"You have twenty minutes," he informed her.

"Twenty minutes?" I said loudly, causing Dimitri to look at me for the first time since entering the building.

"Can I help you?" he asked, taking a threatening step forward.

"Leave him alone, Dimitri. That's my boyfriend," Callie said, earning both of us a sharp look from Dimitri.

"*That* (something clearly derogatory in Greek) is your *fílos*?" Dimitri spat out, using the Greek term for "boyfriend."

*What did he just call me?*

"Dimitri! How *dare* you! *Yes . . .*" Callie said, followed by something else in Greek.

By her gestures and his response, she not only set him back on his heels, but sent him to the car as well.

*Mental note: do NOT piss her off!*

"So, what's going on?" I asked as Callie walked over to me.

She sighed. "Nothing."

"Nothing?"

"I told him to go wait in the car."

"What about the twenty minutes?"

"He wouldn't budge on that. I'm sorry. I didn't know he was coming. I thought we'd have more time."

Tears formed in her eyes, and then she collapsed into my arms.

"Shhh . . . it's okay, babe. I'm going to be seeing you on Monday, remember?" I whispered.

"Yeah, but . . ."

"I know, I know. It's okay. We can talk every day. Call me tomorrow. I'm working tonight."

She hugged me tight and said she would, then she added, "I love you so much."

"I love you, too, Callie. I love you, too."

We reluctantly broke apart, and I headed for the door.

I made it about three feet before she pounced on me. She grabbed my shoulders and spun me around. She then wrapped her arms around my neck and planted a warm, passionate kiss on my lips.

"Well, that should keep you until I see you on Monday," she said.

"Uh-huh, and then some," I replied in a daze, earning a laugh from her.

I waved goodbye and left her dorm, heading for my car in the student parking lot. Out of the corner of my eye, I saw Dimitri getting out of the Benz. He immediately made a beeline in my direction.

"Eh, excuse me, filos! You! Over there. Wait a minute," Dimitri yelled, snapping his fingers and pointing at me.

I made the "Who? Me?" gesture.

"Yes, you. I need to talk to you."

*Oh great. Here we go.*

# 54 - Unexpected Ally

I stopped as Dimitri made his way over to me. Based on his pace, I didn't know if he wanted to talk to me or beat me up. I wasn't prepared for either, and since I'd already had my ass handed to me once this year. I really didn't want a repeat performance.

"What do you want?" I asked with a bit of edge in my voice.

"I want to talk to you, that's what I want. And don't be a smartass. I've got to take it from them. I don't need to take it from you."

"Okay, so what do you want?"

"Who are you, and who gave you permission to date Miss Christos?" he asked, poking his index finger into my chest.

*Ow!*

"What business it is of yours to ask?"

"I'm Mr. Christos's personal driver and bodyguard. That *makes it* my business. Now, I won't ask you again. Who gave you permission to date Miss Christos?"

He poked me again. This time harder.

"First, stop poking me in the chest," I said, slapping his hand away.

Then I poked him back, and it felt like poking a brick wall. He just looked down at my finger, like he would bite it off, and smiled, so I retreated it immediately.

"And second, Callie gave me permission. Last time I checked, that's all the permission I need. Listen, I gotta go. Later."

I turned to walk away and made it two steps before Dimitri blocked my path. I tried getting around him, but every time I tried, he would block me and shake his head "no."

*Seriously, dude?*

"You will stop dating Miss Christos immediately, if you know what's good for you."

I jerked my head back. "Oh, really? I don't think I will."

"If Mr. Christos hears that his youngest daughter is dating a . . ." He then said something in Greek. I guessed it was a racial slur of some sort, based on the expression on his face. A cross between a sour lemon and a stinky fart.

He didn't need to finish his sentence. I caught his drift.

"Look, I'm not going to stop dating Callie, no matter what you say. And if I were you, I'd keep my mouth shut, if you know what's good for you."

"Oh, really?" he said, looking amused.

"Yeah, really. If you think Callie was mad inside, you *don't* want to see her pissed off."

As we were talking, an unexpected ally came to my side.

"Everything okay here?" Matt asked.

*Matt? What the hell is he doing here?*

I didn't know who to focus on. The Greek brute in front of me, or the Cuban brute to my right. I took a step back to keep an eye on both.

"Yeah, everything's fine," I said.

"No, everything is not *fine*." Dimitri countered.

"*Dimitri*! What are *you* doing?" Callie yelled from the doorway of the dorm, designer luggage in hand.

*Oh, crap. Here we go. I warned you, dude.*

Callie dropped her suitcase, pounced down the steps and immediately got into Dimitri's face, yelling at him in Greek. She shoved him back toward their car as she let loose a hailstorm of words and gestures.

Dimitri walked backward with his hands held up, seemingly trying to defend his actions, which caused Callie to yell louder, gesturing back at me as she did so.

My guess was that he made the mistake of telling her his opinion of the situation. She was all up in his face, probably knowing that he wouldn't do anything to her. Unlike me, she was *protected* . . . by him.

It was truly a weird scene.

"What was that all about?" Matt asked.

"Nothing. Just some guy being a jerk."

Matt winced a bit at that comment.

"Oh. All right. Well, see you 'round."

He started to walk away, but I wasn't going to let him off that easy.

"So, what? You're talking to me again?"

This stopped Matt in his tracks. His shoulders fell, and he said, "I'm sorry dude. I'm really sorry. I didn't mean to hit you."

I was dumbfounded. An actual apology from Matthew Salvatore. Was that even possible?

"Are we cool?" he asked, extending his hand.

*Damn.*

"Yeah, we're cool," I said, taking his hand.

He did that stupid grin of his, and I smiled back.

And just like that, the band was together again. Well, sort of. Gill and Matt were still on the fritz.

Callie approached, looking incredulous at the scene before her. She gestured with her chin toward Matt.

"Hey, Callie," he said.

"Matthew," she replied shortly.

Clearly, Callie was still steamed from her conversation with Dimitri.

"Callie, um, listen . . ."

"I'm listening."

*Damn, girl, give him a chance.*

"I'm really sorry about, well, you know," Matt said, gesturing toward me.

"Uh-huh. And?"

"Uh, and . . ." Matt looked confused.

"And for acting like a jerk, right, Matt?" I said, throwing him a lifeline.

"Yeah, yeah, for acting like a jerk."

"And you're okay with this?" Callie asked me with a raised eyebrow.

"Yeah, I guess so. I'm tired of watching him mope around campus."

"I haven't been—oh, I get it," he said when he saw my expression.

"Okay. If you're okay with him, then so am I. But if he does it again, I'm going to have Dimitri come back here and beat the shit out of him."

"Okay. Easy, babe. Easy," I said, taking her by the shoulders and walking her toward the dorm to retrieve her luggage.

"I mean it," she shouted over her shoulder.

After calming her down, we talked about Dimitri.

"Don't worry about him. He's harmless. He won't say a word."

"I don't know, babe. He seemed pretty adamant that we stop dating."

"Don't worry about it. I told him that if he said anything to my father, I'd tell my father about the time he hit on my older sister. I'd then tell him about his various adventures in the city or back in Greece, with strippers in the car, when my father's not around."

*Damn. She's tough!*

She finished with, "So, don't worry about him. He needs his job. Plus, his father would kill him."

"His father?" I asked.

"Yeah, his brother and father run one of our olive groves back in Greece."

"Gotcha, so we don't need to worry about him."

She smacked me in the stomach. "Exactly. I know where to hit people where they live. So, don't get on my bad side."

"Who, me? It'll never happen, babe. Never," I said, taking her in my arms and tickling her sides.

We said goodbye a second time and made sure to kiss in front of Dimitri as he held the door open for Callie, which made him wince.

*Suck it, driver-boy!*

I then met up with Matt, who waited for me in the parking lot.

"Need a ride home?" I asked.

"Yeah, I could use a ride."

"Sure, come on. The beast is in the parking lot," I joked.

"The beast, huh? Cool. It's been a while since I rode in the beast."

*Yep, the band was back together.*

# 55 - Brothers-in-Arms

It felt good to rekindle my friendship with Matt. Instead of just dropping him off, I wound up hanging out with him at his house for a while. His mom was very happy to see me walk through the door with Matt.

"Hey, look what I found hanging outside?" Matt announced as we walked into the kitchen together.

"Ai, hijo de mi vida! What are you doing here? Ven aquí and give me a hug!" Mrs. Salvatore said.

"Hey, Mrs. Salvatore," I replied as I received my hug. "Someone needed a ride home, and I pulled the short straw."

Matt and I grabbed a couple of sodas and hung out in his room. It was just like old times, before all the nonsense started. We seemed to pick up our friendship, right where we left off, which was strange, but in a good way.

We bantered back and forth, talking about sports and girls, and everything in between.

It was good to have my confidant to talk to again. I mean, I loved Callie, but it wasn't like I could talk to her about . . . her. I brought him up to speed on everything. And I do mean *everything*.

Before I left, he went to his sister's room and returned with a box of condoms in his hand. He tossed them to me.

"Merry Christmas. Just in case."

*Jesus!*

I immediately put them into my jacket pocket, mostly out of embarrassment.

When I got home, Mom and Dad were surprisingly happy to hear that Matt and I had made up. While they still didn't approve of what happened, they knew Matt was important to me, so, they decided to look past this *incident*, and chalk it up to youthful indiscretion.

The rest of the weekend seemed to fly by. Sunday morning, Callie called, and I brought her up to speed on everything, except the condoms, of course.

She proceeded to tell me about her ride into Manhattan with Dimitri on Friday. Apparently, she spent the two-hour drive into the city threatening him and dressing him down. When he attempted to put up the barrier between the front and back seat, she'd put it back down and continue yelling at him.

*Poor bastard. Mess with the bull, you're gonna get the horns.*

"He had the nerve to say, he was just looking out for me, because he knows my father."

"What do you mean?"

"You saw him. He's a jerk. Plus, if he found out we were dating, he'd flip out."

"So, he *still* doesn't know about me?"

That question seemed to set her back on her heels. She got real quiet on the phone, which spoke volumes.

"So, what, you're *ashamed* of me or something?"

"*What? No!* Not at all! I *love* you, you know that!"

"So, what is it then? Is it because I'm brown? Because I'm Hispanic?"

"No, no, not at all. Listen, you're putting words in my mouth."

"So, why doesn't he know about me?"

"I just haven't had the time to tell him."

"Uh-huh."

"I planned on telling him about us over break."

"Mm-hmm."

"I am. Let's not fight about this, okay?"

"You think I want to fight about this? At least you know my parents. Hell, I think my mother likes you more than me. I'm surprised she's not letting you call her Margie."

"Can you blame her?"

"I guess not."

"Listen, if it'll make you feel any better, I *have* told my older sister about you."

"Oh, yeah?" I asked.

"Yeah."

We spent the next few minutes doing the long-goodbye stuff.

"I'll see you on Monday. I love you, Captain."

"I can't wait. I love you, too, babe."

# 56 - Callie's Castle

Everything started out perfectly that busy Monday morning. The trains ran on time, and I met Callie at Penn Station as planned. After receiving my long-awaited kiss, we hit the ground running. Callie had planned everything. She wanted to show me her version of Manhattan.

"And check it out," she said, taking a black credit card from her purse. "Dad's credit card. He left if for me, and I plan on maxing it out it today."

*Uh-oh. Well, he did leave it for her to use. Who am I to argue?*

We tore through Manhattan. We kissed at the top Empire State Building, walked around Greenwich Village, circled back to the Twin Towers, where we shared another passionate kiss at the top before heading to FAO Schwarz, the world's greatest toy store.

Callie and I giggled our way through the entire toy store, starting at the top floor and working our way back down, playing in just about every section, including the Barbie section, *but don't tell Matt.*

"Oh my God, I don't think I've ever laughed that much in my entire life," I said as we exited the store. "So, where to next?"

"You'll see," she said, then stuck both pinkies in her mouth and whistled for a cab like an old pro.

Next stop was Rockefeller Center, a midtown Manhattan landmark. The moment we stepped out of the cab, we were greeted with the sounds of Christmas. In the immediate distance stood the huge world-famous Christmas tree, which overlooked the equally famous skating rink.

"Shall we?" she asked.

We spent the next forty minutes spastically skating our way around the rink. While both of us were athletic, neither of us would make it onto the Olympic skating team anytime soon. It was a miracle that we never fell and broke a bone.

We stayed long enough to see the Christmas lights turn on. Callie and I took in the beautiful display, holding tightly to one another. If there were other people there, we didn't know it. It was as if we were alone in our own little world.

From there, we hit the observation deck of Rockefeller Plaza, which overlooked Manhattan. The view was breathtaking, and so was the city.

I couldn't keep my eyes off Callie. Her face glowed, and her blue eyes shimmered in the reflection of the city lights and early-evening sky. I couldn't help but smile.

"What are you smiling at?"

"You."

"What about me?"

"Everything."

I took her in my arms and kissed her as a cool wind whipped around us. Her lips seemed to melt into mine. When we came up for air, we declared our love for one another for the umpteenth time.

She stepped back and looked at me with her warm eyes.

"Ready to head back to my place?"

"I was born ready," I joked, which earned me a giggle.

Next stop, Callie's place.

***

After another crazy cab ride, we pulled up to a castle located on the Upper West Side, overlooking Central Park West. At least it looked like a castle to me.

I'd never seen a building like this outside of a comic book or movie. It was huge. It had, what appeared to me, four turrets along the top of this ancient-white architectural marvel.

A doorman, dressed warmly, in a formal coat, black-striped pants, hat and elbow-length gloves that I'd only seen in the movies wear, opened the cab door for Callie and me.

"Good evening Miss Christos, welcome back. I see you have a guest with you."

"Hi, Bryan. Yes, this is my boyfriend."

"Yes, very good, ma'am. Enjoy your evening."

"Thanks, Bryan. You, too. Try to stay warm."

"Thanks, ma'am. I'll do my best."

Callie and I held hands and walked into the interior lobby, which was as breathtaking as the exterior. It had vaulted ceilings with crystal chandeliers and what appeared to be a hand-painted masterpiece across the entire length of the ceiling. It was like we had walked into a Roman palace.

The entire lobby was decorated for the holidays—Christmas trees with presents underneath it, menorahs, red velvet ribbons and bows, and other holiday-themed decorations. Off to the side, as we entered, sat a guard, monitoring a closed-circuit television display.

"Good evening, Miss Christos. Welcome home."

"Hi, Max."

*Jesus, how rich is she?*

It didn't take long for me to find out.

We stepped out of the elevator and onto the seventy-fifth floor: the penthouse. Callie pulled a set of keys from her purse, unlocked the front door, and opened it for me.

"Come on in."

*Holy shit!*

I felt like was stepping into Cinderella's castle or a museum, only shinier and with more glitz and sparkle.

"Make yourself at home."

"Yeah, uh, thanks."

The opulence of the place took my breath away. There were vaulted ceiling and stone pillars. You name it, they had it.

"Callie, this place is, uh, wow."

"Thanks. I think it's a bit much, but my father likes it."

"Wow, is that a picture of your mom?" I asked, walking over to a portrait of an elegant looking woman overlooking a fireplace.

"Yeah. That was done a few years ago, before she got sick," Callie said, her voice soft.

"She was really pretty, Cal."

"Thanks. She really was."

Callie had her mother's fierce, blue, almond-shaped eyes and the same nose, pouty mouth and olive-colored skin. The only difference between the two was her mother's age and hair color, which was a shade darker.

She was elegantly seated, dressed in a regal blue gown that complemented the color of her eyes. She wore a diamond necklace and diamond bracelets. The only thing missing was a diamond tiara. The woman was simply stunning.

That wasn't the only artwork in the place. Across from the fireplace hung a family portrait. Even in the portrait, her father looked like an arrogant douchebag. He had this smug look on his face, while the rest of his family smiled warmly. It was like he had conquered life or something. Maybe he had,

I suppose.

"Thirsty?"

"Sure. I'll have whatever you're having."

I followed her to a ritzy kitchen, where she poured us a couple of sodas in clear etched-crystal glasses.

"Here you go. It's sour cherry. I think you'll like it."

"Thanks, Cal."

"Come on. Let me show you around."

*Jesus, how big* is *this place?*

"That's my father's side of the apartment. His offices and bedroom are down that way." She pointed down a hallway that seemed to go on forever toward the left side of the building.

"This way is our sitting room. That room over there is the library. And down that hallway, we have our dining room and balcony, which wraps around the entire floor and overlooks Central Park."

As she gave me the cook's tour, I couldn't help but notice all the gold-colored furnishings. The couches, chairs, tables, and lamps all were gold or accented with gold flair. Even the fireplace had gold accents.

"Wow."

"Yeah, it's not warm and homey like your house, but it's . . . home."

We next stepped through a massive pair of French doors onto the balcony. She wasn't kidding about the view, either. You could see the entirety of Central Park along with most of Manhattan.

I was speechless as we stood on the windy balcony.

"Here, put this on," I said to Callie, placing my jacket around her shoulders.

"Thanks, but won't you get cold?"

"Nah. Not with you in my arms." I said, adding, "Callie, this view is amazing."

She just smiled. I felt a shiver run down her body.

"Come on. Let's get you inside before you get sick."

Closing the doors behind us, I asked, "So, what's down that way?"

"That's where my bedroom is. Want to see it?"

Callie bit her French-manicured thumb, raised one of her shapely eyebrows, and gave me that sly smile.

*Gulp.*

*Yes, please.*

# 57 - My Christmas Gift

S he took my hand and led me down a long, winding hallway, passing two other bedrooms on the right along the way. Hers was at the end on the left.

Her room was about the size of my parents' master bedroom. Unlike the rest of the apartment, her room was tastefully stylish, like the girl I loved. The walls were accented in pinks and reds, and she had the type of plush white carpet that begged you to take your shoes off and walk across it.

She had a king-sized chateau-style sleigh bed and matching dressers. Her linens and pillows were either white or cream or a mix of both. Her comforter looked thicker than the carpet. Her bed looked so comfortable, I was surprised she ever got out of it.

Hanging on the wall was a portrait of a young ballerina, dressed in white, gracefully posing on her tiptoes for the picture. There was something about the way she held herself and the look in her eyes that seemed familiar. When I looked closer, I realized it was a portrait of the girl standing behind me.

"That's you?"

"Yeah. I was like ten. You like it?"

"Wow, yeah."

She looked so fiercely delicate and beautiful. Just like the girl today.

Callie walked up behind me, wrapped her arms around my waist, and placed her chin on my right shoulder.

"What do you feel like doing?" she whispered.

*Seriously?*

"I don't know."

"Want to listen to some music?" she asked.

"Sure."

"Well, why don't you put something on? I've got to step into the bathroom for a moment."

"Yeah, okay."

After she glided into her personal bathroom, I thumbed through her record collection. She had a wide selection, from Motown classics to modern rock.

I took out *Marvin Gaye's Greatest Hits*, Billy Joel's *The Stranger* and Dire Straits' *Brothers in Arms*, loaded them on the turntable and sat on Callie's bed, patiently waiting for her to return.

I was staring at the sweet picture of her as a young ballerina when I heard, "Hi, Captain. Merry Christmas."

I flipped my sights to the beauty before me and was speechless. Standing in the doorway was Callie, twirling the belt of a ruby-red, silk bathrobe. To make it even hotter, she wore a pair of black thigh-high stockings.

"Whoa . . ." I choked out.

"Does that mean you like your gift?"

"Uh-huh." I was stunned. I didn't know what to do.

"Well? What are you waiting for? Come here and unwrap your present."

I immediately shot off the bed like the Road Runner from the cartoons. *Meep, meep!*

All that was missing was the puff of smoke I'd left in my wake.

I took her into my arms and kissed her passionately. Her lusty perfume enveloped us as our pheromones filled her spacious bedroom.

"You like?" she whispered.

"Oh my God, yes!" I replied in a husky voice I hardly recognized.

I lifted her into my arms and gently placed her on the bed. As I leaned over her, I couldn't help but smile. She looked so . . .

"Callie, I—"

"Shhh. Just kiss me."

As we kissed, she slowly slipped her tongue into my mouth, which I readily accepted. In the background, I heard Marvin Gaye singing soulfully:

*I've been really tryiiiin', baby, tryin' to hold back this feeling for so long. And if you feel like I feel baby, then come on, oh come on . . . let's get it on . .*
.

I became lost in the moment. I ran my right hand up and down her warm, sultry body, amazed and excited that she was mine. I'd never seen anyone looking this sexy in my life. Not in the movies, not on cable, not in person. Never.

Her lacy red bra barely hid what lay behind it. I skillfully undid her bra and devoured what waited for me underneath.

My nostrils flared, filling my senses with her intoxicating perfume.

"Yes, right there," she moaned.

I nearly collapsed on the spot. But I didn't stop for even a breath. I felt her hands reach behind me and pull at my shirttails. I took the hint, stood, and quickly removed my clothes. In a matter of seconds, I went from winter-ready to nothing but a pair of white BVDs.

While I was stripping down, Callie pulled back her thick comforter, exposing the luxurious sheets and matching pillows.

She then slid between the sheets, tossed her robe to the floor, and motioned for me to join her.

*Meep, meep!*

I leapt onto her bed and crashed into her, causing us both to giggle.

I couldn't believe what we were doing, or, at least what it appeared we were about to do.

"How long have you been planning this?" I asked.

"Does it matter?"

*Nope.*

# 58 - Movies Lie

I pressed my warm body into hers and slipped the tip of my tongue into her mouth. As I did this, my hand began exploring her magnificent body.

Callie would exhale periodically as I slowly applied pressure to certain parts of her body. She arched her head back, exposing her swan-like neck, which I began kissing. Sliding her hands down my lower back, she pulled me even closer.

"Did you bring anything?" she whispered.

"No. I'm sorry. I did know we'd be . . ."

She just smiled knowingly and slipped out of the bed—wearing nothing but the thigh highs. I felt like such an amateur. But I was willing to learn.

*Damn. Get back here!*

"I'll be right back."

Moments later, my half-naked Greek beauty returned with a smile on her face and a pack of condoms in her hand.

"They're my brother's. I don't think he'll mind, since he doesn't live here anymore."

She hopped back into bed and lounged on her back, her arms flung out to the sides, as if saying: *Take me, you fool.*

Her brown hair was feathered out on the pillow. Her blue eyes seemed to shine brighter than I'd ever seen them, and her lustful smile stretched from ear to ear.

"I don't think you'll be needing these any longer," she said, placing her index finger into the waistband of my BVDs.

I immediately slipped out of my tightie-whities, tossing them onto my pile of clothes, and flopped onto my side so I could take in the precious jewel before me.

"Are you sure?" I cautiously asked.

She nodded and bit her lip in a nervous gesture.

"Okay."

I'd love to say I was an old pro at this. Unfortunately, I wasn't. I'd never done this before. It was my first time. And regardless of her confident planning and lustful bravado, it was Callie's first time as well.

I took the package of condoms from her and used my teeth to rip open the plastic wrapper, tasting some of the spermicide.

*Eww . . . that's disgusting!*

Callie and I got quiet as we stared at the latex condom. The reality of the moment hit us both, like a ton of bricks. This was really happening. We were really going to do it.

"Are you sure that you're sure?"

"Yes."

"I love you, Calista Christos."

"I love you, too, Mateo Nelson."

I don't know why I used her formal name. Maybe, it was the reality of the situation, or maybe I just needed to make an official declaration of my love to her and the universe. Or maybe I was *terrified*.

Callie smiled at me as she lay back on her fluffy pillows. I covered my erect partner-in-crime with the slick condom, praying all the while that I was doing it correctly.

I positioned myself over Callie, who slowly spread her legs for me. I soon realized that the movies lie. The act itself wasn't as easy as it looked.

I thought I would simply slip it into her and start pumping away until we both hit an earth-shattering climax that they'd write about for ages. They'd write songs about it. They'd erect billboards in our honor.

It was nothing like that at all. After Callie helped me find my target, which took what felt like an eternity, there was still a barrier to penetrate. An act that would cause her "mild discomfort," I'd heard.

Callie winced and groaned as I tried to, well, you know . . . *get it in there.*

"Ow. Okay, yeah, right there. Ow."

"Oh my God, are you okay? Am I hurting you?"

"No, no, it's okay, just keep . . . Ow. Okay, yeah, just like that. Right there."

I eventually felt something give inside there.

"Are you sure?"

"Yeah, I'm fine. It's okay. Just keep going."

"Okay."

I was a four-pump chump.

After four pumps, I filled the condom and collapsed on top of Callie. I'd love to tell you she was glowing after that awesome performance. I'd love to say that I left her satisfied and that I was The Man.

Sadly, I didn't, I hadn't, and I most certainly wasn't.

I rolled off her and stared at the ceiling, catching my breath as I reached for her hand.

"Are you okay? Was it okay for you?"

"Yeah, it was, uh, great. I'll be right back."

Like a jackrabbit, she hopped out of bed and ran to the bathroom, leaving me lying there in all my glory, confused.

*What the hell just happened?*

*What did I do?*

# 59 - Broken Glass

While Callie was in the bathroom, I replayed everything in my mind, not knowing what to do at that point. I looked over at her side of the bed and noticed a blood stain, which immediately made me feel terrible.

*Oh, fuck. I did hurt her.*

I slid out of bed and walked to the bathroom door. I stared at it for a few seconds and then took a deep breath and knocked.

"Callie? You, uh, okay?"

*Really, idiot?*

"Yeah, I'm fine. I'll, um, be right out."

"Are you sure? Do you need me to get you anything?"

"No, I'm okay. I'll be right out."

"Why don't I get you something to drink? I'll be right back."

"Yeah, okay. Thanks."

"Um . . . I love you."

"I love you, too."

I made my way back down the long hallway to her kitchen. As I came around the corner and entered the spacious kitchen, I noticed the light was on. I also discovered that I wasn't alone.

Standing at the other side of the kitchen island, holding a bottle of wine, was Callie's father. Our eyes met immediately, and both our jaws dropped.

His jaw wasn't the only thing that dropped, however.

The wine bottle shattered, spraying red wine all over the kitchen.

The only two things between Daddy Grumpy-puss and me was the kitchen island and a rather full, thin layer of latex.

Yeah, that didn't sit too well with Daddy Grumpy-puss either.

Callie must have heard the bottle shatter because she came running into the kitchen.

"Oh my God, what happ— *Father?*"

And the only things between her father and his youngest daughter was the kitchen island and a silky pair of black thigh-highs.

With the fury of a lion, he pointed his finger from me to her and back to me again, then grabbed a steak knife from the butcher block. He could barely choke out his words: "You . . . you . . . *sonofabitch!* I'll kill you!"

I stumbled backward and tripped over Callie.

She yelled, "Father, no! Leave him alone! It was all my idea! Leave him alone!"

I scrambled back to her room with her father hot on my naked tail.

Slamming the door shut behind me, I immediately locked it, my pulse racing faster than it'd ever raced before. I scanned the room for my clothes, all the while trying to think of an exit plan.

I dressed quickly, not caring if my clothes were inside out or properly buttoned. Callie's father pounded on the door.

"Let me in there, you sonofabitch! I'll kill you!"

"Father leave him alone! *I love him!*"

Her father proceeded to yell at her in Greek. She shouted back. This went on for a few minutes, giving me time to catch my breath and plan my escape.

*Boom! Boom! Boom!*

"Let me in there, you sonofabitch! Let me in there! You're going to pay for this!"

*How the hell am I going to get out of here?*

I looked out Callie's bedroom window for the balcony, but there wasn't one. She'd lied about it wrapping around the entire floor. And since I didn't bring a parachute, I couldn't jump out the window.

*I'm screwed!*

As the minutes ticked away, I knew the only way out was through her bedroom door. So, I did what any red-blooded American would do. I said a quick prayer and began to time his door pounding.

I counted down.

One. *Boom!*

Two. *Boom!*

Three. *Boom!*

The next time he pounded, I was ready. I yanked the door open and watched as he tumbled past me into the bedroom, with a mostly-naked Callie landing on top of him.

As I ran out the door, I looked back and mouthed to Callie, *I'm sorry.*

"Go!" she shouted.

"I love you!"

"I love you, too!"

I made it to the living room before I felt Callie's father practically breathing down my neck. I could hear the steak knife swishing behind me as he tried to hit his target: me.

"Get back here, you . . ."

*Sonofabitch. Yeah, yeah. I know! I know!*

I faked left as he took a swipe at me with the knife. And then I swerved right, causing Mr. Christos to trip and fall over the couch. Thankfully, the knife flew in the air, landing behind a pillar in the distance.

*He's at the fifteen . . .*

"Get back here!"

*He's at the ten . . .*

"When I get my hands on you . . ."

*He's at the five . . .*

*Click, click, click . . .*

*Open . . .*

I thought I was getting away scot-free. No such luck. I had five yards to go when the front door opened, revealing none other than my old pal and favorite driver-monkey, Dimitri.

"Dimitri! Get him!"

I put on the brakes, doing everything I could not to crash into him. I quickly dodged him and avoided his grasp.

"Come here, you. I warned you to stay away from her."

They had me trapped behind one of the stone pillars in the foyer, terrified. I did everything I could to stay out of their reach. Fortunately, I had backup.

"Leave him alone!" Callie shouted, coming out in her silky red bathrobe and black thigh-highs.

I don't know if it was the way her hair flowed, or the way the bathrobe hugged her body, or simply the fire in her blue eyes, but Callie immediately caught Dimitri's attention, and he did a double-take.

That was my moment. I dove past Dimitri and made it to the front door. Just before it slammed behind me, I looked back one last time to catch one final glimpse of my beloved queen.

Her pouty lips mouthed, *I love you.*

# 60 - The Rest of the Year

I never saw Callie again. Mr. Christos immediately yanked her from school and, apparently, sent her back to Greece. Rumor had it that he'd made her take a pregnancy test, and then sent her to a convent, but knowing our rumor mill and Callie, she probably wound up going to live with her brother or sister and finishing out the year at a local high school.

I waited for a call, a letter, or even a carrier pigeon, but nothing ever came. I just wanted to know that she was okay. I was heartbroken. Even my parents were sad. They'd really grown fond of Callie, especially Mom.

I never had the heart to tell them what had really happened. It's not the type of story you share with your folks, you know?

*Yeah, so, after losing my virginity to Callie, her father found me standing there naked in his kitchen, with the condom still dangling from my baby-maker, and then all hell broke loose.*

"Um, I don't think you'll be seeing Callie around here anymore."

"Why not? What happened?" Mom asked.

"I don't want to talk about it."

"Oh, sweetie. Did you two break up yesterday?"

"Yeah, something like that."

"Oh, mijo, I'm sorry."

"Me, too."

The following day, I tracked down Matt and told him the whole thing. He listened without interruption, which was surprising.

When I finished my monologue, he said, "Wow. I can't believe you got away."

"Tell me about it."

"Do you think they're going to track you down?"

"I have no idea, dude."

"Well, don't worry about it. I've got your back."

By March, I started receiving acceptance letters from college, so I basically skated by as best I could the remainder of the year. Without Callie there, I decided not to try out for the musical, much to Aaron's sadness.

I continued to think about Callie and missed her terribly. It hit me hardest during our annual talent show in the spring, when Emilio brought the house down with his tribute to his beloved B.

He sat there at the piano, pouring out his heart and soul, with a slideshow playing in the background. He was singing "She's a Rainbow" by the Rolling Stones, and my heart ached for Callie.

*Callie was* my *rainbow. My renaissance. My queen. And I was her captain.*

Life at home took an interesting turn. In February, with no job prospects in sight, my father became extremely depressed. My mother was at her wits' end with him.

While she was on a lunch break at work, she'd read about the burgeoning food truck movement happening out in California. She went to the library to research it.

"Look, you hated your job, and you *love* cooking."

"Yeah, but . . ."

"Yeah, but nada. Listen, everyone loves your food, honey. *Everyone!* I love you. And we *can* do this. We have my 401K money saved, and worse comes to worse, we will apply for a second mortgage."

"A second mortgage?"

And then she said the magic words that every spouse longs to hear from their partner.

"I *believe* in you."

By March, we had an old ice-cream truck sitting on blocks, in our driveway. By May, Dad transformed it into a food truck, complete with a few gas grills, a couple of refrigerators, a freezer and a permit.

He christened it *"The Tomcat,"* after one of the aerospace programs he worked on at Grumman.

After a couple of failed attempts—first, being parked in a bad location, and the second, having too fancy a menu—The Tomcat took off.

He found a location near his old office building, and when his former coworkers found out, they lined up to get a taste of what the Tomcat had to offer. After that, word spread like wildfire and lines began forming down the block. While he wasn't an overnight success, he was able to grow a steady business, one that runs to this day.

Dad took his own advice and stepped out of his comfort zone, spread his wings, and tried something new while he still could. Not only did he accept his true calling, he found his renaissance, and we couldn't be prouder.

*Way to go, Dad!*

# 61 - Hello, Captain

My college years were uneventful. After graduation, I got an accounting job on Long Island and dated a few girls, eventually marrying someone I'd met at work.

I'd love to tell you my marriage lasted, but it didn't. We became a statistic. The good news is my ex-wife gave me four outstanding children. Even greater news is she and I are better friends now than when we were married.

We even go out to dinner periodically.

I'm still living on Long Island in a house a few blocks from where I grew up. My eldest daughter, Jessica, took over the Tomcat from "Gramps," as she calls him, and lives with me. My other kids live with their mother in Smithtown, but I still see them as often as our schedules allow.

My curiosity got the better of me the day after looking at Helen Doherty's Facebook post. I wondered what had become of Callie. Was she still alive? Did she ever get married? Did she join the family business, like her overbearing father wanted? Did she have any kids?

After unsuccessfully searching for her on Google and across social media, I broadened my search to include her father's conglomerate. Much to my dismay, the only Christos's listed were her ancient-looking father, listed as CEO Emeritus, and her older brother, Nicholas, listed as the current CEO.

I took one last stab with social media, this time searching Facebook for Nicholas Christos. I figured if her siblings were anything like my children, Callie would show up in family pictures.

Much to my surprise, I found her.

It was in an album labeled "Christmas 2015." She was wearing an apron and standing at a counter, laughing and surrounded by children. They were making kourambiethes and baklava. I smiled as a flood of memories came rushing in.

There she was, making a mess and having the time of her life. As beautiful as ever.

*Calista Romani.*

Her brother had tagged her, so I clicked on her name and was brought to her Facebook page. Even though it felt a little stalker-ish, I couldn't help looking through her personal photos posted.

There was something cathartic about seeing her blossom from a young lady to a grown woman.

Her beauty never faded. Sure, she had crow's feet at the corners of her still fiery blue eyes, and a few strands of silver peeked through her dark wavy hair, but who cared? Certainly, not me.

It appeared she was married, living in Greece with her husband and four children, three boys and a girl, who was the spitting image of Callie.

Callie looked . . . happy.

My cursor hovered over the *Add Friend* button for a few minutes, before throwing caution to the wind.

*Screw it! What's the worst that can happen?*

*Click.*

A week later, via Facebook Messenger, I received a ping.

"Hello, Captain!"

***

A month or so later, we met in Manhattan, not far from the *scene of the crime*, her old apartment building. She was in town for business and had a free night, so we met at a trendy Manhattan bistro.

I don't know which one of us was more nervous. She looked even better in person than online. Simply stunning. After an awkward hug and kiss on the cheek, we had drinks at the bar, followed by a pleasant dinner.

We brought each other up to speed on our lives. She wanted to know about my parents and wasn't surprised to hear about my father's success.

"He was such an excellent chef."

After telling me about her life, I broached the elephant in the room: that fateful evening.

"So, what happened?" I asked.

She confirmed that her father had made her take a pregnancy test, but had not made her go to a convent. He'd also fired Dimitri because he felt he was disloyal for not letting him know about our relationship.

Instead of a convent, her father sent her back to Greece to live with her older sister for the remainder of her senior year. After high school, Callie went to college and studied performing arts, much to her father's chagrin.

That was where she met her ex-husband, Mario, an Italian boy from Naples, who went on to become a famous actor in his native Italy.

*I'm sorry . . . did you say "ex"?*

Her youngest son, Giannis, was getting married the following spring to a lovely girl from Connecticut. They were having the wedding and reception in Manhattan.

"Do you want to come with me to the wedding?"

"Callie, are you serious?"

She shrugged and gave me a wry smile. "Sure, why not? I need a date."

*That's my Callie.*

# EPILOGUE

## The Wedding

"**L**et *go of me*! I'll *kill* him!" old grumpy-puss yelled as Callie and some of the wedding guests held him back.

"Father, sit down, and stop being ridiculous! That was years ago!" Callie shouted.

I don't know if it was her words or his ninety-something-year-old exhaustion, but he begrudgingly sat back in his chair, huffing and puffing, shooting daggers at me with his eyes, as the wait-staff cleaned up the mess.

"I'll kill that sonofabitch," I heard him grumble.

An embarrassed Callie walked me back to our table, shaking her head.

"I guess he remembers me."

"Apparently."

"Well, I *am* unforgettable."

She laughed. "Yes, you are. God, I've missed you, Captain."

"I've missed you, too, my queen," I said, kissing the back of her hand.

*More than you know.*

I made sure to stay away from the old man the remainder of the reception, which went off without a hitch. Callie and I laughed, danced and had a great evening.

After the bride and groom left, and Callie said her goodbyes to family and friends, she asked me, "Want to walk me to my room?"

"Sure."

Callie slipped her hand into mine, and we went back to her hotel room.

Unsurprisingly, her suite was enormous. As we entered, she took off her heels and excused herself. "I'll be right back. There's wine in the refrigerator, if you want to pour us a couple of glasses."

"Sure."

*Cabernet Sauvignon. Christos Vineyards. Why am I not surprised?*

Callie soon returned, wearing a plush, white bathrobe and a matching pair of slippers. After pouring two glasses of red wine, I joined her on the couch, where I proceeded to rub her sore feet. We drank our wine and laughed about the evening.

"I really thought he was going to get me this time."

"I thought so, too." She laughed.

"He's pretty spry for an old man."

"Yes, he sure is. What about you? Are you still spry?" she asked with an arched brow.

It may have been thirty years later, but I knew that look. I hungered for it.

I just smiled and inched closer.

Her lips tasted as good that evening as they had thirty years prior, and she felt even better in my arms. Without saying a word, she led me to her bedroom.

She flopped backward onto the bed, and I took a moment to gaze at her. Her eyes were still that fiery blue, and her whole essence . . . beautiful.

"Remember this, Captain?" she whispered as she opened her robe, revealing herself.

"Oh, sweet Jesus! Callie."

"Are you going to stand there all night, or are you going to join me?"

*Meep, meep!*

Join her I did.

Unlike my teenage version, I took my time getting reacquainted with this beautiful Grecian queen. Our bodies may have changed a bit over the years, with a stretch mark here and a scar there, but our passion hadn't.

We made sweet love well into the early morning. Between *sessions* and glasses of water, we held one another, chatting and laughing like a pair of young lovers.

As the sunrise peeked through the thick curtains, it made me think of this new chapter in my life. After all these years, I had my Callie back. My sunrise. My renaissance. My queen. Looking simply perfect as she lay warmly in my arms. That moment, I knew we'd spend the rest of our lives together. And we did.

"So, let me ask you a question?"

"Sure."

"Better than the last time?"

"Much." She giggled with a satisfied smile and snuggled into me.

*Best reunion ever!*

~ Fin ~

# ABOUT THE AUTHOR

**P**hillip Vega has always been a storyteller, but he'd never put pen to paper until a few years ago. Suddenly, he had a publishing contract for his debut novel, *Last Exit to Montauk*. In the midst of the vortex of marketing, analytics, refining, and continuing to write, he discovered what he defines as his true calling, his passion. He is now fully and happily immersed in the whirlwind that is the publishing industry, even as he diligently continues his work in software sales. The *Captain & the Queen* is his second novel with more in the works

Phillip is a Long Islander with Hispanic roots, now living Florida, and it is from those memories of summers in Long Island that he crafts his stories. Now he can't stop his brain from working through new ideas.

His hobbies, aside from enjoying his ongoing work as a published author, include many of the other art forms: singing, performing, and reading. The beach is always home to him . . . and laughter, whether his own or someone else's, is an unsurpassable joy that he embraces whenever possible.

Phillip lives in the Tampa Bay area with his wife of twenty-five years. He has four sons and "two and a half dogs," which actually is four dogs, but three out of the four are Chihuahuas while the fourth is a shepherd mix. So he calls it at "two and a half."

Comfortable in a room full of people or one on one, he welcomes opportunities for guest appearances, interviews, and book signings.

You can reach Phillip directly through his website: www.phillipvega.com, his publisher www.thewordverve.com, and a plethora of social media sites for either. He treasures the feedback he receives from his readers and looks forward to hearing from you.

www.ingramcontent.com/pod-product-compliance
Lightning Source LLC
Chambersburg PA
CBHW070609170726
48291CB00003B/756